To Mr ... tts

I hope

Book as much

writing it. Thanks for

giving it a look.

Dan Pick...

ACCIDENTAL COP

Dan Pickens

ISBN: 1494224542
ISBN 13: 9781494224547

1

ACCIDENTAL COP

October, 1954

Sally Daro screamed as two black Fords closed in on the Daro's '54 Cadillac. Her father fought the steering wheel as Sally and her mother were violently thrown about. The deeply rutted road narrowed into a trail, ending in a brushy cul-de-sac. Mr. Daro's hoped-for escape route turned into a trap.

"Lock your doors!" he shouted as he punched his door lock. Frightened, but furious, he slammed the car into reverse and floored the accelerator. He was rewarded by the screech of crumpling, tearing metal. The violent impact took out the lead car's bumper, grill, and headlights, crunching into the front fenders.

Seven young men piled out of the two following cars "You old son-of-a-bitch," yelled the driver, "Look what you done to my car."

All wore blue jeans and leather jackets. Three of the seven giggled insanely.

Sally's terror increased when she saw a length of heavy motorcycle chain dangling from each man's hand, one end wrapped in tape to make a handle. With eyes like a frightened doe, an anguished, "Daddy?" squeaked from between Sally's bloodless lips.

A chain smashed through Richard Daro's window. By instinct he threw up a hand to guard his face, but too late to prevent the flicking tip of the chain from destroying his left eye. Reaching in through the shattered window, three of the punks roughly pulled his struggling body across the jagged glass and threw him to the ground.

Sally and Evelyn Daro watched in horror as Mr. Daro tried to ward off the blows. He caught much of the assault on his arms and hands, but it was over quickly. In a matter of seconds resistance ceased, his face a mass of cuts and welts, his left arm broken.

Turning their attention to the mother, three of the group ran to the passenger side and began rocking the car.

"Open the door, bitch!" yelled a voice.

Frozen in fear, Mrs. Daro didn't respond. The sound of chain on glass covered her scream. Sharp pellets hammered her, several embedding in her face as her window burst. Fumbling the door open, evil hands dragged her from the car toward a patch of grass.

Two men held Mrs. Daro down while another straddled her. Flicking open a switchblade, the third man licked his lips as he watched the dawning terror suffuse Evelyn Daro's face. He slowly slit her dress, moving next to panties and bra. Seconds later he unzipped his trousers and brutally entered her.

When he finished another took his place. One by one the others took their turn as a dark silence fell. Her diminishing cries finally ceased, leaving only seeping tears.

In the back seat of the car Sally tried to roll herself into a ball as she muffled her sobs. Soon prying hands dragged her from the car. She fainted, a suppressed scream frozen on trembling lips. Sally was sixteen years old. She'd never even had a date.

The leader heard tearing cloth as some of the young men had apparently decided to sample Sally's wares as well.

"Leave off, dumbass," growled a voice. "We're gettin' good money for this one. Make damn sure she ain't marked up."

Grumbling, the wolf pack backed off. While the unconscious girl was rolled in a blanket and placed in the trunk of the second car, the leader separated from the group.

Pausing above Mrs. Daro he flicked open a stiletto and plunged the thin blade into her chest. As detached as though watching their mothers carve a pot roast, the other six waited for the seventh to artfully finish his work.

Detective Charlie Golden's watch read 4:00 AM when he and his partner, Jim Killean, got the call. They drove out Harry Hines Boulevard to Parkland Hospital and entered the emergency room through the south entrance. Both men knew the hospital staff, but the usual pleasantries were missing. The normally gregarious trauma team seemed strangely subdued.

Making their way to the morgue the detectives were met by three uniformed cops, T.T. Tyler, Carlos Tudsdale, and Sergeant JD Potter. 'Goldie' Golden winked at the six-two, 210 Potter, surprised at how pale his former partner looked. JD had a haunted look around the eyes as he raked strong fingers through thick black hair.

Goldie still wished that JD and his now married sister, Clara, had gotten together. She still said that JD was the best looking man she'd ever known. Goldie couldn't see it, somehow.

Golden watched as an obviously disturbed JD unconsciously fingered the three inch horizontal scar on his right cheek, a souvenir from an off duty fight at the It'll Do Club several years before. Scuttlebutt circulating inside the police department about Potter's wife, Helen, made the marriage suspect, but the wiry detective still didn't know what to believe. Golden had met Helen; so beautiful she hurt his eyes. But beyond the superficial he knew nothing. Still, where there's smoke?

Goldie nodded at Tudsdale and the six-five Tyler, a good three inches taller than either Potter or Tudsdale. Goldie judged T.T. to go two-thirty, maybe two-thirty five. A muscle in Tyler's jaw kept working as he chewed on an ever-present toothpick. He looked like a man with something stuck in his craw.

"How's it going, JD?" Golden asked.

"Bad, Goldie. The chain gang hit again."

"Same as before?"

"Worse."

"Who got whacked?"

Potter shook his head. "Don't know yet."

JD's normally well modulated baritone sounded tight with suppressed anger as he continued, "The man's wallet and the woman's purse were gone. When the lab boys got all the pictures they wanted we moved the bodies here. The lab is going through the car and we're running the plates now. We should know something soon."

Golden and his partner Killean had seen it all during their ten years on the force, especially after they made detective. So familiar was he with the way his partner worked that Golden could tell almost to the second when Killean slipped on his protective emotional armor, steeling himself against the outside world.

Unconsciously, Golden drew in a breath as both men stepped into the morgue for a quick look at the bodies. Even so Goldie was not prepared for what he found. Seconds later he hurried out for some air; Killean followed shortly.

"You okay, partner?" asked Killean, his stocky frame all but blotting out the light from the emergency room door.

Golden swallowed hard. "Yeah; they just reminded me of my folks. They're about the right age and all. How could anybody do that?"

Killean chewed his gum and shrugged. "Damned if I know. Makes you think the whole world's a bucket of shit, don't it? You want me to take the report?"

"No. Just give me a minute."

"Sure." Killean turned and went back inside. In a moment, Golden followed. His six foot, almost painfully thin frame seemed bent and weighed down, a lock of light brown hair falling over his forehead.

Spotting Potter inside the emergency room, Golden motioned him over. "Who found 'em?"

Potter hooked a thumb toward Carlos and T.T., "They did, about 1:30 this morning."

"Any witnesses?"

Potter shook his head. "Nope; it was a quiet night. Their squad was just ratting around up in the north part of town. Neither one are real familiar with the territory."

"Where'd they find 'em?"

"Off of Inwood Road, way up past Royal Lane. There's a dirt trail into the woods where the kids go to make out. You know, rubbers laying all over. T.T. was riding shotgun and spotted some skid marks and a Ford hub cap near some broken glass on the street. They got curious. Found 'em about a quarter mile inside the woods where the road peters out. Poor bastards got themselves trapped."

Golden frowned. "Damn! They'd have been a lot better off to try to make a run for it straight up Inwood."

Potter shrugged. "Yeah - just not thinking, I guess."

Golden took a small, spiral notebook from his inside coat pocket and began to jot down some notes. "Worst thing they coulda done. What kinda car were they drivin'?"

"Fifty four Cadillac Fleetwood," JD said. "Nice car before the bastards beat it half to pieces."

Golden's eyebrows shot up. "They trashed the car, too?"

Potter nodded. "Yep. Every glass knocked out, and there's hardly a square inch that hasn't got a ding in it someplace. The lab's going over it before we tow it in."

"Damn, that's a first," Golden said. "Why the car you reckon?"

Again, Potter shrugged. "Who knows how crazies think? The back end and bumper is pretty banged up and there's a whole bunch of glass and metal on the ground behind it. It looks like they deliberately backed the Caddy into the car that was chasing them. Looks like they busted up the front pretty good from all the stuff that was on the ground. Don't know if it got the radiator, but that car's gonna need a lot of work."

"You ready to take a look?" Golden asked, motioning with his head toward the morgue.

Potter drew a deep breath. "I guess - let's get it over with."

JD and Charlie Golden strode side by side through the metal-faced, double doors. Dr. Paul Montgomery had just completed his preliminary examination, walking away from two bodies which were silhouetted beneath white covering shrouds. The Doctor's pale blue eyes stared at the two officers through an old pair of US Army style steel-rimmed glasses. A surgical mask dangled from his neck as Montgomery stripped off his gloves and wiped a gnarled hand through thin gray hair. At the double sink, the doctor turned on the wing shaped water tap with a bony elbow and began to wash up.

"Doc, after you get through, can we talk?"

"Sure, Goldie." Montgomery selected a fresh towel and dried his hands and arms. "Let's go to my office."

"Okay, but I need to see the bodies first. You ready, JD?"

"Let's do it."

Bowel odor assailed Golden as he got closer to the slain couple. He didn't know why, but every time he saw the morgue he always thought of glacial ice, the cold gray stainless steel tables giving the impression that the shrouded bodies were frozen to the metal. He pulled both coverings aside, but in spite of his preview, Golden matched JD's gasp.

Judging from the body the man looked to be in his late fifties, but the woman was so mutilated that there was no way to even guess her age. Both breasts had been hacked off, one stuffed into her mouth, the other into her vagina. A thin, almost surgical cut ran from her crotch to the base of her neck. To the left of her sternum, about where the heart would be, a thin rivulet of dried blood trailed down the rib cage from a small, slit-like, puncture.

Tears sprang to Potter's eyes as he turned and left the room. Moments later the detective followed.

"Well," Golden said, swallowing hard, "let's go see the Doc."

Not trusting himself to speak, Potter nodded.

When Golden and JD joined him, Killean had just finished interviewing the nurse who first saw the bodies. He snapped his book shut and thanked her as she walked away.

Typical, thought Golden. Even though his partner's mind was occupied with a murder investigation, he knew that Killean couldn't resist checking out the nearest pretty female. Sure enough, Killean's eyes were locked onto the pretty brunette's backside as she bounced down the hall.

"Anything?" asked Golden.

"Nah - nothin'," said his stocky partner.

Golden frowned. "Shit! Well - Montgomery can talk to us now."

The trio shuffled down the hall and stepped into a small, glassed-in alcove. The three cops had been through this many times, but Golden especially would never get used to the smell of a morgue - a cross between alcohol and formaldehyde. They took seats as Montgomery looked up from a file.

Dr. Montgomery shook his head and massaged his temples with long, bony fingers. "It's a bad one."

"Yeah," said Golden. "You got anything, Doc?"

"Not much, but I've only done a preliminary. There was an unmailed letter in what was left of the man's inside coat pocket. After I saw the return address, I realized that I know these people. Their name is Daro; Richard and Evelyn Daro. I knew them slightly."

Potter's brow furrowed. "Daro - I know that name. Did they have a son?"

"I think so; a son and a daughter. You know them?"

"Maybe the son," JD said. "It's not a common name. I had a teammate in high school named Danny Daro. Hell of a football player - played left tackle."

The Doctor shrugged. "Could be. Anyhow, they were active in several local charities. Quite wealthy. Owns a company that makes small appliances - toasters, waffle irons, that sort of thing. Been in business many years. As for their murder, it's the same drill as the last three, except this time they cut off her breasts and placed them in -uh - strategic spots. I don't know how that figures in."

"The sons-of-bitches are just getting meaner I guess," Killean said. "Anybody that'd do that is a real sicko anyway. Find anything to help us catch these dirtbags?"

"Some fingernail scrapings, sperm samples, hair, and the like. I can't point any fingers till you catch someone, though. Maybe not then."

"You're not being much help, Doc," Killean said.

"I know, and I'm not real thrilled about it either. There may be more later, but I doubt it."

"Can you even tell us how many we're dealing with ?" asked Golden.

Montgomery shook his head. "Not for sure - at least five, maybe eight or ten. It's like a whole army raped and sodomized her."

The doctor's more detailed description put Potter further into shock. He cleared his throat and looked away to see Tudsdale round the corner and crook a finger at him. JD excused himself and went into the hallway to hold a whispered conversation with his half English, half Spanish officer.

Montgomery took off his glasses and wiped the thick lenses with a tissue. "You think maybe these guys are already working on an insanity defense in case they get caught?"

"How you figure?" asked Killean.

"Like you said, they have to be nuts to do something like this. Maybe they're just trying to make it look like they're crazy."

Killean shook his head. "Nah, I doubt it. I'll bet they ain't that smart. Besides, that might work in California with all them liberal judges and fat assed, flannel mouthed shysters, but it ain't gonna fly in Texas. We catch 'em, we fry the sons-a-bitches. They gotta know that."

Montgomery nodded. "I suppose you're right. At least I hope so. The Daro's were good people. I know - er - knew them well enough to know that at least."

JD looked even more pale when he and Tudsdale finished talking. He hurried in to join the doctor and two detectives.

"We've got a problem," he said.

"What's that?" asked Golden.

"The lab boys just found another purse in the car, jammed underneath the back seat. It's got to be the daughter's. Name's Sally. The ID makes her sixteen."

Both the doctor and Killean had pinched looks as Golden lowered his head into his hands.

Sergeant Potter punched the doorbell and stepped back from the ornately carved oak front door of the big house on Turtle Creek Drive. His watch read 7:03 AM. Absentmindedly, Potter scanned the front of the immense house. It reminded him of pictures he had seen of southern plantations.

Potter was not happy at being elected for this mission. Since he probably knew the son, however, he was a natural to carry the bad news. He punched the bell a second time and heard a faint rustling behind the door. Shortly, a small peephole opened giving him a look at two narrowed eyes and part of a face. The eyes widened when they saw his uniform.

"May I help you, officer?" asked a cultured, British voice.

"Yes - I'm Sergeant JD Potter. Is this the home of Mr. and Mrs. Richard Daro?"

The eyes narrowed again. "Indeed it is, but they are asleep."

It was Potter's turn to be surprised. "They are?"

"I am quite sure they are; usually until about eight thirty. I can wake them if it is important."

"If you wouldn't mind. It's very important."

"Just one moment, please." The peephole closed and the door whispered open on well oiled hinges. "Follow me, please; I will show you to the library."

Potter was even more impressed with the inside of the huge house, certain that he could put his entire home inside the mansion's foyer. Suspended overhead hung the biggest crystal chandelier he had ever seen. Against the right wall a staircase climbed upward and made a ninety degree, left hand spiral before joining the second story landing. The butler led Potter across the entrance hall to a double door on the left. Sliding the doors open, the butler motioned him inside.

"If you will please wait here I will summon –

"Randall?" interrupted a voice from the top of the stairs.

Potter looked up to see a tall, muscular man about his own age standing on the landing, tying the belt on a pale blue robe.

The man's hair, still worn in a flattop, was black except for a genetic white streak in front. From this distance Potter could not see his oddly colored amber eyes, but the face was the same; good looking, but too rounded to be considered classically handsome. The man's face gave the impression of kindness and softness, but as many could attest, he was anything but soft. Potter recognized his old football chum, Danny Daro.

"Yes, Master Danny?"

"Is something the matter?"

Potter cut in. "Hi Daro, long time."

The man squinted, focusing on the intruder. As he started down the stairs his face broke into seemingly hundreds of wrinkles. "JD? Is that you?"

"You bet. I haven't seen you for a hundred years."

Daro laughed. "Well, maybe just eighty. What on earth brings you out at this time of the morning?"

"I came to see about your folks, but your butler tells me they're still asleep."

"I suppose so. The doorbell woke me. You need to see them?"

"Yeah."

"Just a minute and I'll get them."

Taking the stairs two at a time, he went back to the landing and down a hallway to the right. Potter heard a muffled knock, then another. In a minute an agitated Danny Daro was back at the top of the stairs.

"They're not in their room. The bed isn't even disturbed."

"Do you have a sister?" Potter asked.

"Sally? Sure."

"Would you check her room too?"

Obviously panicked he hurried away. In a moment he was back, slamming down the stairs.

"She's not there either. What's going on, JD?"

"Can we go in here?" Potter asked, indicating the drawing room.

Daro shouldered past Potter and the butler, closing the doors behind them.

Potter couldn't help remembering how often he had followed those shoulders through a hole in an opposing football team's line. With the six-four, 220 Daro at left tackle and his other friend, the six-three, 235 Chief O'Neal at the right tackle slot, there was hardly a safer place on earth to be than in the backfield during a football game at his high school alma mater.

"It's bad news, isn't it?" Daro asked.

Potter knew of no way to soften the blow. "I want you to get hold of yourself, Danny. There's been an accident. Your folks were assaulted."

"How bad is it?

Potter paused. "I'm so sorry, Danny. They were killed."

Daro looked as though he had been slapped. "Sally?"

"She's missing. We don't know where she is."

"Dear God," he said. He collapsed into a high-backed chair next to the fireplace. Looking down on them from above the mantle was a portrait of father, mother, sister, and brother; a handsome family. And if the painting was accurate, Sally was a very pretty young lady. Potter could only pray that she still was.

Neither man spoke. Daro stared, unseeing, into the cold fireplace as Potter sat across from his one-time teammate trying desperately to wish away his friend's pain. Several minutes passed.

Daro cleared his throat, his voice almost a whisper. "Where are they?"

"At Parkland."

"I want to see them."

Tears sprang to Potter's eyes. "No you don't."

Daro's head jerked up. "What are you saying?"

Potter hesitated. "Danny, uh - this wasn't a car accident. It was a cold, calculated murder. The worst I ever saw."

Daro's tears joined JD's. "All the more reason, then - I want to see them. I want to know."

Potter sighed. "I'll take you."

"No. I'll go in my own car. You go ahead. I'll meet you there."

"Okay," Potter said, his voice resigned. "And, Danny, I can't tell you how sorry I am. But I want you to know this - we'll get these bastards. And we're doing all we can to find Sally."

"Yeah, thanks."

He escorted Potter to the front door and asked Randall to assemble the staff. In minutes, four obviously apprehensive servants gathered in the library. With as little emotion as possible, he told them about his father and mother.

More like family than employees, the staff's tears were as real as his. The youngest at fifty three and last hired was William, their combination chauffeur and gardener, an employee of twenty three years. There was Randall, the butler, and Mildred, his wife who doubled as cook, both in their mid-sixties. Last, quite pretty and a few months older than William, was Emma, the maid.

From each of the servants Daro felt a special loss and concern, but sensed uneasiness about what might come next. None knew it of course, but his father had already provided a pension for each of them. The worst that could happen was retirement on a fully paid annuity at eighty percent of their present salaries.

Daro asked William to bring his car around. Apparently relieved at being assigned a familiar task, the sometime chauffeur jumped into action as a numb, sole surviving son dragged himself upstairs to dress.

Daro loved his new, 1955, two-tone black and white Ford Crown Victoria, the first in Dallas. When he got behind the wheel this time, however, he wasn't thinking about the car.

Cranking the special order, V-8 interceptor engine to life, he pulled the shift lever into drive and punched the accelerator with a 13B. His body was in the car, but his mind was elsewhere as he bounced onto Turtle Creek and headed for Parkland Memorial Hospital.

He felt strange that most of his thoughts were about Sally instead of his parents. Dear little sister, born late in his mother's life, particularly welcome since his folks thought they couldn't have any more children after he was born. He remembered how shocked he was when his folks told him that his mom was pregnant.

It bothered him at first seeing his mother grow bigger each day as this unwanted, larval intruder thrust its way into his world. How could they be so happy? After all, he was almost fifteen years old. A baby? Ridiculous.

But the strangeness quickly went away. During her birth at Baylor Hospital, Daro waited alongside his father, sweating it out just as though he had some real part in the process. After several hours, there she was, squirming and crying as a masked nurse held her up behind the glass encased nursery for them to see. There were several other babies, all much prettier he thought, but his dad kept saying what a beauty she was. To him she looked like a bright red prune. He didn't say so, but he also thought she was the ugliest thing he'd ever seen.

But in a matter of hours the prune turned gorgeous. Almost from the first day, Sally was an almost perfect baby, hardly waking at night even for her bottle. Daro developed a proprietary feeling toward this fat, bubbly charmer with the soft brown hair and eyes. She wormed her way into his heart and soul more surely than a well aimed bullet.

And now she was missing. Dear God let her be well.

Engrossed in his thoughts, he almost missed the turn into Parkland. He wheeled the Ford around behind the yellow brick hospital and parked in the only vacant spot, one reserved for police. When he hurried inside he found Potter waiting.

"Let's go see Dr. Montgomery," Potter said.

"Is that where my folks are?"

"In the same area."

"I want to see them."

"In a minute, Danny. Let's see the Doc first."

Daro gave him a grim-faced nod and Potter led the way to Montgomery's office. The doctor was waiting, sad eyes behind the old-fashioned steel frames. He extended his hand and grasped Daro's in a warm, firm grip.

"I'm so sorry, Danny. I knew your parents. They were fine people."

"Thank you, doctor. Do you know anything yet?"

Doctor Montgomery flashed Potter a knowing look. "I'm sorry, but my report is incomplete."

Daro's eyes narrowed. "And when do you think it might be complete?"

"Not for several days, I'm afraid."

"I see. Where are they now?"

Both Dr. Montgomery and Potter squirmed.

"In the morgue, Mr. Daro," the Doctor said.

"I want to see them."

"I most strongly advise against it."

"I appreciate your concern, Doctor, but they are my parents and I will see them - now, please!"

Montgomery sighed. "Very well; follow me."

Daro didn't remember the drive up Highway 77. He literally attacked the road, foot to the floorboard, as the Ford knifed through a gusty head- wind. The interceptor engine strained to keep the speedometer needle above one hundred.

Snapping back to reality just south of Lewisville, Texas, he glanced at the rear view mirror. A struggling Department of Public Safety cruiser lagged far behind, its red, top-mounted cherry spinning madly.

Forcing calm He pulled to the roadside just over a small rise and waited. In less than a minute the DPS unit screamed past, the Doppler Effect lowering the siren's wail almost a full octave.

Seeing his prey parked off the shoulder, the lone State Trooper locked the brakes, almost swapping ends. After his cruiser slid to a stop, the officer backed up and placed his car to the rear and slightly to the left of Daro's similar Ford.

"Pisswilly son-of-a-bitch," muttered the DPS Trooper, as he bolted from the sedan and stomped toward Daro's car, ticket book in his hand.

Three stripes on his sleeve and a shiny, stainless steel plate pinned above the right shirt pocket with 'Nigliazzo' etched in black into the metal announced the name and rank of the scowling cop. He could feel himself get madder with every step. Even the most casual observer would have recognized his expression as that of a man about to get a big chunk of the nearest available ass.

"Mister, I was doin' over a hundred and wasn't gettin' a whiff, what you got to say about that?"

"Not a thing, officer, you are exactly right, I was driving like an idiot."

Unused to such honesty the Sergeant was taken aback. He looked closer at his captive and saw the bloodshot eyes and haunted look.

Too, there appeared to be tear-streaks down the man's face. Nigliazzo sensed that there was more here than just the normal pisswilly out to see how fast his car would go.

"Mister, is there someplace you've gotta be in a hurry?"

Daro's chuckle sounded bitter. "No, Sergeant, I was trying to run away from something, not toward it."

The enigmatic answer only confused Nigliazzo more. "I see. Well then, let me have your operator's license."

"Sure." He fished out his billfold and took his license from behind a clear plastic tab, handing it to the trooper.

"Is this your correct address?"

"Yes."

The Sergeant scanned the license. Daro? The name nibbled at his mind. Where had he heard it, and not long ago either?

Nigliazzo's expression cleared. "Uh - Mr. Daro, are your folks - uh –

"Yeah," He said, his voice gruff and choked.

The sergeant handed Daro's license back. "Do me somethin', will ya? Slow this thing down. I'm real sorry, Mr. Daro. There's an all-points out for them dirtbags, but there's not much to go on."

"Yeah, I know. I spoke to Sergeant Potter and Dr. Montgomery at Parkland."

"You know JD Potter?"

He nodded. "We played football together."

"He's good people. Tell 'im Nig says hello."

"Sure, Sergeant, and thanks."

Nigliazzo pointed his finger at Daro and dropped his thumb like the hammer on a pistol. "You slow down, now, ya hear?"

"Yeah, and thanks again."

With a wave, the trooper got back in his car and sped off north toward Lewisville.

A moment later, He made a 'U' turn and began a slow drive back toward Dallas.

• • •

2

A demoralized staff greeted Daro when he got home. The best he could do, however, was tell them that the police were hard at work and hoped to have answers soon.

Several hours passed before he thought to ask how long it would be until he could make funeral arrangements. After consulting the telephone directory, He called Dr. Montgomery. The doctor had left, but Potter was still there.

Potter's familiar baritone came onto the wire. "You okay, Danny?"

"I've been better. Do you know when Montgomery will release my folks?"

"No, I don't. It usually takes several days." Daro shook his head. "I just wondering when to schedule the funeral."

"Uh - look, Danny; I don't mean to tell you your business, but why don't you turn it over to the funeral home and let them worry about it."

"I hadn't thought of it. Thanks." For some reason Daro remembered the message from Sergeant Nigliazzo. "By the way JD, Nig said to tell you hello," he said, and hung up.

Could he have seen Potter's face, he might ordinarily have laughed at his friend's puzzled expression, wondering how Daro could have gotten such a message from Potter's Department of Public Safety friend.

Five days later on October 15, 1954 the funerals for Richard and Evelyn Daro were held, the interment taking place in the family plot at Restland Memorial Park Cemetery. There was still no word on the killers or Sally's whereabouts. Daro's already low spirits sank even lower, bringing him close to a breaking point. There was nothing he could do about his dead parents, but the thought of where Sally could be and what might be happening to her nearly drove him insane. Time seemed frozen, the clock's hands stuck on doom.

He was moved at the sight of so many friends. He was particularly stunned by the number of people he had never seen before. Not only was the crowd diverse, many of whom were prominent members of the Dallas social register, but it appeared that the entire work force of Daro Industries had turned out to pay final tribute to their beloved boss.

Dressed in mufti, JD Potter stood beside two men in Dallas Police uniforms, the shorter of the two wearing Sergeant stripes. It took a second for it to register that they were, Jim "Chief" O'Neil and Tommy Lee "Storm" Raney, two more friends from his high school football days. Daro nodded and looked away, blinking tearful eyes.

The service was short, but it would not have mattered. Daro felt submerged in a sea of timeless grief. He knew that when the service was over he would have to turn his thoughts toward Sally. The living - at least he hoped she was still alive - took precedence over the dead. After the benediction he made his way through a sea of sympathetic well wishers, walking over to Potter.

Potter spoke first. "Hi, Danny. You okay?"

"I'll make it."

"Remember Storm and Chief?"

"How could I forget?" he said, shaking hands.

Storm still had the same look of devilment in his blue eyes and on his heavily freckled face. His flaming red hair looked like lava trying to leak from beneath his policeman's cap. At five-eleven and a trim 175, Raney looked almost tiny sandwiched between Potter and O'Neal. But the big Cherokee had changed the least. He remembered how inseparable the three had been in high school.

"I didn't know you guys were on the police force."

Potter smiled. "Storm's idea. I'll tell you about it sometime."

"Yeah, any word on Sally?"

Potter sobered and shook his head. "No, I'm sorry."

Daro sighed, looking at the ground. "I don't know how much more of this I can take."

"Hang in there my friend, we'll get the bastards," Potter said.

"Yeah. I just hope it's soon."

"Look, Danny," chimed in Raney, "How's about ridin' back into town with us so's we can do a little catchin' up?"

"I don't know," he said. "I came out in the limousine."

"I'll take care of it," Potter said. He walked over to the funeral home limo and held a whispered conversation with the chauffeur. The man nodded, looked toward Daro, and gave him a half salute as he got into the nine-passenger Cadillac and moved off down the drive. There was something sad in the gesture. Potter realized for the first time that Daro had come to the cemetery alone and would have left alone. It had not occurred to him that Daro had no other family.

The thought made Potter shudder under his suit coat. Daro seemed to be living Potter's life in reverse. Adopted when he was ten, two years after the auto accident that took his folks, Potter completely related to his big friend's pain. He also knew that Daro had not yet felt the full impact of his loss. He would heal, but it would take time.

Storm, Chief, and JD had come to the cemetery in Raney's squad car. The foursome piled into the cruiser as Storm cranked the V-8 to life. Raney picked up the microphone and popped the transmit button. "Sixty in service" he said, giving his radio call-sign.

"Roger Sixty," came the tinny reply. "Sixty, call the station on a land line, code two."

"Sixty, Roger."

"Code two?" asked Daro.

"That means get your ass in gear," Raney answered as he sped out of the cemetery to find the nearest telephone.

Raney hung up the receiver, his lips compressed into a thin, bloodless line as he stomped back to the car. Daro was talking to O, Neil in the back seat. Raney got behind the wheel, raising an eyebrow at Potter. Potter could tell it was bad news.

Raney turned half way around, his arm draped over the seat back. "Danny, I've gotta go to Parkland. Can you come with us?"

"Sure. I'm in no hurry. What's it about?"

"Oh - I've gotta meet a couple of detectives. They'll fill me in when we get there." Storm stuffed the gear box into low and headed for the hospital.

Pulling into Parkland Hospital, Raney parked in a police slot and started to get out of the car when Daro stopped him.

"You want me to wait here?"

Raney paused a second. "No. Why don'tcha come on in with us."

The four of them trooped into the emergency room and down the hall toward Dr. Montgomery's office. The thin, bespectacled doctor was waiting at his desk. He got up as they entered his alcove.

"Danny," said the doctor, extending his hand. "Have a seat."

There was something foreboding in the doctor's voice. For the first time Daro became uneasy.

"I'm not just along for the ride, am I doctor?"

Montgomery shook his head. "No, I'm afraid not. We found Sally. There is no way to soften the blow. She's dead."

His emotions already raw, Daro had hardly any reaction, realizing that he had expected this all along. An unaccustomed feeling of helplessness enveloped him.

"How did she die?"

The doctor cleared his throat. "She was strangled."

"I see. Mutilated?"

"No. She was at least spared that."

"Then it's not the same as my Mom?"

The doctor sighed and looked away. "No, but it was bad."

"Raped?"

"Uh - yes, I'm afraid so."

Daro's hand trembled as he brushed it across his two-tone flattop. "Do you know who did it?"

"Not yet."

"I see." Daro got to his feet and turned to Potter. "Take me home, please."

"Sure, Danny," Potter said.

Potter borrowed the keys to Raney's prowl car and Daro walked with his friend to the parking lot. They were half way home before Potter spoke.

"Is there anything I can do, Danny?"

Daro nodded his head. "Yeah. Bring me their balls on a plate. Better yet, bring them to me. There'll be no need for a trial."

Potter whacked the steering wheel with the palm of his left hand. "Damn it! I feel so helpless. Nothing like this ever happened so close to home before. You expect it to happen to others, but not to you or your friends."

Potter pulled up to the front of the mansion and Daro got out. As he closed the car door, Potter asked, "You gonna be okay?"

Without speaking, Daro nodded and walked up the front steps. Potter sighed as his friend's stooped figure entered the front door. An equally helpless JD Potter headed back to Parkland as Daro went to the study to make a telephone call. There was a feeling of deja vu as he once again asked the funeral home to arrange for a burial.

Looking back on it Daro figured he'd been on overload. After Sally's burial he stayed in his room for two days, not even eating. Time meant nothing; neither night nor day. Several people called, but Randall either took care of it or put them off, telling them that Master Danny could not be disturbed. The staff had no idea what was going on. Each in their own way was visibly disturbed.

Three days later at 9:00 AM, Daro came out of it. Suddenly ravenous, he picked up the house phone and buzzed downstairs.

In the kitchen, having coffee with his wife, Randall almost dropped his cup when the sharp, unexpected ring startled them. He picked up the telephone. "Yes, Master Danny."

"Randall," Daro said, his voice sounding tired, "Will you ask Mildred to make my breakfast, please?"

"Right away, sir. The usual?"

"Please."

A smiling Randall hung up, rubbing his hands together. "A good sign, Mildred. A rasher of bacon, eggs, toast, and coffee, if you please. I shall see to the table."

Mildred jumped to the task.

Although unshaven and still in his robe and slippers, Daro looked alert when he entered the dining room, a definite improvement over the past several days. As usual, Randall placed the morning paper by Daro's plate, retiring to the small alcove behind the kitchen door in case he should be needed.

Daro ate slowly and scanned the news. His sister's death was already relegated to page five, his parents long since dropped entirely. He rang the small silver bell by his plate and Randall entered through the swinging doors.

"Yes, Sir?"

"Randall, has Mr. Dinsmoor called?"

"Oh, yes, several times. He has been urging me to ask you to contact him at the earliest possible moment. There are some legal documents that require your attention."

"Will you get him for me please?"

"Of course, sir, right away." Randall went to the hallway and dialed the lawyer's office. When Dinsmoor came on the line, Randall took a telephone to the dining room and plugged it into a jack, handing Daro the receiver.

"Hello, Lionel, I understand you need to see me."

"Yes, by all means," came the aged, almost breathless reply. "How are you?"

Though Dinsmoor was only a voice on the telephone, Daro was reminded of the smell of ancient leather. He shrugged and brushed a big hand over his face. "I'll be okay I guess. I'm still not sure I believe all this has happened."

"I know," said the fragile, white- haired lawyer, "I have a hard time with it, too. May I come out today?"

"Sure, just give me about thirty minutes."

"I will come straight away."

He hung up, leaving the table to clean up before the family lawyer arrived. He asked Randall to deposit Dinsmoor in the study.

Forty five minutes later a freshly showered and shaved Danny Daro descended the stairs to the combination library and study. The wizened old lawyer was already seated in one of two high backed chairs, a battered leather brief case precariously balanced on his bony lap. He started to his feet when Daro entered the room, but he waved him back to his seat.

He smiled. "No need to stand on ceremony with me, Lionel. I'm the new kid on the block, remember."

The old man returned the smile, his face breaking into a sea of dry wrinkles that tugged at his thin cheeks and forehead.

"That was last week," said Dinsmoor. "Today you are Mr. Danny Daro, owner of Daro Industries, Incorporated."

Almost choking on his words Daro said, "Good grief, Mr. Dinsmoor, what am I going to do? I've lost everything."

Dinsmoor's voice was suddenly soft and youthful. "I'm sure it must seem that way, but you must keep the business going. Many families are depending on you."

It was a new thought. "I guess that's true," he said. "What do I do first?"

"Very little, actually. Your father and mother had everything held in what is called an Inter Vivos trust, sometimes called a living will. What that means is that they had already passed all property, including this house, the business, the stock and bond portfolio, all bank accounts, in fact everything, to you and Miss Sally to take effect at the instant of their death. There are tax considerations, of course, but we can take care of that."

Dinsmoor pulled a folder from his briefcase and spread papers out for Daro to see. "The trust documents also have the provision that if either of you - er - that is either you or Miss Sally are not living, the survivor gets everything. Since you are the sole survivor, everything goes to you. I cannot tell you exactly what that amounts to at the moment, but it is in the vicinity of twenty millions."

Daro looked deflated. "I'd give up every dime to have them back, even just Sally."

"I know," Dinsmoor said, softly.

"Lionel, I'm not the businessman my father was. I'm an engineer. Do you know if that bunch that tried to buy Dad out last year is still interested?"

"As a matter of fact, they are. Why, just last week–"

Daro interrupted. "Sell it."

"But, Sir, the offer was only eight million. The business is easily worth ten, possibly twelve."

"Call them and tell them ten million, in cash, by the end of next week or no deal."

Dinsmoor smiled. "Yes, you are your father's son all right. I will tell them and I'm pretty sure they will accept."

Sally's funeral was more deja vu, right down to the crowd which included Potter, Raney, and O'neal. Daro got through it in a sort of fog, once more suppressing his emotions until he could be alone. As best they could, his three rediscovered friends tried to help, but he was convinced that no one had ever felt such pain.

Because of his friendship with one of their own, detectives Killean and Golden held off questioning him and the staff until after the two funerals. Several days later however the pair showed up at the Daro mansion. Randall installed them in the study and called Daro on the house phone.

"Sir, two detectives are here."

"I'll be right there," he said. Putting down his old K&E slide rule, Daro jotted down a final figure and brushed a hand through his closely cropped hair. He washed up in the small lavatory by his office before going downstairs to what, he knew, would be a painful experience.

The detectives and his staff stood when Daro came into the study. As usual, the stocky Jim Killean's face settled into the poker- playing expression he used before every questioning. Charlie Golden, always the good cop, even when he and his partner were not playing 'good cop, bad cop' with some dirtbag, rolled his face into a sympathetic smile.

He nodded at the pair. "Jim. Goldie."

Apparent from their faces, he'd surprised them with remembered names.

Giving each a warm handshake, Daro said, "It's good to see you again."

"Uh - yes, Sir," said Killean. "Us, too."

Daro went to the high backed leather chair behind his desk. "Please everyone, take a seat. I'm sure this isn't a social call."

The detectives and employees settled down as Killean began. "Usually when we question people we do it separately. The reason is that sometimes one or more of the people we're questionin' are suspects, but not this time. We figure that what one of you says might make some of the others remember somethin' too; somethin' they might of forgot."

Daro leaned back and crossed his arms. "We're at your disposal."

"Do you know where your folks were goin'?"

"Yes, they mentioned the Petroleum Club for dinner and afterward they were going to see a movie."

"Where?"

"They didn't say."

"Uh, Master Danny, I heard Miss Sally say something about the Majestic Theater," Randall said.

Killean turned to William. "You're the chauffeur?"

"Yessir." It came out as one word. William chewed his words, his west Texas twang thick and rich.

"Why weren't you drivin'?"

"Well, I was more gardener than driver. Most generally Mr. Daro'd drive his ownself, 'less it was to work, then I mostly would. I'd use the big car when I done that – the Rolls. I'd take him in to the office of a mornin' and fetch him home at night so's he could work in the car goin' both ways. Once in a while Mr. Danny would go with us, but most generally I'd drive Mr. Daro - and Mr. Danny, he'd drive alone so's he could have his car if he needed it."

"But you didn't drive them?"

William shook his head. "Nosir."

"Did they say anything at all that would explain what they were doing in the north part of town?" asked Golden.

Five blank faces looked at each other as heads shook.

Daro was having a hard time with the questioning. His mind kept returning to the first moment he saw his folks in the morgue at Parkland. The scene had seemed unreal. He remembered being unable to connect his mother and father with those devastated tissue masses laid out side by side on cold, stainless steel tables. A sense of deep seated, abiding anger began to replace the hurt.

Daro had no way of knowing that both Killean and Golden sensed it the instant he began to replace grief with fury. He couldn't see, as they could, the blaze which crept into his unusual, amber eyes. When the anger suffused him, his face became almost as surreal as the morgue scene. The two cops gave each other a knowing look.

Golden continued, "Can anyone think of anything else, anything at all?"

"I have a question," said Daro, his voice rough. "Who's in charge of this case?"

"Jim and I are now, and will probably stay on it," answered Golden. "If there's a change, our boss'll make it. His name's Herman Talmadge - Lieutenant Talmadge, that is."

"Should I contact him or you?" Daro asked.

Both detectives bristled. "Well," said Killean, "If you figure we're doin' a bad job, I reckon you'd best call the Lieutenant. You'd might wanta wait a little though 'cause he's in the hospital right now - got hisself hurt the other night chasin' some dirtbag across a roof."

Disgusted with himself, Daro shook his head. "I've done this very badly. I'm not upset with either of you. It's just that I don't know the procedure. I didn't mean to offend you."

Both cops relaxed. "I understand, Mr. Daro," Golden said. "Believe it or not a case like this affects us, too. But I'll promise you this; Jim and I will give it all we've got."

Daro smiled, further softening his words. "Thank you. I can't ask more."

"Anything else?" asked Killean.

There were blank looks all around and then Mildred put up her hand.

Killean raised an eyebrow. "Yes, Ma'am?"

The old cook's eyes were moist. "Miss Sally always had the Lobster Armoricaine when they went to the Petroleum Club," Mildred said, her British accent blurred behind a crumpled white handkerchief. "The dish was her favorite. I never did quite learn to make it properly."

Days dragged into weeks and suddenly two months were gone without so much as a clue. Frustrated, Daro hired a private detective agency to enter the case. But by the middle of January, 1955, all he had to show for the detective agency's efforts was a stack of bills.

He felt like he was wearing a straight jacket. The only relief he got was when he threw himself into his work, and even that ended in late January. The only bright spot was his renewed friendship with Potter, Raney, and O'Neal.

But Dinsmoor was right about selling the business. The group which made the initial eight million offer raised it to ten. After several weeks of wrangling over secondary issues, the final papers were signed. One of several contract stipulations required Daro to finish his present project, a new type of ultra accurate thermostat to be used in a production controller system he had developed and patented in his name.

As it turned out the controller had many industrial applications beyond those he originally envisioned. A few preliminary telephone calls to some business associates indicated that a secondary market was sure to develop. On paper at least, these new markets threatened to outstrip the original business, certainly from the standpoint of income.

"Just what I need," Daro muttered, sarcastically. "More money."

He finished his work in late January and found himself suddenly adrift. For some time he'd been thinking about the mansion, skulking down hallways, seeing shadows and hearing phantom voices, mostly Sally's. He both loved and hated the place.

But what did one man need with such a home? He could afford it, but money wasn't the point. There were too many memories, too many stalking haunts. He had already decided to sell his home and retire the staff, but he had no idea where to go; maybe a nice apartment or possibly a small house in one of the better parts of town. He assembled the staff and broke the news. He was surprised that they were expecting it.

Two days later a nervous Randall came to see him. William, the gardener, and Emma, the maid, wanted to get married, and they wanted to have the wedding in "their home" before they left. He not only gave his permission, but gave the bride away in a private service held in the drawing room. He even arranged for a small party to be held afterward, catered by the House of Kassim. The four servants appreciated the gesture, but Daro had no idea how uncomfortable it made the two couples to be served in the house they had kept and cared for so many years.

In late February, Daro contacted a real estate firm and a realtor came to inspect the house. The agent, Mrs. Phips, was quite impressed, but warned him that large estates did not tend to move as rapidly as smaller places. Mrs. Phips was assured that it did not matter since he was still sorting things out. Besides, he needed time to find a place. The possibility of two commissions did not escape the sharp-minded realtor.

"Mr. Daro, do you know in which part of town you would like to locate?"

"No Ma'am, I haven't really thought about it. Probably the north side, but not too far out."

"I see, must it be in Dallas or would you consider Highland or University Parks?"

He shrugged. "I suppose either would be all right."

Mrs. Phips' smile reminded him of his mother. The memory cut him.

"I do know of a place coming onto the market," she continued. "In fact it hasn't even been advertised yet. It's on Bryn Mawr on the western edge of University Park; a quite large two bedroom stone cottage, but it also has a roomy servants quarters attached to the two car garage. Would you like to see it?"

"Sure." He liked this slightly pudgy, gray haired lady. "I won't need the servant's quarters, but I'd be glad to look."

She went immediately to work, arranging to show him the cottage the following day. While she was at it, she arranged to show another prospect the Daro mansion.

The first property seen is never the right one, but this was an exception to the rule. Daro saw the cottage and fell in love, as did the prospect that saw his house on Turtle Creek. Both made an offer, the offers were accepted, and Daro found himself with sixty days to move.

Sixty days seemed hardly enough. But since the police had nothing to report, time weighed heavy on the young engineer. At least the sudden flurry of activity took his mind off Sally and his folks.

Through the old lawyer, Lionel Dinsmoor, Daro found a firm that took care of estate sales, inventorying and cataloging, appraising, and even arranging for the sale of items. He had already separated out the memorabilia, but he never had much appreciation for his mother's antiques or his father's extensive wine cellar.

Before the inventory started however Daro conspired with Dinsmoor's secretary to discover when the old man was born. Remembering the many times he had heard the old lawyer and his father argue the relative merits of various wines, Daro went to the cellar and found a bottle each of Chateaus Lafite-Rothschild, Margaux, Latour, Haut-Brion, and Mouton-Rothschild, selecting the first five bottles of the Medoc wine classification of 1855. Each bottle carried the date of 1880, the year of Dinsmoor's birth. That evening in the library he presented the dusty bottles to Dinsmoor. The old gentleman broke down.

With a trembling hand, Dinsmoor carefully brushed the dust from the seventy five year old Mouton label and read, 'Premier je suis, Second ne daigne: Mouton suis.'

In a choked voice, Dinsmoor translated, "First am I, Second I will not be: I am Mouton. Oh, Mr. Danny, you could not have selected anything that would have pleased me more. Your father and I –"

Completely overwhelmed, Dinsmoor couldn't continue. Later, Randall carefully wrapped and packed each bottle while William placed the wines in Dinsmoor's car. Daro would have been pleased had he been with the old gentleman as Dinsmoor drove slowly home, crooning over the bottles as though they were beloved children.

• • •

3

The move from the big house to the cottage went without a hitch. A moving company did the heavy hauling and the few things Daro wanted were ferried over in the old 1936 Rolls Royce his mother had loved so much.

He never liked the car. As a boy, he remembered people's stares as they drove by. Their gawking made him feel like a bug under a microscope. He wanted to sell it, but Randall was so horrified by the prospect that Daro decided to keep the old bus until after the move and present it to Randall as a gift. The thought of his butler owning a Rolls amused him as much as he imagined it would dismay Randall.

By the middle of April, almost two weeks before the sixty day deadline, Daro was moved into the cottage. The now married William and Emma lent an air of finality to the change by saying their goodbyes and leaving on a European honeymoon.

Daro had just completed a final tour through the Turtle Creek house when Randall and Mildred approached him.

Sir," said Randall, an obviously nervous Mildred by his side. "Have you a moment?"

"Of course." Daro looked around for somewhere to sit and found none. He smiled. "Looks like we'll have to talk standing up."

With an extended arm and open hand, Randall indicated the stairway. "Why not here, sir?"

He nodded. "Why not, indeed."

The three sat down on the second step, their feet resting on the floor, as Randall began. "Master Danny, Mildred and I began working for your father almost from the moment we arrived in America over thirty years ago, the year he married Madam. We have been ever so happy here. Mildred and I want to stay with you."

Daro was touched. "Thank you, Randall, I appreciate that, but I should be able to fend for myself."

"That is true," Mildred said, her chubby face crinkling into a smile. "But the servant's quarters at the cottage are larger than our present room. It even has a Pullman kitchen. I could fix it up quite nicely at a very modest cost. Besides, sir - and I mean no disrespect - you have not so much as boiled an egg in your entire life."

He laughed, his first since the funerals. "That's a fact, Mildred, but I can learn."

She nodded. "True - you could. But you might also become quite hungry in the process."

He laughed a second time, this time lightly touching Mildred's arm. "I might at that. But you two have worked so many years. Wouldn't you rather do something you've wanted to do and didn't have the time. You could travel, or fish, or whatever you like."

Randall's expression sobered Daro. As though he might cry, the old man's jaw worked several times before he spoke. "What we would like, sir, is to continue to serve you. I hope this is not presumptuous, but when your parents and Miss Sally were killed, you became all that is left of our family. We have no one in the UK, nor do we own property there. We would like nothing better than to stay with you."

A fist sized ball formed in Daro's throat and he couldn't speak for a moment. He finally croaked, "Thank you, Randall. I'd like that."

Daro was right about space. The cottage's rooms were good sized, but putting away all they had brought from the mansion was a tight fit. The three of them were busy for the next week getting things sorted out and put away, after which the Salvation Army was pleased to get the overflow. If there was any doubt as to whether having Randall and Mildred with him was a good idea, such thoughts were quickly dispelled.

The mid-sixties couple seemed happier than they had been in some time. Mildred was the bubbly one, but even some of Randall's reserve seemed to melt once they were away from the big house. When they found themselves in a less formal atmosphere, it was as though the couple gave each other permission to enjoy life. One day Daro even caught the butler softly whistling to himself as he went about his chores.

A few days later a concerned Randall came to him. "Sir, we have a problem."

"And what's that?" asked Daro.

"Always before, when we needed supplies, Mildred made a list and William either took her or went to the grocer's himself. Mildred cannot drive."

"You can, can't you Randall?"

"But of course. I maintained my driving certificate in case William was otherwise occupied and one of the family needed a driver."

Daro tossed him the keys. "Take the Rolls."

Randall's mouth fell open and he sputtered. "But, sir, the Rolls? I could not possibly take the Rolls."

"Why not?"

Randall pulled himself up to his full five-seven. "Sir, the Rolls Royce is the finest automobile in the world. Butlers do not drive them."

For the third time Daro laughed and placed a hand on his butler - turned friend's - shoulder. "Tell you what, Randall. Why don't you just put on some regular street clothes and take Mildred to the grocery store. It'll just be our little secret."

A daily routine soon developed. Daro made a small office out of the guest room and submerged himself in work. In less than two weeks he drafted an idea for a new production controller which did not infringe on the old patents, would operate unattended, and could be monitored and controlled from a remote location using a standard telephone line. The electronic design alone was formidable.

Even though he was under no obligation to contact the new owners of Daro industries, he felt it was the moral thing to do. After the patent was registered, he made an appointment to see the CEO. When the meeting began, and Daro outlined his plans for the new device, tempers flared. He restored calm by making it clear that he was not there to start a competing business, but to make a new arrangement. It was obvious to those at the meeting that the new controller had many more applications than did his older device. It could be produced at lower cost and could be sold for considerably more. All present seemed stunned that he was all but giving the controller to them under the same deal he had made with them in the first place. He instantly went from a pariah to fair-haired boy. What they had missed in the euphoria was that the new proposal negated the original contract provisions which would have allowed the company to deliver ten systems without compensating him for his original patent. Already wealthy, his financial situation would take a quantum leap.

Once the team hammered out the final design, Daro had nothing else to keep his mind busy. Ever since the murders he'd had trouble suppressing his fury. Work had been a temporary antidote, but now that was gone.

At first he made daily contact with his policeman friend, JD Potter. And JD never failed to return his calls - so far only to tell him that there was nothing new. He was not aware of it, but the uniformed divisions were rarely privy to criminal investigations. When he called, Potter contacted either Killean or Golden, then passed the word back to him.

After all these months of nothing, Potter didn't tell his friend that the longer a case wore on the less chance there was of solution. He felt sure that Daro intuitively knew.

Daro had just finished hearing his friend tell him that there was nothing to report when JD asked, "Did you get moved?"

"Yes, finally."

"Your phone number's the same exchange as mine. What's your address?"

"I'm on Bryn Mawr just inside University Park's western boundary."

Potter smiled. "Small world neighbor; I'm on Stanford. If it wasn't for the old railroad bed between us I could walk to your place in less'n five minutes."

"Well – that sounds like a good excuse for a house warming dinner at my house with you, Storm, and Chief," Daro said. As an afterthought, he added, "And everybody's wife, too, of course."

"Chief and I are married," said Potter. "But you know Storm. To quote our redheaded bard, 'He ain't about to buy no cow when milk's free.'"

Daro laughed, his round face breaking into a hundred crinkles. "I had forgotten that. Well, he could bring a friend."

"Look, Danny, I really appreciate the invitation, but getting three cops together that work different shifts is all but impossible."

Daro paused a moment. "I know this is going to sound like begging, because it is. I'm about to go nuts, JD. I really need a friend to talk to right now."

"I could make it Friday night."

"Great. Six thirty?"

"See you Friday."

The week dragged by. Daro was little inclined to work and it occurred to him that life had become doggerel. In fact, now that the plans for his controller were completed, he had no assigned place or time to go to work, nor even a project.

What he really wanted was some good news about the murder investigation. But as time went on even he knew that the prospect of catching the killers was becoming exponentially remote; that the moment, if there ever was one, had slipped away. But it was also clear that he would never rest until the murderers were caught. Such intuitive knowledge caused him much frustration and rage. He had the rest of the week to build quite a head of steam.

At 6:20 PM Friday the doorbell rang at the Bryn Mawr cottage. "Good evening, Sergeant Potter," Randall said as he opened the door. "Please come in."

"Thank you, uh - Randall, isn't it?"

"That is correct, Sergeant Potter," Randall said, bowing slightly. At Daro's insistence, the butler was wearing a plain gray suit instead of his accustomed livery.

Daro strode into the living room, rubbing his hands together, a bright smile on his face. "Thanks for coming, JD."

Potter returned the smile and nodded. "My pleasure."

"Any news?" he asked, turning serious.

Potter shook his head. "No. I checked just before coming over."

Daro frowned and looked down at the floor. "Damn; I don't know what to do."

"I really do understand," Potter said, clapping his taller friend on the shoulder. "There's not much anybody can do right now. Time. It takes time, often lots of it."

Daro indicated that his friend take a seat. "But there's got to be something, JD. I've always heard there's no such thing as a perfect crime."

Potter plopped down on a gold and black couch in front of the small, native rock fireplace and ran his hand over the velvet-like arm rest. To Potter's right, Daro seated himself in one of two matching brown leather chairs placed on either side of the sofa in a semi-circle facing the hearth. Staring down at them from above the mantle was the same painting he'd seen at the big house - too large for the space where it now hung - a portrait of the Daro family; father, mother, son, and daughter. A shiver ran over Potter when he thought about losing an entire family. At least he'd lost his natural parents in an automobile accident and not a terrible murder. Even though he couldn't fully understand, Potter was sure that most of the feelings he'd gone through before his adoption would apply.

Daro clasped his hands in his lap. "What can I do?"

"The hardest job of all, I'm afraid - wait."

He grimaced. "I'm not sure I can do that."

Potter opened his hands toward his friend. "What else can you do, solve it yourself?"

He gave Potter a mirthless grin. "And just how would I go about doing that?"

"I don't know." Potter paused a moment. Jokingly, he said, "Become a cop, maybe?"

Daro sat back in his chair and spread his hands. "Just like that, huh? Become an instant detective and solve the case when the pros can't?"

Potter had been kidding, but something in his head snapped into focus; why shouldn't his friend become a cop? Doing something positive might be just the catharsis Daro needed.

"No, seriously, Danny, what are you gonna to do now that you've sold the business?"

"I don't really know. I haven't given it much thought."

"Well, I've been thinking about it and, although I wasn't serious about solving the murders, you're a good man and I know from personal knowledge that you like to be physical - unless you've changed since high school, that is. You've been sitting around here on your ass with nothing to do but brood over your family and you can't keep running your life that way. You're young - plenty young enough to get on the force - so there's no reason in the world why you shouldn't join up. Why not be a cop? It can really be rewarding. And think of all the money you would make."

Daro chuckled. "Yeah, there is that. But you're talking crazy; I'm an engineer. I don't have a clue about police work."

"So what? Most don't 'till they sign up. We've got lawyers and all sorts of different people. My major at SMU was business administration. I don't think one lone electrical engineer would mess things up too much."

Frowning, Daro said, "But, I don't know anything about the law - and the Army can tell you that I sure don't know anything about firearms. I damn near shot myself in the foot several times."

Potter grinned. "That'd make our range officer, old Gooseneck Brooks, real happy. One of Brooks' favorite sayings is that he'd like for every new cop never to have even seen a weapon much less fired one. He says that it's always harder to un-train a trigger finger with bad habits than it is to teach good habits to someone who's never fired a pistol before."

"Gooseneck?"

"Yeah - motorcycle accident, broke his neck when he rammed his head into a 1922 Chrysler touring car some thirty years ago. He carries his head funny. All he does now is run the pistol range and teach cops how to shoot; I sure wouldn't want to meet him in a dark alley. The guy's a pure menace with a pistol."

"Is he as good as you?" Daro asked.

Potter's eyes narrowed. "What do you mean?"

"Come on, JD. I read about you when you got home from the service; one wounded soldier, armed with an Army 45 taking out a whole squad of Germans? How many guys got a Medal of Honor, much less lived to tell about it?"

Potter looked embarrassed. "I only started with a pistol. Besides, if I hadn't been driving a General nothing would have happened."

"Yeah – well, if a frog had wings he wouldn't bump his butt when he jumped, either," Daro said. "But you *were* with a General and he's the guy who put you in for it."

"That was a long, painful time ago, Danny."

"I'm sure it was, in fact I know it from personal experience."

"Well." Potter said, "Enough of this. We need to talk about you and your future."

Daro clasped his hands together and eyed his friend. "JD, are you really serious about this cop business or are you just playing some kind of game?"

"I'm real serious," he said, shifting to a more comfortable position. "I didn't come over here with that in mind - in fact, hadn't even thought of it before, but it makes sense. The Dallas PD needs good men and I can sure testify about you. You haven't gone soft, have you?"

Daro broke into his wrinkle faced smile. "I don't think so. I keep in pretty good shape; run some, pump a little iron."

"Then you think about it."

Before he could answer, Randall announced dinner.

A little after ten o'clock, Potter left Daro in deep thought, seated on the couch in front of a cold hearth. The servants had cleaned up and retired to their quarters leaving him alone. He picked up a book and ran his hand over the soft, leather binding and held the volume unopened on his lap.

A cop? Not even remotely feasible. He didn't know a thing about the job or about the law for that matter. But what else would he do now? Start a new company? Work for someone else? Thankfully, he wouldn't have to worry about the salary. When was the test going to be given? Two weeks?

Laying aside the book, he went to take his shower before going to bed.

On the day of the exam for police officers, Daro found himself in the basement auditorium of City Hall on Harwood Street. He had no way of knowing that the faded, peeling white paint was unchanged since Potter, Raney, and O'Neal had taken their tests in the same place.

Without counting, there appeared to be almost a hundred people milling around, some already in seats, the others knotting into small groups talking quietly.

Promptly at 9:00 AM the rear doors banged open and in strode three uniformed officers, a pudgy lieutenant followed by two sergeants, one of whom was Sergeant JD Potter. As they mounted the stage, Potter spied his friend and smiled. Daro grinned back.

"Okay, people," said the lieutenant. "Settle down and find a seat."

When order returned the pudgy officer spoke. "I'm Lieutenant Brody and these are Sergeants Thompson and Potter. We're here to administer the test. That'll take about three hours.

"Oh, before I forget, how many of you did NOT bring your high school diploma, birth certificate, and your military discharge papers if you were in the service?"

Seven hands went up.

"Okay. You need to know that you can't be processed any further unless you get those to us." Brody smiled. "That is, if you pass the test. If you don't then it doesn't matter anyway. Now - down to business."

In less than three hours Daro completed the test and strolled out the door, pleased with his score. He had missed two questions. Seated at a desk in a small alcove office across the hall to his right sat a police Captain. Holding a folder, Potter stood facing the desk. Daro turned to walk away.

"Danny!" shouted Potter toward his retreating back. "Come here a minute. There's someone I want you to meet."

The Captain stood, a smile tugging at his weathered face, and extended a graceful hand with long, tapered fingers. The grip was firm from this six - one, 165 pound officer on whose shoulders rested the green patches of the Radio Patrol Division.

"Howdy, son. Why don't you come in and have a seat."

"I don't want to disturb you, Sir," he said.

The Captain waved it off. "Don't think nothin' of it. I'm Captain Louis Spencer."

The trio took seats as Spencer filled his pipe, stoking it to life with a wooden match. He fiddled with the briar longer than necessary, using the time to size Daro up.

Spencer liked what he saw, the black hair with the white streak in front, cut in a military style flattop; the intelligence that peered back at him through amber eyes. It surprised him though how Daro's face could be so wrinkled when he smiled, but so smooth otherwise.

"JD here tells me that you're thinkin' of joinin' the force. You mind tellin' me why?"

"Well, sir, has JD told you anything about me?"

Spencer blew out the match and tossed in the ashtray. "You mean about your folks?"

Daro nodded. "Yes, sir, things like that. I suddenly find that I have nothing to do. I'm an engineer, but I don't want to work for someone else, and the other night JD asked me to consider becoming a police officer. It was certainly a new concept. Later, the more I thought about it, the better I liked the idea."

"How old are you, son?"

"Thirty one."

Spencer nodded. "No problem. Thirty five's the limit. You in good shape - you look to be."

"Yes, sir, pretty good. I still weigh 220, the same as high school."

"How tall?"

"Six feet four."

Spencer swiveled his chair toward Potter. "Damn, JD, don't you know anybody small?"

Potter laughed. "Not hardly, Cap. I liked 'em big when they were protecting my ass on the football field. Of course, Storm's kinda puny by comparison, but his only job was trying to catch my sorry passes."

Spencer chuckled and struck another match touching flame to tobacco. As he coaxed his pipe back to life the aromatic smell of a good blend of perique and Latakia filled the cubicle. "Can you think of any reason that you'd not pass a good physical?"

"No, sir, why?"

"Just checkin'. You heard of the murder board?"

"Oh, yeah," Daro nodded. "JD told me all about it."

"Well, you pretty much just had it right now 'cause I already know more about you than anybody oughta know - JD's seen to that. After your physical you'll meet with a five man panel; me, JD here, Dade Reich, Pokey O'Malley, and Lieutenant Brody. So far as I know there ain't none of 'em that JD hasn't been bendin' their ear about you. A blackball could keep you out, but that's not likely."

Everything was happening too fast. "You mean I'm in?"

The Captain smiled. "If you pass the physical it sort of looks that way."

Two weeks later Daro found himself at the Dallas Police Academy. Like Raney, O'Neil, and Potter before him, he shoveled in information like a fireman stoking a steam engine. The only time he felt odd was when Potter was his teacher. He would have been surprised to learn that Potter felt as strange as he did. Eight weeks later Officer Danny Daro, badge number 1293, took his place alongside his three friends.

Put on the midnight shift from 11:00 PM to 7:00 AM, Daro worked with a new partner every night during his first weeks. It was during the third week that he was paired with Jack Perkins. The meeting was instant dislike.

Perkins always hated it when his regular partner, Jeff Liggett, had even one night off much less a two week vacation. Getting used to working with Jeff was bad enough, but when he worked with other cops, especially a rookie, Perkins felt almost physical discomfort. It wasn't that Perkins was shy, quite the opposite. If nothing else, he was an arrogant, ignorant, loud mouthed, opinionated misanthropist.

But then, Perkins had always been that way, especially around anyone new. As a result, most people didn't like him and he didn't have the mental horsepower to understand why. After all, he didn't kick dogs or beat children, not that the thought hadn't occurred to him. There was just something about Perkins that struck a sour chord with almost everyone, the few exceptions being a certain type of woman. Had he been the least bit sensitive, even Perkins could've seen that he was about as smooth as steel wool.

On several occasions, Perkins had tried being one of the guys, but it never worked out, the proof of which was contained in the latest incident in the recreation room. Perkins was kibitzing a lively domino game called Moon when Sandy Thompson, a small, red headed motorcycle officer, walked by on the way to his locker.

"Hey, Sandy," Perkins shouted, his coarse voice carrying even into the showers, "I hear you got married last week?"

Thompson's face flushed as he gave Perkins a shy smile. "That's right, Jack, sure did."

Perkins winked at the Moon players, his big smile showing large, slightly yellow teeth. "Tell us all about your weddin' night."

Thompson's face got even redder. "That's a little personal don't you think?"

Perkins lightly punched Thompson on the shoulder. "Nah, little buddy, we're just curious. Hell, even I was married once. I don't mind tellin' you that I tapped that sweet thing six times on our weddin' night. How about you?"

Thompson's face looked like a bull fighter's cape, but there was a twinkle in his eye as he shook his head. "Just one time for me, Jack. But you gotta understand - my wife wasn't used to it."

It was Perkins turn to flush and sputter as Thompson walked away amid a growing chorus of guffaws.

Although Daro had not met Jack Perkins, he was pointed out to him during his first week of duty. The officer doing the pointing referred to Perkins as "Ape" prompted by his body hair, so thick that it looked like a black pelt. Daro looked the stocky officer over, dismissing the square jawed, 205 pound, five eleven Perkins as someone to distrust, a rare sensation for him to snap-judge someone so quickly.

When their names were called Daro tried to catch Perkin's eye, but Perkins refused to look his way. As soon as their detail was dismissed, Perkins was out the door and on his way to the police garage to pick up the car, leaving Daro to bring up the rear.

Perkins was already with the senior partner from the previous detail when Daro arrived. He caught part of the conversation as he listened to Perkins question the previous shift's officers.

While waiting to introduce himself, Daro scanned the line of squad cars lined up at the curb on Canton Street. Beside each vehicle, small knots of four harness bulls - a term he had learned meant uniformed officers - stood quietly talking as they exchanged information about activity in their district. Beside each group of four, the squad car waited, gassed and ready to go in case of an emergency. Half of the squads came in at a time, thirty minutes apart, so that the streets would always have cops available to take calls.

When Perkins finished with the previous squad he stuck out his hand. "My name's Daro."

Perkins looked at the offered hand as though it was unclean. "Yeah, I know who ya are. I've seen your kind before, some rich asshole that thinks he can come in here and save the world."

Perkins switched his eyes up to Daro's face, the five inch height discrepancy more obvious when standing this close. He began to poke Daro's chest to punctuate each word. "Well let me tell you somethin', mister, I – "

Daro grabbed his partner's finger and bent it away. Perkins winced and stepped back, scowling. "You son of a bitch, you like to of broke my finger."

Daro's lips compressed into a thin line as he managed a tight smile. "Tell you what, Perkins. You ever touch me or cuss me again I'll kick so much shit out of you Captain Spencer can send you home in a match box."

Perkins' face went from scowl to hate. "Why you pip squeak, son-of-a-bitching, rookie, I'll – "

Perkins never knew what hit him. Daro's right fist crashed into Perkins' chin, his full 220 pounds behind the blow. The first thing to hit the pavement was Perkins backside, followed shortly by the back of his head. Several cops turned toward the commotion and two of them ran over when they saw Jack on the pavement.

"What the hell happened?" asked one of the officers.

Daro didn't know the cop who asked the question. He opened his mouth to answer just as Perkins groaned, shook his head, and sat up rubbing his jaw.

"You okay, Jack?" asked another cop.

It took a few moments for Perkins' eyes to focus. "Yeah, Tim, I think so." Perkins ran his hand over his head and looked at his bloody palm in astonishment.

"Damn, Jack, that looks bad," said the cop as he examined Perkins' scalp. "There's a deep gash back here. You gotta see the doc."

Sergeant Wilcox sauntered over, took a look, and ordered Perkins into his car. A quick crank of the V8 and Wilcox took off for Parkland Hospital leaving Daro not knowing what to do. It didn't dawn on him until that moment that he was without doubt in deep trouble.

"Hey, Daro!" yelled Sergeant Bruno.

He turned. "Yes, Sir."

"You go with Baker," the sergeant said, indicating a car with only one officer in it. "He was gonna be twenty two, car two, but we'll yank him off that district and put him on twenty one instead. You'll be his partner this shift."

Daro touched the bill of his cap with one finger. "Sure, Sarge. Thanks."

As he walked past, Sergeant Bruno asked, "What happened?"

Daro shrugged. “Beats the hell out of me, Sergeant. Perkins must have stumbled.”

Bruno laughed. “Yeah, right. I saw him do it.”

Daro introduced himself to his new partner and they headed out toward district twenty one.

Daro and Baker answered several minor calls and were cruising out Maple Street when a green, 53 Mercury two door slid up beside them at the stoplight at Knight Street. Daro was closing out their last call in the book and Baker was watching for the light to turn when they heard a honk.

In the Merc sat two rather pretty women in their mid thirties, both grinning at the officers. The driver of the Mercury motioned for Baker to turn into the parking lot of the drive-in grocery on the corner. As requested, Baker swung in and stopped, followed by the two girls. The driver got out and came up to Baker’s side of the cruiser.

“Hey, Baker, how ya been?” asked the dark haired driver, parking her ample bosom on the rolled down glass.

Daro caught an almost overpowering whiff of gardenia perfume as the woman stuck her head into the car and gave his partner a wet, probing kiss.

“Real good, Estelle,” answered Baker, after the kiss ended. “Especially now that you’re back. What’s the matter with Lucy, she gone shy on us?”

Estelle laughed. “Shit, her shy? You gotta be kiddin’. We just didn’t recognize your compadre here,” said Estelle, looking Daro over.

“Well, ‘scuse the hell out of me,” Baker said. “This is my partner for the night, Danny Daro. He’s a rookie, so you girls be gentle with him. He don’t know about you two.”

“No time like the present I always say. You game?”

Baker laughed. “You ever see me when I wasn’t?”

“That’s my boy,” Estelle said. “Follow me.”

Estelle turned and trotted back to the Mercury, her overripe behind bouncing from side to side. Cramming the Merc into gear she sped down Maple, hooked a right on Oak Lawn, and headed toward the warehouse district off Industrial Boulevard. Turning into one of the back streets she pulled into a cul-de-sac behind a darkened building. It was obvious she had been there before, apparently with Baker since he seemed to know the way.

The instant Estelle parked, the passenger door opened and the blonde came strutting back to the squad car at the same time Baker hurried toward the Mercury. Blondie plopped her butt in the back seat behind Daro, waited a moment, and said, "Well?"

Somewhat shocked, he turned and asked, "Well, what?"

"Are you gonna get your ass back here, or not?" she said, pointing at the seat beside her.

He was glad it was dark and she couldn't see his face redden. "I don't know what you're talking about, Ma'am."

"You really are fresh meat, aren't you, Hoss?"

"I'm new on the force, if that's what you mean," Daro said.

There was just enough light to see two outlines in the car parked ahead of them. As if by their own will, clothes seemed to be flying off both Estelle and Baker as they stripped for action.

Blondie sighed. "Look, we don't have a hell of a lot of time here and I'm horny. All I'm lookin' to do is get laid. If you think you can handle that then get your butt back here."

More than shocked he turned toward her even further. "Lady, I don't even know you."

"Well, we can fix that," said the blonde. "My name's Lucy and I like gettin' laid. Besides, you look like a clean cut guy. We could have some fun."

He couldn't believe his eyes or ears. Parked in front of them, the Mercury began rocking furiously, its springs squeaking in loud protest.

"Whoa, lady," Daro said. "You've got the wrong boy. I'm sure you're real nice, but I'm not interested in a quick grope in the back seat of a squad car."

He could barely see Lucy shrug in the dim light. "Have it your way," she said, taking out a cigarette and lighting up. After several deep drags, she laughed. "I usually have one of these after, not instead of."

Loosening up a little, he chuckled with her.

"At least you've got a sense of humor," Lucy said. "Lotsa guys don't, 'specially some cops I know. What's your name, Hon?"

"Danny. Danny Daro."

With a longing look at the rocking car in front of them, Lucy sighed again. "Well, Danny, I guess you know that Estelle's gonna be one up on me 'cause a you and I probably won't hear the end of it for a week."

"You could always lie," he suggested.

Lucy threw her head back and laughed again. "I like you, Hoss. Are you real sure you don't wanta come back here with me? I'll haul your ashes real good."

He shook his head. "Thanks, but I better pass."

They were quiet for a moment while Lucy finished her cigarette. Finally, Daro's curiosity got the better of him. "May I ask you something?"

"Sure, babe, ask away."

"Why do you do this?"

"You know, everybody asks that. My old man has lots a money, but he's over seventy and he can't get it up no more. Now, me," Lucy said, leaning back and exposing her breasts for him to get a better look, "I'm still young 'n healthy and I really like blockin' some good ole boy's hat."

In spite of himself, Daro sneaked a peek at the offered treasures. "But why cops?"

"Another easy one. Most cops are clean and they're safe. Hell, most of 'em are married so they ain't gonna fall in love and complicate my life. Ya see, I ain't looking for a permanent man, just the loan of one for a few minutes. Besides, I've not found any one man that could keep me happy more'n a few days at a time, but I figure the whole police department oughta be able to cut it - no pun intended."

Daro smiled and nodded. "I guess there's some perverse logic in there somewhere, but at the moment it escapes me."

Lucy tossed her cigarette out the window and smiled. "Well, I don't know how you are in the back seat of a squad car, but you sure talk pretty."

Baker's tryst with Estelle lasted some ten minutes before the beefy cop got out of the Mercury and began to tuck in his shirt and put on his Sam Browne belt. He strolled down the alley to relieve himself behind a large wooden crate before heading back to the cruiser.

"Well, Danny, it's time to go." Lucy said, starting to open her door. "Would ya do me one favor?"

Only a little hesitant, he said, "Sure. What?"

"Lean your head back here."

When he did, Lucy planted a warm, passionate kiss, probing his mouth with her tongue. She laughed when she pulled away and saw the confusion on his face.

"No big deal, Baby. Just a sample of what might of been," she said. "Who knows, one a these days we might just meet again."

When Lucy got out of the car and walked seductively away, he noticed that in addition to nice breasts, Lucy was built a lot better than Estelle. He remembered how long it had been since he'd been with a woman and felt himself stir. Maybe he had passed up a great opportunity. But on the other hand, maybe he'd missed a trip to the doctor's office for a series of shots.

"How about it, Partner?" Baker asked, getting into the car. "You ready to get back to work?"

"Sure."

Baker picked up the radio mike and popped the transmit button. "Dispatch, have twenty two meet twenty one at Lemmon and Oak Lawn."

"Roger twenty one," came back the reply.

"What's that all about?" Daro asked.

Baker grinned at his partner. "Estelle and Lucy'll keep our appointment with twenty two for us. That's the way it works, Partner, share and share alike."

Baker started the car, blew a kiss to the two girls, and waved them on their way. Before their shift was over Daro heard a similar message put out to bordering districts of twenty three and sixty three. If his math was correct, Estelle made it four times to Lucy's three.

Daro hoped he hadn't ruined Lucy's evening.

• • •

4

No one could figure out how Herman Talmadge even got on the police force, much less how he made Lieutenant in charge of Homicide. Universally disliked by both peers and citizens with whom he came in contact, Herman - or Herm as he liked to be called - had the tact of a battleship, the sensitivity of Adolph Hitler, and a brain about the size of a desiccated pea. Even after two failed marriages, he could not understand why people reacted toward him as they did, especially women. Almost without exception, ladies rejected him in utter loathing. After many rebuffs, he consulted his mirror trying to see what others saw. He could find nothing wrong. Of such monumental pride, Herm was unaware that he was seeing himself through a rose colored ego.

Still, by some quirk of a tiny, but unfathomable mind, Herm had steadily made his way through the ranks and various departments, biting and stabbing backs with unbridled glee until he got to be Chief of Section. His astonishing success could be attributed to his two talents, an intuitive knack for taking tests, and the ability to look at a set of rumpled bed sheets and tell you whether it was done for love or money. In short, when it came to solving puzzles, Herm was a real whiz.

In spite of his shortcomings, Herm was a virtual savant when it came to solving murders. For this reason only, he was tolerated. But test taking abilities aside, everyone but Herm already knew that he had attained as much rank on the police department as he ever would, particularly since all higher positions required at least a modicum of tact and diplomacy. It was common knowledge that he had neither.

But he didn't much care. He was where he could "feel the pulse" of his men and his Section. Besides, he could be a plague on every aspect of his subordinate's lives so much more effectively at the working level than he could at a higher grade. Within the circle of almost all who knew him the words "Herm" and "asshole" had become synonymous.

Very few things bothered him, nothing that is except his left hand which was missing the outside two fingers. After the accident one of his men dubbed him "chicken foot", so reminded was he of that particular appendage on a hen. Not that Herm was chicken - far from it. Talmadge did not have that kind of sense. As a matter of fact the old saw about fools rushing in where angels fear to tread could have been coined with him in mind. Already he had donated his two missing fingers by way of proof, having left them beneath a piece of angle iron when he vaulted a brick wall between two adjoining roofs. As he went over the wall, his fingers stayed behind, jammed between metal and wall, a grim testimony to the lengths he would go in the single-minded pursuit of his job. Needless to say the two dirtbags he was chasing got away.

Herm seldom allowed anyone to see the angry looking injury, jagged flesh cut diagonally to the left of his three good fingers and angling back almost to his wrist. He held himself in such a way that it was natural to have his hand in his pocket, under his other hand, or in some way hidden from view. In fact, he didn't even realize that it bothered him, the thought never penetrating to that secret, almost sterile place where, in most people, human thought processes grind away until conscious concepts surface. In all cases but making money and solving murders, Herm's mind didn't grind.

It was early August and he was already in his office, all 240 pounds of solid bone and flab weighing heavily on his small-boned, five-ten frame. Rolls of fat kept trying to ooze through the rungs of his swivel chair as he reviewed for the third time the night's arrest reports.

Whether residue or gearing up for another scorcher, Commerce Street smelled of warm, acrid asphalt as Daro trotted across and climbed the stairs two at a time to the Homicide Division. It was already hot inside the decrepit red brick building. To make matters worse there was no air conditioning.

At the top of the stairs Daro removed his cap and brushed a large hand over his flattop as he turned down the hall toward the detective offices. His steps took him directly past Lieutenant Talmadge's door.

"Hey, you!" yelled Talmadge, "Where the hell do ya think you're goin'?

The uniformed Daro stopped, his amber eyes narrowing as he stepped into the Lieutenant's office. "You talking to me?"

"Damn right, two-tone," the Lieutenant said, apparently referring to Daro's hair. "You can't just waltz your ass in here off the street and walk down my hall. Who the hell do you think you are?"

Daro was repulsed by the balding, mousy brown haired officer, dressed in a rumpled, too-tight, seersucker suit. Even worse was the man's mouth, an effeminate circle of thick pouting flesh, puckered as though in permanent disapproval. His close-set eyes were almost colorless, sunken deep in their sockets, reminding Daro of a fat snake peering from inside a culvert. To heighten the illusion, Herm's long, narrow tongue darted out to wet his lips.

"May I ask who you are, sir?" Daro said.

Herm waved a pudgy arm in an expansive gesture. "I'm Lieutenant Herman Talmadge and I run this here outfit, Officer, now you answer my question."

"Sorry, Lieutenant, I'm Danny Daro. I just came up here to see how Goldie and Killean were doing on a murder case."

"What the hell business is it of yours?"

Daro reddened. "My family was killed last October."

Herm's brow wrinkled in thought. "Oh, yeah - Daro - I didn't know you was a cop. Anyhow, they can't tell you nothin' and I don't let nobody roam around disturbin' my men, see."

"If it's all the same to you I'd just as soon hear it from them."

"Well, it's not all the same to me. I want your ass out of my shop, see. My men got better things to do than answer some pisswilly's questions."

"Sir, I don't know what your problem is, but until the murderers of my family are caught I intend to keep in touch with the detectives assigned to the case. Now, you may be able to get me fired, but that won't stop me. Maybe you forgot, but in addition to being a rookie cop, I'm also the victim of a crime."

Herm struggled out of his chair, stretching up to his full five-ten. "Now I'll tell you something, Rookie, you haul your ass outa here right now or you'll be in your detail commander's office before a cat can lick its ass, see."

Daro nodded and gave Herm a thin-lipped smile. "Give it your best shot, Lieutenant." Daro turned on his heel and stomped off down the hall. He was hardly out of sight before Herm was on the phone.

The hallway ended at a large open room cluttered with desks. Golden and Killean sat facing each other, their desks efficiently placed back to back. Goldie looked up as Daro came in, his face blank until he recognized Daro. He smiled and stood. "Well I'll be damned. When did you join up?"

Daro stuck out his hand. "Hi, Goldie. Just a couple of months ago. You're looking at a real fresh rookie."

Killean, who had been reviewing a file, also stood and shook hands. "Damn, Mr. Daro," he said, "Why the hell did you wanta do somethin' like that - a man with all your money?"

He laughed. "I'm not Mr. Daro any more, just one of the troops. Besides, money has nothing to do with it."

They took seats as he told them what he had been up to since they last had a face-to-face. He also asked about Lt. Talmadge.

Killean snorted and shook his head. "He may be our boss, but he's still dumber than a sled load of shit."

"How do you put up with it?" asked Daro.

"We mostly just ignore him," continued Killean. "He rides everybody's ass somethin' fierce. The best thing to do is just stay the hell outa his way."

"Now you tell me," Daro said. He explained what had happened in Herm's office.

"Who's your detail Captain?" asked Golden.

"Spencer."

"You pretty tight with him?"

Daro shrugged. "Not really. I hardly know him. Potter's a good friend, though. He talked to the Captain about me and the Captain went to bat for me with the murder board."

Golden tapped a Lucky Strike against his thumbnail and lit it with a Zippo. Leaning back on the rear chair legs he blew a plume of smoke into the air and said, "You ought to be okay. Spencer doesn't like the asshole any more'n we do."

"I sure hope you're right. Anyhow, I hoped that now I'm a cop you could tell me more about my folks and sister."

The two detectives looked at each other, then nodded.

"Yeah, members of the club get more advantages than other people," said Golden. "You've got to promise us something though."

"Anything."

"Don't think you're gonna come in here like gang busters and try to solve the case. We don't need you muckin' around messing things up for us, especially if Talmadge found out. Besides, most cops wouldn't even think of you as a harness bull yet, much less a detective."

Daro leaned back in his chair. "No sweat. I'll admit the thought crossed my mind, but I know there's no way I could do it. But since I sold the business, and Potter started questioning me about what I was going to do, it did get me to thinking. JD's the one who got me pointed toward being a cop, and all of a sudden I liked the idea. Anyhow, you have my promise."

"Okay," continued Golden, "We got six good fingerprints off the car and three other partials. Two of the prints were the same. That means we've got five good prints that may be from different people or they could all be from the same two or three. There's no way of telling."

Daro frowned. "But if they are different aren't they from different people?"

"People have ten fingers, dumbass," chimed in Killean. "They could all be from the same guy."

Daro smiled. Already the Mr. Daro was behind them. "Some detective I'd make, huh?" he said.

Golden shrugged. "It takes time."

Daro ran his hand through his hair, unaware that Lieutenant Talmadge had unknowingly already given him his nickname. "I don't understand. If you have the prints, isn't it likely that they're on file someplace?"

"Sure," said Killean. "But do you have any idea how many sets of fingerprints are on file in this country? There's millions. But you gotta multiply that by ten."

Golden chuckled. "Yeah, except for guys like Chicken Foot."

Killean joined the laugh. They explained the name to Daro.

"There's only one place that keeps a print file for single fingerprints," continued Golden. "That's the FBI. Even then it's only for the most wanted people, not just the top ten, but not for more than maybe the top one or two percent.

"What we've done is scan the prints of all likely suspects that have been arrested since all this started. Not everyone, just those that figure to be about the right age and all. If you remember from the Academy, fingerprints are classed by patterns; you know, loops and whirls and the like."

Golden paused, thinking, "So if we get one that's the right type we have Jimmy Booker look at it. Booker's the best. Went through the FBI training for fingerprint analysis; you don't get nothin' past The Book."

Daro shook his head. "You'd think something would have turned up by now."

"Yeah," nodded Golden. "But it hasn't. One of these days we'll catch a break 'cause these dirtbags aren't that smart. They'll slip up, they almost always do. And when they do we'll be on 'em like a duck on a June bug. Honest, Daro, we haven't been sitting on our ass on this one. But sometimes you've just gotta wait."

Daro sighed. "Yeah - anything else?"

It was Killean's turn. "Yep. Not much, but some. We got tire tracks, chain impressions, blood types, footprints, even a hubcap we think's off the car. It's a 54 Ford. I've about wore my damn neck out looking at cars to see if they was missin' one. Matter of fact we think there might'a been two cars instead of just the one. No idea what the second one might be."

"How do you know the hubcap is from the right car?"

Golden shook his head. "We don't, but when your folks turned down that dirt road, the Ford - at least we think it was the car with the murderers in it - had to brake hard and was still braking when they turned off the pavement. As soon as they were off the road the right front tire hit a big rock then rolled through a small mud puddle and left a track."

Golden pulled a photograph from the file and handed it to Daro. "This is a picture of it. The hubcap was in the right place for it to have come off at that time. There was some more tracks identical to that one at the murder scene. We're as sure as we can be without bein' there when it happened."

"And another thing," said Killean, "From all the glass and stuff on the ground we're pretty sure there was a lot of damage to the front end of the dirtbag's car. What we ain't found is where they got it fixed – assumin' they took it to a commercial shop. Course they could'a fixed it their ownselves or even taken it outa town someplace. We've even been takin' a look at car dealerships to see if they been sellin' anybody parts they'd need."

Daro's face was pale as he handed the photo back. Although months had passed the memories came flooding back. He shook his head and lowered his eyes to the floor. In a few moments he looked up. "I want to thank you guys. You didn't have to tell me all this, but I sure appreciate it."

"Hey," said Killean, "No sweat. Brother officer and all that. You just be sure you remember not to go runnin' off chasin' the bad guys. You're part of the posse, but you ain't the Sheriff, okay?"

Daro smiled and stood up to leave. "Okay, Sheriff, I will honor my promise. Scouts honor."

The two detectives returned to their work as Daro clumped off down the hall. Herm didn't even look up when he passed his door.

Captain Spencer was still at his desk when Daro walked back across Commerce Street and strode down the ramp into the basement of City Hall. He turned left through the double doors toward the jail and walked past the Desk Sergeant's office on the right. As he glanced in, two Radio Patrol officers were telling Sergeant Olney about their prisoner - why he was under arrest and why they should be allowed to take him upstairs for booking. Olney, a tall cadaver of a man, was nodding his head in time to the officer's voice, his brow furrowed as though deep in thought.

"Okay, take him up," Olney said, thrusting a thumb toward the elevator which hauled prisoners to the lockup several floors above.

A trustee held open the door to the ancient elevator as the officers helped the drunk inside and propped him against the wall to keep him from falling. The trustee closed the accordion like cage across the front and Daro heard the whine of the lift motor as he rounded the corner to the right and walked down the hallway to the Detail Captain's office.

Spencer looked up when Daro tapped a knuckle on the door jamb. The Captain took off his reading glasses, tossed them on the desk, and leaned back in his chair, rubbing his face with a tanned hand.

"Shit fire, son," Spencer said, his voice low and level. "Why didn't you just take a baseball bat and whack a hornet's nest?"

"Cap, I'm sorry if I've caused you any grief, but Talmadge really pissed me off telling me that I couldn't talk to Goldie and Killean."

"I understand that, son, but you've gotta simmer down here. If I was gonna give the world an enema I'd insert it in that particular gentleman, but that's beside the point. He's a Lieutenant in the Dallas Police Department. Rookies are not generally encouraged to give Lieutenants a ration of shit."

Daro's face was already red. Although his time on the force was short he really loved the job. He could almost see the printing on his walking papers. He wondered how long it would take to clean out his locker.

"What happens now, Cap?"

"I told Chicken Foot that I'd eat your ass out, so consider it done."

Daro didn't realize that he'd been holding his breath. He let it out in a whoosh. "You mean I'm not fired?"

Spencer frowned. "Hell no, boy. If I fired everybody that got cross-ways with Chicken Foot there wouldn't be nobody left to drive the cars.

Now, why don't you get outa here so's I can get my work done and go home to get some sleep before some other uniformed clown comes up with a new way to make my life miserable?"

Daro's face broke into a wrinkled smile. "Thanks, Cap. I really appreciate it."

"Think nothing of it, Two-Tone," he said with a wave.

Daro was half way to the locker room before it dawned on him what the Captain had said. Talmadge had used the term and the Lieutenant must have told Captain Spencer. He would have been happier with a different nickname, certainly one with more panache.

Several months later Daro learned that the old axiom about police work being hours of boredom interspersed with a few seconds of excitement was true. His partner for the night was Lyle Lesher, a five-nine, 175 pound, sandy haired cop of over fifteen years service. It was quiet for a Sunday midnight shift. He and Lesher had cruised their Oak Cliff district for over two hours when the radio came to life.

"Eighty one, family disturbance in progress, Ninth and Vernon. Code two."

Riding shotgun, Daro grabbed the mike. "Eighty one, Roger." He had been on the department long enough to know that a code two, red light run could spell lots of trouble. In theory there was only one call worse, a code three which included siren. There was, in fact, another category - Officer Needs Help. Simply put it meant - do what you have to do to get there yesterday. Or as one of his first training officers had described it, "That means balls to the wall, Rookie."

"Oh, shit," Lesher said as he pulled the emergency lights. "I hate them damn calls. You never know if it's a shouting match or they're swapping artillery rounds. You be ready for anything, Partner."

Daro felt his heart rate go up and he automatically checked his holster, testing the grip on his new Smith & Wesson, 357 magnum revolver. He wrote the address on his call sheet as Lesher goosed the prowl car and careened down Jefferson Street, red lights flashing.

In less than two minutes they arrived to find a bathrobe clad, middle aged woman standing in her yard waving at them with a white handkerchief. Lesher pulled to the curb and stopped. Both cops warily got out of the car.

"What's the problem, Ma'am?" asked Lesher.

The lady was wringing her hands. "I'm not sure, officer. It's quiet over there now, but there was a terrible fight next door a little earlier. I thought I ought to call you. The kids are okay; I've got 'em at my house. Irene brought 'em over before the screamin' started."

"Irene?" asked Lesher.

The lady nodded toward the house next to hers. "Irene Potty. She's the lady I was talking about."

"Were any shots fired or anything?"

Her eyes widened. "Goodness, no. Just another fight, I guess. But this one seemed worse than before. There were several men over there earlier. I don't know for sure, but I think they left. I saw a pick-up leave just after all the screamin' stopped. Sometime after that there was just this sort of whacking sound. I didn't know what to make of it - but I thought I ought to call."

A lone light shone in the back of the house that the lady pointed toward.

"May I have your name, Ma'am?" Daro asked.

Her eyes widened even more. "Do I have to give it?"

He smiled. "No Ma'am. I understand."

"Let's go, Partner," Lesher said.

Daro felt nervous sweat pop out on his back and soak through his shirt as they climbed the stairs onto the porch. Even though the description of the trouble didn't sound too bad they still had no idea what they might face. Both men automatically unsnapped the black leather restraining strap which looped over the hammer of their revolvers.

With Daro to the right of the door and his partner to the left, Lesher tapped a knuckle against the glass pane.

They waited.

In what seemed like an eternity a light came on in the front room, followed by the porch light. Both cops tensed as the curtain pulled to the side and an eye peered out. The curtain fell back in place, a key rattled in the lock, and the door swung open.

She was tiny - a blonde of about five feet, maybe eighty five pounds, and she had a bloody baseball bat trailing from her right hand.

"Come on in officers. Ya'll oughta have this address memorized by now," she said, her hill country accent evident.

She turned away from the door still dragging the bat, the large end leaving a trail of what appeared to be blood across a small, faded gray carpet in the center of the living room.

Lesher looked at Daro and shrugged. They stepped inside.

"Ma'am," started Lesher, "We got a call about a fight goin' on over here - good lord, what happened to you?"

The woman had turned giving them a look at her face. Her right eye was swelled shut, the left side of her face bruised, and her lip was split in two places, one so badly that it looked like a tooth had punched through.

As she collapsed into an overstuffed chair the bat handle dropped to the bare floor, like a drum roll tapping out several rapid staccato beats before bouncing to a stop. "My husband beat me up again, but he'll not do it no more."

Lesher gave Daro a funny look. "Whatdaya mean, Ma'am?"

She tried to smile, but the pain must have stopped her as a cut on her lip popped open again. "Can I just tell you what happened?"

"Yes, Ma'am," Daro said, "May I have your name first?"

"Sure. It's Potty. Irene Potty."

He wrote it on his call sheet as Lesher nodded for her to continue.

"Ralph come home drunk again last night. It happens ever Saturday night, sometimes durin' the week. Like always he starts cussin' me. He don't always whip on me, but as often as not he does. This was one of them times."

"Where is Mr. Potty, Ma'am?" asked Lesher.

She pointed toward the back of the house. "Back in the bedroom."

"Would you mind calling him out here?" Lesher asked.

The pain didn't stop her laugh this time. "Wouldn't do no good. He's dead."

Both cops paled and Lesher said, "Check it out Partner."

Daro went down a short hall to an open door. The bed was on the left as he stepped into the room. Lying on the bed was what must have once been Ralph Potty. Daro might as well have been looking at a meat display case in a butcher's shop. Potty had been beaten into a pulpy mess. He could barely recognize the remains as human.

Almost sick, Daro stumbled back to the front room. "You better have a look, partner."

Lesher was gone only a minute. "Daro, get on the horn and get the coroner and a detective squad out here." Lesher turned back to Irene Potty as Daro went out to the car radio.

"What happened, Ma'am?"

Irene shrugged and picked up an eight by ten photograph from the table by her chair. It showed a couple in wedding dress, a diminutive blonde, the top of her head barely coming up to the chest of a dark haired, not particularly handsome, but very big man. The man appeared to be at least six-five or more and go almost three hundred pounds. With her one good eye Irene Potty stared at the picture for a moment then looked up at Lesher.

"I've been told I was pretty when I was younger. And I'm only thirty five now. Lookin' at me that's hard to believe, I know. But takin' as many whippin's as I have, a girl ain't likely to keep her looks. It's been hard, what with the kids and all. We've got three. I sent 'em over to Mrs. Neff next door."

Daro came back inside. "On the way, partner." He took a seat on the couch to Irene Potty's left and picked up the call sheet.

Lesher nodded and grunted. "Go on, Miz Potty."

She sighed. "Like I said, Ralph come home drunk. But this time he had two friends with him. I had a case of beer all cold in the icebox like I was told, and they started drinkin' some more. I was afraid there might be trouble so I took the kids next door to Mrs. Neff's and went on to bed and went to sleep. The next thing I know, Ralph wakes me up. Them two guys is with him."

Daro entered Mrs. Neff's name on his call sheet as Irene Potty choked up, tears squeezing from both her good and her swelled eye.

"Take your time, Ma'am," said Lesher.

She shook her head. "I don't know if I can tell this. It's so bad I don't know if I can."

Mrs. Potty took a handkerchief from the pocket of her white, blood -spattered, terrycloth robe and began to worry it between folded hands. When she spoke again her voice was as soft as angel's hair.

"Ralph had a bet with his friends. He'd bet 'em that I was better in bed than their women, and that he aimed to prove it. They was all real drunk."

Irene looked first at Lesher, then at Daro. Both men were too stunned to speak. In a moment she lowered her head and continued. "I thought it was some sort of a sick joke. There ain't no man, no matter how sorry, that'd let his friends have his wife on a bet. But I was wrong. Before I knew what hit me, Ralph and one of his friends held me while the other'n got on. After he got done, the other'n had me too. Ralph didn't take a turn. I got most of this," Irene said, indicating her beaten face, "while I was trying to fight 'em off. I'm so ashamed I could die."

Daro was particularly shocked. The images of his mother and sister came pouring back into his mind. Neither man spoke as Irene Potty silently cried, her small, childlike body shaking in the large chair. She looked like a tiny stuffed animal a child might cherish.

"Miz Potty, where are these men now?" asked Lesher.

She shook her head. "I dunno - went home I reckon."

"Can you identify them if you see them again?"

For the first time her spine stiffened and her voice was strong. "Oh, yes, I can recognize 'em. If it takes a thousand years, I'll know 'em. Ralph called one of 'em Earl and the other'n Jeeter."

Lesher shook his head. "Can you tell us what happened after they – they, uh ?"

Mrs. Potty cleared her throat and nodded. Her voice was again soft, but understandable. "They come in the livin' room here and had another beer, laughin' and talkin' 'bout me like I wasn't even human, much less in the same house. They each pulled ten dollars outa their pocket and give it to Ralph. One of 'em - I think it was Jeeter - laughed real big and said that he might like to prove it again some time. My lovin' husband just laughed right along with him. I knew right then that he'd sold me for money. I've took a lot, but that was too much no matter what was gonna happen to me and the kids."

Mrs. Potty picked up the baseball bat and both cops stiffened.

"I waited for Ralph to go to bed," she continued. "We've been in different beds for a long time, but he come in to me whenever he was of a mind to. After I heard him snorin' I got my son's bat here and the first place I hit Ralph was right between the eyes, you know - to make sure he stayed out. Then I beat him till I got tired.

"I come in the front room here and rested awhile. But the more I thought about it, the madder I got, so I went back and beat him some more. I ain't a bit sorry the bastard's dead."

"Neither am I," muttered Lesher. Daro was thinking the same thing as his rage returned. He was surprised at its strength and speed.

"Will I have to go to jail?" she asked.

"Yes, Ma'am, I think you probably will, but we need for you to go to Parkland Hospital for an examination first," said Lesher. "Can your neighbor keep the kids or will we need to make other arrangements?"

Irene nodded. "Mrs. Neff's good people; she won't mind. What's the hospital for?"

Lesher leaned forward. "Ma'am, it's real important, particularly in this case. You were raped and the doctors have got to look at you and make tests and all. But there's something more important than that. I'm gonna swear my partner to secrecy and tell you something before anybody else gets here. It's gonna be hard, but you've got to listen to me – you listen real good and you've gotta do what I tell you, okay?"

She nodded her head, blinking her one good eye.

"Good. Now - don't say nothin' to the detectives, don't give 'em more than your name. Don't under any circumstances volunteer information. They'll try to get you to chat with 'em, but don't do it. Tell 'em you were raped by those two birds and you need a doctor, but when they ask about Ralph in there, tell 'em nothing. Just keep saying you want a doctor and you want to talk to a lawyer - can you remember all that?"

"Yes, sir, don't tell 'em nothin' and I wanta see a doctor and I wanta talk to a lawyer."

"Okay, good. Now, they're gonna try to rattle you. One of 'em will act like a good guy and the other one a bad guy, expecting you to spill your guts. Don't play their game; they're pros. And since you don't know what to say, don't say anything. I can tell you right now that over ninety percent of the people in the jailhouse got there because of their own big mouth, so you just pull the zipper shut on yours."

Even though her features were battered, both men could see Mrs. Potty's puzzlement. "Why are ya'll doin' this for me?"

Lesher sighed and rubbed his hands together. "Ma'am, I'm married over fifteen years now to a wonderful woman. She's given me four fine kids, runs the house good, and she's the best cook I ever saw. Now, those aren't the only reasons I love her, but they'll do for openers. She's good people, but good or bad, nobody ought to get beat the way you were. And sure as hell ought not get raped. I take it real personal and I'm as sorry as I can be about it. This is the only way I know for me to do something to help you out."

Irene was quiet for a moment. She quietly lay the bat on the floor, got to her feet, and walked over to the seated Lesher, gently kissing him on the forehead. "You're a good man, officer. I'm real glad it was you that come over."

Pleased, Lesher flushed a bright pink. "Thank you, Ma'am."

Just then they heard brakes squeak at the curb and several car doors close with a thunk. Moments later two detectives stomped across the porch.

It was more than two hours before Lesher and Daro went back on patrol. Daro used the radio to put them back in service and then turned to his partner. "Lesher, when is your next night off?"

"Next Saturday, why?"

"Got any plans?"

Puzzled, Lesher shook his head. "Not that I know of."

"You and your wife ever been to the Petroleum Club?"

"Shit no, partner, are you nuts? On a cops pay?"

"Well, you're going now. I'll meet you there about seven thirty."

Lesher looked at his rookie partner like he really was crazy. "Are you serious?"

Daro nodded. "You bet. You, your wife, and all four kids. The tab's on me."

Lesher's mouth hung open. "You mean to tell me that all that shit I've been hearing about you is true - you really are rich?"

Daro laughed. "Well, let's just say that I can afford to take all of you to the Petroleum Club. What you did back there was right, and I know it could get you in deep trouble. That kind of bravery is rare and should be rewarded."

"Well I'll be damned. The only thing is, I doubt if Carol will let the kids stay out that late even on a Saturday, especially not the little one, but we'll sure as hell go." Lesher paused for a moment, smiled and shook his head. "I was worried about you, Daro. I mean, we don't know each other. You - or me for that matter - could have been nine kinds of a horse's ass without the other one knowin' it."

"True. But I guess we know now."

Yeah," nodded Lesher, "I guess we do. How about you and me partner up?"

It was Daro's turn to be surprised. "Isn't that a bit unusual? I mean, I'm brand new and it would mean that Captain Spencer would have to pick me up on his detail."

"You let me take care of that part."

Daro thought a moment. "Under one condition."

"Name it."

"If you find out later you've made a mistake you'll tell me."

"Deal," said Lesher as he stuck out his hand.

A smiling Danny Daro shook his new partner's hand.

• • •

5

Daro liked being on Captain Spencer's detail and having Lesher for his regular partner. He already knew what kind of a man Lesher was and now all he had to do was get to know how Lyle liked to work and what he expected from his rookie partner.

He thought he was doing a reasonably good job considering the short time he'd been on the force, but he constantly speculated as to whether or not he had the right stuff to cut it as a cop. Only time would tell.

Daro finished out the month on mid shift then changed to swings, and finally to days. Even though their time together was short, teamwork improved as he and Lesher knocked the rough edges off their partnership, much like newlyweds must do. As with any good 'marriage' they began to develop a rapport, getting to know how the other man liked to work. Within days they seemed to read each other's minds. Such intuition is necessary between partners since one small slip could cost both men their lives. In a short time Daro came to understand what being a cop was all about. Often boring, police work was sometimes like being perched on the muzzle of a 12 gauge shotgun about to go off.

They had been on days only a short time before Daro discovered that he preferred swings. The day shift pace was too slow for his taste. Besides, it was at night when all the slugs came out from beneath their rocks where the cops could get at them. Arresting bad guys reminded Daro of the time he and another kid sprinkled salt on some snails to watch them shrivel up. He found it to be profoundly satisfying to put a bad guy in the jailhouse.

In addition to being busier, working evenings gave him time to take care of business during the day. He went to work at 3:00 PM, got off at 11:00 PM, and was usually home and in bed shortly after midnight. Still, if after work he was in the mood for a beer, he had time to go out to one of the favorite police hangouts, such as Mom Brand's, or the It'll Do Club on East Elm Street. He usually opted for the latter.

The It'll Do catered to a wide variety of ages from the early twenties to thirties. There were usually many people his age. Besides, he could get there before the midnight cut off for serving alcoholic beverages, and he had grown accustomed to having a beer after a swing shift.

At first Daro called the midnight alcohol cutoff law into question. It seemed much more reasonable to have a later time for those who liked to party. But one of his earlier partners had reminded him that, "Anybody that can't get drunk by midnight just ain't trying."

While normally true, the statement did not take into account that people who worked until 11:00 PM were getting a late start. Besides, he had never been drunk in his life and he had no understanding of those who couldn't take or leave alcohol. What really surprised him was to discover what a serious problem drinking was within the police department. With all the evidence of what alcohol could do to individuals and families, especially those who had too much to drink, then got behind the wheel of a car, he would have thought it impossible for a cop to become an alcoholic. Twisted lives and twisted metal were almost always eventual companions.

The first time he saw the blonde was at the It'll Do. She was tall, about five-ten, maybe 130, with below-the-shoulder, honey colored hair that fell in soft waves on either side of her face. He couldn't tell from where he sat, but he guessed her to be about thirty. He loved her full lips, and he'd bet that she had blue eyes. When he caught her staring at him, instead of looking away they locked eyes. After a long moment she arched her right eyebrow as if asking a question.

It was an odd time to think about it, but Daro realized that he had not had a date in almost a year. He wished he had more time; the girl was beautiful. He left a dollar tip, put on his jacket, and strolled out the door. He imagined that he could feel her eyes boring into his back and he chuckled. "You wish," he muttered to himself as he made for his car.

"Hey, Daro!"

It was the following evening after shift and Daro was in the basement of City Hall. He turned and saw Storm Raney, still in uniform, loping toward him. "Hi, Storm, what's up?"

"Nada, just going out to the It'll Do to pick up my girl. I saw you leaving last night when I drove into the parkin' lot."

"She waits up that late for you?"

"She works there. Waitress. Name's Betty Cop. Ain't that a great name for a policeman's girl?"

"I think I know which one she is. I heard the bartender call one of the girls Betty and the other one Eva."

"Yep, that's right," Storm said, taking his cap off and running a comb through his thatch of red hair. "Tell you what, why don't I meetcha there? I'll change and be out in about fifteen minutes."

"Sure, I'll buy you a Pearl."

Storm wrinkled his nose. "Skunk piss. I'll buy you a Miller."

Daro laughed. "Why don't we argue this out later?"

"Why not?" said Rainey. "See you in a few minutes."

When Daro walked into the It'll Do she was there, the blonde from the night before. Dressed in a beautifully cut, light brown skirt and matching jacket over a frilly white under-blouse, she had parked herself near his usual table. His eyes went to her shapely, crossed legs. She was openly looking him over.

He wondered if she deliberately chose to get closer or if it was just an accident. He decided it was an accident. She could obviously have all the company she wanted. All the unattached males in the place were eying her like hummingbirds sniffing out nectar. She lent weight to his impression by rebuffing a nice looking man who asked her to dance.

Before he could consider her further the smaller of the two waitresses, a diminutive but well built girl with brown hair, came for his order.

"I'll have a Pearl, please," he said.

"Sure thing." She had a bright smile, showing small, very white teeth.

"Are you Betty Cop?"

She looked puzzled. "Yeah. How'd you know that?"

"Storm's a buddy."

"You've got good taste. Who might you be?"

"Danny Daro. Would you do me a favor?"

"Sure, what?"

"You see that lady over there?" he said, motioning toward the blonde. "Give her another of whatever she's having."

Betty grimaced. "If you want, but she won't take it. I'll bet she's turned down over a dozen just tonight."

He shrugged. "Give it a try anyway."

"Okay, babe, it's your money."

Ten minutes later Storm came in, waving at people, stopping at the bar to exchange some chit-chat with the bartender and the other waitress. The other girl - the one he'd heard called Eva - was older and not as pretty as Betty Cop, but there was something about her that stroked the hormones. A big girl, about six feet tall, small of bust and wide of hip, but when she moved there was a feline grace about her. He filed the thought away for later examination.

"Hey, Hoss," Storm said, taking a seat, "who's that blonde over there looking you over?"

"Where?" Daro asked. Just as they had the previous night, their eyes locked when he looked her way. She held up the drink and mouthed, "Thank you."

He smiled and nodded, for some reason embarrassed.

"Well, well," said Storm. "From across a crowded room, huh; no need askin' how you're making out, is there?"

"Come on, Storm, I don't even know her name."

"You come on. You ain't gonna find it out sitting here on your dead ass. Give the girl a break. Go over and blow in her ear or somethin'."

Daro started to answer when he caught movement out of the corner of his eye. He turned his head to find the blonde standing by their table.

"I've got a question," she said.

Both men stood. "Sure, what's the question?" he asked.

"Just what does a girl have to do to get noticed by you? I've done everything but send up a flare and you haven't turned a tap."

He smiled, his embarrassment gone. "I must be color blind, I didn't see the flare. Won't you join us?"

She dimpled. "I don't know. I'd hate to be responsible for breaking up this all-male tete a tete."

In her high heels, she was taller than Storm. Raney had an appreciative gleam in his eye. "Tell you what," he said, "This part of the tete is leaving so my friend here is gonna need a replacement. Why don't you have a seat?" he said, gallantly pulling out a chair.

She placed a hand on his arm. "Please don't go. I don't even know your name."

"I'm Storm Raney, Ma'am, and this here little fellow is Danny Daro. You be real good to him, you hear. He's fine people."

Her smile got bigger. "Little fellow, huh? How do you know he'll want me to be good to him?"

Storm gave her his lopsided smile. "Well, Ma'am, he may be dumber'n dirt, but he ain't blind and stupid. See you Daro. You kids have fun now, ya hear?"

With that, Raney left, threading his way through the overly small tables to the bar.

"Your friend is quite a character," she said, watching Storm's departing back.

"Yeah, and he's not likely to change either. Have a seat."

"Thanks," she said, tucking up her skirt before placing herself just so in the small chair. He heard the swish of silk against silk as those long, beautiful legs crossed again. She took a sip of beer and sat the glass on the table. "My name's Janette Colmer."

Daro was already smitten, lost in her eyes. Sure enough he had been right. They were blue - an unusual shade. Sort of like heavy smoke in sunlight.

"Pretty," he said. "The name, too."

She dimpled again and bobbed her head. "Thank you, sir. Are you one of those silver tongued devils my mama warned me about?"

He broke into his smile. "Devil – maybe - silver tongued -not hardly. But I do say what I think, and I think you are a very beautiful lady."

"Keep it up and you'll turn my head."

"Right - I'm sure you've never heard that before."

She tipped her head back and a musical laugh came from between rich, full lips. He loved the curve of her smooth, graceful neck.

"I can see right now that you're going to be refreshing, if not downright fun," Jan said.

Last dance was called and he took Janette onto the floor. She fitted nicely in his arms and was tall enough to place her forehead next to his cheek. Her right hand lightly cupped the back of his neck and the soft, subtle fragrance of her perfume seeming to move as she did. The scent suited her perfectly. She was the most sensuous woman he'd ever danced with. He resisted the urge to bury his nose in her hair.

They didn't talk during the dance, allowing the rhythm to pull them around the floor. Once she started to speak, but stopped as though afraid to break the mood. After the record was over they held each other on the dance floor, neither seeming to want to break contact.

Finally he said, "Guess what?"

'What?"

"The music stopped."

"Ask me if I care?" she said, her breath brushing against his ear. He shivered and she smiled.

Daro laughed. "I really don't want this to end. Could we go somewhere and talk?"

"Yes. I'll even make you a cup of coffee if my place isn't too far out of your way."

"Frankly, I don't care if it's in Fort Worth. Your place is fine. Do you want me to follow you?"

She smiled. "No. I'll ride with you. I don't drive; I take cabs everywhere."

The apartment turned out to be an up-stairs duplex off Preston Road on the edge of the Dallas Country Club. Although close to his original home on Turtle Creek, Daro had not been there since he was a boy, riding around the neighborhood on his bicycle.

Although old, the outside of the building had been renovated. The owners had added a new tile roof and had the brick sandblasted to its original dark red color. Ivy was just now beginning to get a fresh toe-hold, slowly regaining the lost ground it had taken years to originally establish.

Colmer's was the upstairs apartment. She unlocked the lower door and they climbed the stairs to a foyer at the top. A second door, already unlocked, opened into the living room.

He was impressed. The room appeared to have been professionally decorated, modern but not cold. Over an open-front fireplace hung a seascape showing a three- mast schooner straining at the wind, the sails billowing from a brisk breeze.

"Would you like to have a seat or do you want to supervise the coffee?"

"I better have a seat. I never made coffee in my life."

She raised an eyebrow. "Oh? Do you eat out?"

He chuckled. "Rarely, Mildred does my meals."

Janette turned, a quizzical look on her face. "Am I allowed to ask who Mildred is?"

"One of the sweetest women I have ever known," he said, keeping a straight face. "We've been living together for years."

Janette's expression was amusedly suspicious. "I see. Then do you think you should be here with me?"

"Oh, I don't think she would mind. I know for sure that her husband, Randall, wouldn't."

Jan planted a fist on her hip. "Okay, what's going on?"

Daro's laughed. "Randall is my valet and Mildred is the cook. They have worked for my family my whole life."

"Valet? Cook? On a cops pay?"

He started to speak and then stopped. "How did you know I'm a cop?"

For just a heartbeat she seemed flustered. "I asked the waitress who brought my drink. She said she thought you were."

He nodded. "Betty. She's Storm's girl. But you're right. A cop doesn't make much. I used to do something else before I got on the force. I'll tell you the whole story if you like."

"I do like, but let me get the coffee going before you start."

"Sure, Janette, thanks."

"Call me Jan," she said as she disappeared through the swinging door into the kitchen.

He could hear her getting out the coffee pot and cups. Then heard water run and the swish of the spoon as she scooped the grounds into the basket. Shortly there were perking sounds and she returned to plop down beside him on the sofa.

"Now, tell me."

He sighed and began at the beginning, leaving nothing out, even telling her all about Sally and his folks. After a few minutes her face was an ashen mask of concern. As he finished she placed a slender hand on his arm.

"I'm so sorry, Danny. I had no idea. Aren't the two detectives doing anything?"

"Golden and Killean? Sure they are, but there just aren't any decent leads yet. They tell me that these bastards will slip up one of these days, though. And when they do, we'll nail 'em."

He looked at his watch. "Good grief, it's two o'clock. I've got to get home. I should have called Randall and Mildred. They'll be worried."

"Why don't you spend the night here with me?"

They had gotten along so well that her words were not totally unexpected, and he felt warmth flood his loins. He would have liked nothing better, but he wasn't ready. He liked to know a girl's mind before he knew her body, at least that intimately.

"Thanks, Jan. I appreciate that more than you know, but I know you're just trying to be kind. I don't want that."

She shook her head, her husky voice almost a whisper. "It's not kindness, my friend. You're a hell of a lot of man; certainly a lot more than I've known in a long time. No - it's not kindness."

He smiled sadly. "Thanks, but I'm wrung out. I haven't opened up like this to anyone since the murders and it felt good. If you'll let it, I think we can go a long way together - just not tonight."

He could tell by her expression that his words both surprised and jarred her.

"That's really sweet," she said. "I don't see why not." She opened her purse and took out a card, handing it to him. "Here's my number. It's not listed so don't lose it."

This time his smile wasn't sad. "Don't worry about that. I'll give you a call in a day or so."

Once again he took her into his arms, intending to part with a gentle kiss. But she was having none of it. She pulled him fiercely to her and probed his mouth with her tongue. Her passion took him off guard and he responded without thinking, a soft moan escaping from deep inside.

Taken by surprise, he stirred powerfully against her and she shifted her hips, beginning to move against him. In a blur of activity, they were on the couch, locked against each other in a rib crushing embrace.

It was Jan's turn to moan as he moved a hand inside her blouse to cup a heavy breast. He was surprised to find that she wore no bra. Her nipple hardened and popped between waiting fingers. He rolled it as she made a hissing sound, drawing a ragged breath from between clenched teeth. Daro stood up to remove his shirt, but she stopped him.

"I want you now." she whispered as she kicked off her shoes and stepped out of her panties

Pulling down his pants and shorts she grasped his shoulders and pushed him down on the sofa to sit on his lap, facing him. Straddling his legs she pulled up her skirt and guided him into her. As she sank down on him she wrapped her arms about his neck and placed her cheek next to his, making the same hissing sound as before.

Very slowly she began to move and shortly both their faces were pulled into an agonized expression. Seconds later they shuddered and stiffened, and Jan threw her head back uttering a small, barking cry. When her breath returned to normal she lowered her lips to his and kissed him tenderly.

"Thank you," she whispered, her sweet scented breath again caressing his ear. She smiled as she felt him shudder elsewhere.

Tenderly he took her face between two large hands. "You're a funny lady. I get the gift, but you give the thanks. Seems backwards somehow, don't you think?"

She shook her head. "No I don't. We both got this gift."

She lifted off him and dragged her fingertips across his cheek as she padded into the bathroom.

Daro pulled up his shorts and pants and in a minute heard a flush. After a few rustling sounds, she came out wearing a navy blue silk robe. The contrast with her eyes was striking.

"I didn't mean for that to happen," he said.

She smiled up into his amber eyes and brushed a hand across the white widow's peak at the front of his flattop. "But I did," she said. "Actually, officer, you might say that I raped you. You want to press charges?"

"Probably not," he said, answering her smile. "I might want to press something else later, however."

Suddenly she turned shy. In a small soft voice that sounded near to tears she said, "Anytime, my love - anytime."

This time their kiss was as Daro had first intended, soft and sweet, trembling on each other's mouth - like butterfly wings. Reluctantly he released her, and without another word he went down the stairs and out to the car.

Jan watched through the curtains until he drove away before going to the telephone. Without having to look up the number, she dialed and waited. After four, hollow rings a gruff voice answered.

"Yeah?"

"It's me."

"Whatcha got?"

"He doesn't know anything."

"You sure?"

She bristled and it sounded in her voice. "Of course I'm sure, damn it, you're not dealing with some amateur."

"Okay, okay," said the voice. "You don't have to get all whipped outa shape. I want you to keep in touch with him and keep me posted."

Although he couldn't see it, she shook her head. "Nope, I'm not gonna do that. That's it, no more, I'm out."

It was his turn to bristle. "Don't give me that shit, girl. I can make you wish you'd never been born."

"That you can," she agreed. "But I'm willing to bet you won't. We've done a lot of business and can do more, but not on Daro. I'm done."

"Yeah - well," he muttered. "You gone soft on that asshole, have you?"

"Let's just say that I think he's a hell of a guy that you've shit on up to his armpits. Remember what I said - no more."

"Okay," said the voice, "I'll let you off the hook a little bit. You don't have to tell me every move, but if he gets on to something that can hurt me, you let me know."

Jan shook her head. "You're not listening. I said no."

"I can tell you this right now, Kiddo - you ain't about to bag that boy, particularly if I see to it that he gets the word about you. He ain't gonna like hearin' that you're a working girl."

"You'd do that, wouldn't you? How does it feel to be such a complete horse's ass?"

The voice laughed. "Just so you understand me. You gonna cooperate?"

"Do I have a choice?"

"Nope."

Both furious and resigned, Jan hung up the phone. It wasn't until that moment that she realized that she and Daro never did have their coffee. She washed out the pot and put up the dishes, then dialed her answering service to see if any clients had called.

• • •

6

It was two days before Daro called and Jan could tell from his voice that he was a little antsy. She knew he would have gone to the It'll Do the night before, expecting to find her. She deliberately stayed away. After all, you have to keep guys guessing and she hadn't said that she would be there. Besides, being an expert on the subject of men, she also knew that wondering about her would drive him a little crazy. The thought of him driving home after closing the club, only to toss and turn alone in his empty bed, made her smile. Men were so transparent. But she had to be careful. This wasn't one of her Johns. She really liked Danny.

"Hi yourself, Officer," she said, her voice low and throaty. "You got time to come over?"

"As a matter of fact, I do. Are you free for the evening?"

She had two appointments, but was more than willing to cancel them. "Absolutely," she said. "What's cooking?"

"An apt question. We're going out for dinner; my night off you know. Dress nicely, we're going to the Petroleum Club."

She paled. Several of her clients had taken her there. The risk was too great that one of them might see her, or someone who knew what she did for a living might say the wrong thing. No - too risky.

"Would you mind a suggestion?" she asked.

"Of course not."

"There's a place over on Lovers Lane that makes the best charcoal broiled hamburgers in the world. Frankly I'd rather have one than the best lobster in Dallas, if that's okay."

Daro laughed. "You're going to be a cheap date tonight, aren't you? Are you sure you'd rather go there?"

"Yes, I would. I don't get the chance very often. It would be a treat."

She could almost see him bow over the telephone. "Your wish is my command, madam. I'll pick you up at seven."

Daro's watch read five of seven when the car pulled up in front of Jan's apartment. Randall shut down the whisper quiet engine on the old Rolls and started to step out to open Daro's door.

"No thanks, Randall, I'll get it." he said, stepping out and clicking the massive door shut. There was a spring in his step as he strode up the walk and rang the bell at the downstairs door. The door buzzed open, and with a silent whistle on his lips, he bounded up the stairs two at a time to fetch his date.

"Well, well, if you don't look nice," he said as Jan came out of the bedroom, trying to insert a large loop earring in her right ear. She looked exasperated.

"Can you help me with this damned thing? I don't know what it is, but I never can find the hole."

His face broke into wrinkles. "Uh - I wouldn't touch that comment with a fork lift."

Her exasperation gone, she answered his smile. "A wise move, officer; I might have to hurt you."

She wore a pale blue, short sleeved cotton dress with a modified vee neckline and a narrow belt which perfectly showcased her body. Daro had known some well - built girls in his time, but Jan far and away had the best curves he had ever seen. He would not have been so surprised had he known how hard she worked to keep them that way. The feel of her came flooding back and he ached from remembrance.

"Gee, I'd hate to have you do that," he said walking towards her. "But who knows, it might be fun. Here, let's see what I can do with that thing."

He took the gold loop and turned her toward the light as Jan pulled her hair away from her ear. Her perfume gave him that giddy feeling again. He threaded the loop through on the first try and bent down and kissed her neck. Tiny goose bumps quickly formed around the site. She turned her face toward him, offering her lips instead. As he gently pressed his mouth to hers, her lips trembled. It was the most sensual sensation he'd ever felt.

"Do I frighten you?" he asked as they broke contact.

She shyly lowered her eyes. "I think so, a little. I feel like a sixteen year old virgin again. I wish I were."

"Why?"

Still looking down, she shook her head. "I don't know. I've never felt like this before and it scares me. Besides, you can't be real. There aren't any men out there like you."

Daro smiled. "I'm not nearly as good as you think, particularly if you could read my mind right now. Besides, I'll try not to bite, except in places that will feel really good."

She raised her face to his, her eyes glistening from unshed tears. "Promise?"

"You bet," he said, offering his arm. "Shall we?"

"Yes. I'm starved."

A smiling Randall stood holding the door to the Rolls as the pair strolled out. Jan froze in her tracks, jaw open.

"Good evening, Miss," said the liveried Randall. "Where do you wish to go?"

An astonished Jan looked up at him. "A chauffeur, too?"

"Not really," he said. "This was Randall's idea. It's my mother's old car and it's my first date in almost a year and he wanted it to be special. Aren't you sorry now to be taking me to a hamburger joint?"

Her laugh was that of a delighted child. "You just wait. They're better than anything you ever tasted."

Helping Jan into the limousine, Daro settled into the plush seat and held Jan's hand as Randall cranked the huge engine to life and whispered away from the curb toward Lovers Lane.

She was right - it was the best hamburger he'd ever had, big and juicy with just the right amount of fat. The menu said that they ground their own meat and added special ingredients before cooking to get that special flavor. He never had anything like it.

In addition to preparing them a fine meal, the cooks put on a show, breaking up into barbershop quartets and presenting funny skits. A group of four came to their table and sang 'Wait 'Till the Sun Shines, Nellie.' The act was almost as good as the food.

Daro's eyes twinkled. "That would be a nice name for you."

"What?"

"Nellie, of course."

Jan made a face. "I think it's horrible. Cute song though."

When the quartet finished, Jan gave each man a kiss on the cheek. They feigned embarrassment and clowned their way back to the open kitchen in the center of the huge room, continuing their duties at a bell-shaped copper hood strategically placed over the giant grill. Even though the hood tapped off most of the smoke, enough of the delicious aroma escaped into the room to send the most finicky taste buds into a frenzy. Daro found that the smell alone was enough to turn him into Pavlov's dog.

"Would you like another?" he asked, wiping his hands on a cloth napkin. The napkins were a nice touch, he thought.

"Are you kidding? Not another bite - you?"

"Not me," he said, rubbing his stomach. There was a pile of food left on his plate. The French fries were curled up like a pig's tail, brown and crispy. He hated to leave so many.

"What would you like to do now?" he asked. "There are several good movies, the symphony is playing at Fair Park, and I even made a tentative reservation at a dance club if you like."

"My choice?" she asked.

He spread his hands. "Your choice, madam. The night's festivities are entirely under your control."

"Take me home and spend the night."

He was nonplused. "You mean now?"

She broke into her childlike laugh. "You should see your face. Yes, my dear, I mean right now."

"But what about Randall?"

"Let him get his own date. He's a big boy now, Sweetheart."

Daro laughed. "You know what I mean."

Jan smiled in return and reached out to touch his face. "Of course I know, darling. Send him home. He knows you're not a virgin, he won't be shocked."

Colmer was right. Randall dropped them at her door and drove home. Daro could tell from the look on his parting face that his more friend than servant was pleased that his 'boy' had found such a pretty and seemingly charming young lady. He was equally sure that Randall would not have been shocked to see the trail of clothing they left strewn from the top of the stairs all the way into the bedroom.

It had been a long day for Patrolman Marge Johnson and Detective Sam Goren. Marge, a petite thirty year old that could pass for well under twenty, normally worked in Juvenile and Sam in Burglary and Theft. They were on loan to vice, however, working a job in north Dallas. The assignment called for a father-daughter team which made them perfect for the job. Although at thirty two Sam was only two years older than Marge, the lack of hair let him pass for forty. Marge at five-one and 90 pounds, had long, black hair, and easily played the part of Sam's teen age daughter. Goren normally wore a pork pie hat, but was bare headed this night. As the couple walked under the street light at Commerce and Central Expressway South, Sam's bald head look almost chromed, further giving the illusion of age. Standing five feet ten and two hundred ten pounds, Goren stretched his massive shoulders beneath a navy blue sport coat and adjusted the speed rig under his left arm pit where he carried his Model 1911, 45 ACP. He and Marge rounded the corner and walked toward his black, '39 Packard classic. After unlocking the door and seating Marge, Sam went around and scooted beneath the steering wheel. Fumbling with the ignition, he promptly dropped his keys.

"Damn I'm tired," he said, retrieving the key chain from the floorboard. Sam's voice was rough from lack of sleep.

"Too tired?" she asked.

"For what?" Sam asked, smiling through his weariness, but playing her game.

Marge laughed, a tinkling sound on the deserted street.

Sam started the car and rocked out of the driveway onto Commerce Street. Turning west he headed toward the Houston Street Viaduct and their Oak Cliff apartment. It seemed like a week since they had been home.

Sam and Marge lived together, a fact commonly known by almost every cop in Dallas, but ignored by the higher-ups in spite of going against departmental policy. They had been together for three years, the total time that Marge had been on the force. After the first year they decided it was stupid to pay two rents so they moved in together, living as man and wife.

To everyone who knew them, there seemed nothing wrong with the arrangement. They had tried to change the police department's policy so they could marry. But the rule still stood that no two people closer than cousins could be on the police force at the same time. Even then, if they were first cousins, a special dispensation had to be granted from on high. Somehow, in the minds of these shadowy, nebulous rules-maker's, a man and wife team exceeded the most liberal interpretation of departmental kinship parameters.

After a time neither Marge nor Sam thought much about their arrangement. To them they were man and wife and the rest of the world could take a flying leap. Or as Sam was heard to say, "I don't give a rat's ass what the Chief thinks."

They were sitting at the light at Commerce and Akard when a black, '54 Ford crammed with four young men pulled up beside them and tapped the horn. Thinking they had a question, Sam rolled down his window and said, "Can I help you?"

"Yeah, Pop," said the punk by the passenger door. "How about we take your pretty daughter off your hands for a few hours?"

Sam wasn't worried, but he was pissed. "Son, why don't you go home and suck on your bottle."

A chorus of laughs erupted in the Ford as the punk's face flamed red. "How'd you like to try me right here, old man?" the punk asked.

"No thanks. Not 'nough competition," he answered, rolling up his window.

The light changed and they moved off, the Ford falling in behind. Sam still wasn't worried, but a small remembered something began to tug at the back of his mind.

He looked at Marge. "Hey, babe, you remember what kind of a car Goldie and Killean were lookin' for awhile back? Wasn't it maybe five or more guys that coulda killed that couple and their daughter? And weren't they maybe drivin' a fifty four Ford?"

Marge's eyes went wide. "Hey, I think you're right. Did you get a plate?"

Goren was wishing they were in a police cruiser with a radio. "No. Can you catch the front plate?"

Marge turned around in her seat, squinting into the bright headlights. "Can't read it, Hon. Can you drop behind?"

He shook his head. "Better not. There's another car right behind those little farts. I think it's another Ford. We may have two cars after us. It's probably the wrong bunch, but I don't wanta take any chances. You locked and loaded?"

"Damn right," she said, opening her purse to rest a hand on her Walther PPK, 9mm Kurz. Marge kept the weapon in a unique holster Goren had made for her, one which held two extra magazines, giving her fourteen extra rounds for the little pistol. He also hand- loaded her cartridges, calling them his dirtbag specials.

With one eye on the rear view mirror Goren unconsciously checked his 45 and the two extra magazines for his weapon. If called to action, he was ready.

"They still back there?" asked Marge.

"Yep, the second car, too; I think there's three guys in it." he answered. "But they're just followin'. I'd give my left nut to know what they're up to."

"Can you make it to a call box?"

He shook his head. "I ain't about to stop, Babe. If I counted right there'd be seven or eight of those bastards on us before a cat could lick its ass."

"Did you get a good look at 'em?"

Sam shook his head again. "Not really, just the pisswilly that was doing all the lippin' off."

Marge scanned Commerce Street ahead of them. "I wonder where seventy one is?" she said, echoing his thoughts.

"They just went on duty about an hour ago. They're probably still shakin' doors."

In a minute Goren made the left turn to Houston Street and passed the Union Terminal on their right. He kept watching as the two Fords followed them up the ramp onto the deserted Houston Street Viaduct.

The Fords made no moves other than following and they were almost across when Sam took his eyes off the cars for just a second. As luck would have it, the punks picked that exact moment to accelerate, timing it perfectly as they reached the end of the bridge.

Sam sensed rather than saw the car as it raced in front to cut them off. The other pulled alongside to block them in. When Ford number two jinked toward them, Goren swerved to the curb and bounced to a stop. The next thing they knew, four guys piled out of the lead car and three out of the blocker, all running toward them whooping it up and swinging motorcycle chains.

The clock read 4:00AM when the telephone rang. An irritated Jan Colmer answered.

"Miss Colmer," said Randall, "Please forgive me for calling, but it is very important. May I speak with Mister Danny?"

"Of course; just a moment. It's Randall," she said, handing him the phone.

Alarmed, Daro swung his legs over the edge of the bed and sat up. "Yes, Randall, is something wrong?"

"I'm sorry, Mister Danny, but Officer Golden called for you. It seems that the gang who murdered your parents and Miss Sally tried the same thing with two police officers on their way home from work."

Fully alert, Daro asked, "Where's Golden now?"

"At Parkland Hospital, Sir."

"How about the officers?"

"I am sorry, Sir, but I have no more information."

"Oh, shit, I just remembered, I don't have a car."

"Not to worry, sir. I took the liberty of calling a taxi. They will arrive for you in about ten minutes. I will bring your car to you later."

"Thanks, Randall, you always seem to know exactly what to do." Daro hung up and told Jan all he knew as he hurried into his clothes.

Giving Jan a quick kiss good bye, Daro went downstairs to wait for the cab. When the lower door slammed, Jan dialed the telephone and waited through five rings. Finally she replaced the receiver in the cradle and stretched out on her back, staring at the ceiling. Sleep was a long time coming.

Golden was waiting in the emergency room when Daro came storming through the door. A line of uniformed cops were holding back a phalanx of reporters.

"Talk to me," he said when he saw the detective.

"We got the bastards. All seven of 'em; only one's still alive."

"How's he doing?" asked Daro.

"Not worth a damn. The asshole caught so much lead he weighs a ton."

"Damn!" Daro exclaimed. "With seven guys you'd think more of them would make it."

Goldie shook his head. "Not this time. The bastards were unlucky enough to pick on a couple of cops, both expert shots. The bad guys all had chains, but three of the dirtbags were packing iron, too, so it was one hell of a fire fight."

"Where'd it happen?" Daro asked.

"Right at the Oak Cliff side of the Houston Street Viaduct."

"Has the guy said anything?"

"Not hardly. The bastard can't even drool, much less talk. He's been in the operatin' room ever since he got here. I wouldn't get my hopes up."

"Shit!" Daro said, pounding his fist into his hand.

"I know, trooper," Golden said. "It's a tough pill to swallow. But look at the other side. We got 'em. We got the bastards that killed your folks."

Daro frowned. "How do you know that for sure?"

Golden shrugged. "That's easy. I kicked Booker's ass out of bed and he's already run their prints. Every damned one of 'em matches."

"There's no doubt?"

"Absolutely none. I'd trust Book's ID of a partial before I would an FBI lab report on all ten fingers."

Daro plopped down in a chair and put his face in his hands. Shortly his shoulders began to shake. Golden sat down beside him and lightly placed a hand on his back, giving him a comforting pat. Several minutes later the spasm passed.

"It was too easy," Daro said, wiping his eyes and nose on a handkerchief. "I know it's a fantasy, but I wanted my hands on them one at a time. I wanted to cut off their balls and watch 'em bleed to death. At the very least, I wanted them to fry."

"I know, Danny," said Golden, "But we hardly ever get the whole loaf. You're gonna have to make do with whatcha got. And if you stop to think about it, six on ice and another probable is pretty damn good."

"Who got 'em?" Daro asked.

Golden chuckled. "Sam Goren and Marge Johnson. I doubt if you know 'em. They've got an apartment over in Oak Cliff. Anyhow, they had just got off work and were headed home when these assholes in two Fords started messing with 'em."

Golden's grin was huge. "The way we figure it from what one of 'em said to Sam is that they thought it was a man and his daughter, and they tried to curb 'em at the end of the bridge. Sam stopped and all seven of 'em came running at the car swinging chains and laughing and cutting up. After that, both cops get a little hazy. All they really remember is opening their doors and exchanging gunfire until all the bastards were down."

Golden laughed as he interlaced his fingers. "Neither one of the cops got hit, but Sam got two bullet holes through his nice new sports jacket and several in his car. Boy is he pissed. He really loves that old Packard. Anyhow, Sam stayed at the scene while Marge drove to a phone. The rest you know."

"I want to see the bodies."

"What the hell for?" asked Golden, sobering.

"Why not?"

Golden shrugged. "I don't know. It just seems kind of a funny thing to want to do."

Daro's eyes were like a flame. "Wrong, my friend. I want to see their dead asses."

"Okay, follow me," Golden said, leading Daro to the morgue.

All six were laid out on stainless steel gurneys, covered with white sheets, a tag tied to their big toe. One after another Daro stripped off the sheet and looked at them, trying to imagine what pleasure they could have gotten from the brutal murders and rapes they had committed. No answers fell from their lips.

"Looks like every one of them caught at least one slug in the chest," Daro said.

Golden nodded. "Yeah, all but the guy they're operating on right now. He caught at least one from Sam's 45. Marge put three, 380 slugs in him, but that's just a love tap compared to a 45, particularly since Sam loads his own ammo. Marge put two in his chest and one in his groin, just about this far from his pecker," Golden said, holding thumb and forefinger about an inch apart.

Daro snorted. "Too bad she didn't blow it off."

"Yeah," Golden said, smiling and nodding in agreement. "Marge swears she was aiming higher, but I'm not sure I believe her. That's one cool lady."

Daro felt better. True, things didn't turn out exactly the way he'd wanted, but Goldie was right with his half a loaf analogy.

"The other guy is in surgery?"

"Yep, still with the cutters. If he makes it they'll put him in ICU."

"I want to see him, too."

Golden shook his head. "No can do, friend. He's got doctors hanging off every part of him. Man, even a cricket fart could push him over the edge. If he gets better - which I doubt - maybe you can see him then."

"Does Chicken Foot know yet?"

"Not hardly. I woke him up once to tell him about something I thought was important and ended up on his shit list for a month. When he gets to the office this morning is soon enough."

"So all I can do is wait?"

"Yep, afraid so."

August, 1955, gave way to September and each minute brought Daro renewed hope for the seventh chain gang member. He didn't regain consciousness, but the prognosis wasn't quite so dicey as before. At least they were able to give the dirtbag a name; William P. Mitchell, aka Bill Pierce, Will Michael, Mike Wills, and other assorted monikers. His beef sheet read like the ten most wanted. Most of Mitchell's crimes however were committed while he was still a juvenile. He was not yet twenty.

The first glimmer of hope came when Mitchell survived surgery, a circumstance the doctors could not explain. He tenaciously clung to life, fighting for each breath as though the universe was suddenly devoid of oxygen. After the third day his condition seemed to improve. By the fifth day two of the doctors were giving him a fifty-fifty chance.

Daro couldn't have been happier. His fondest hope was that Mitchell would survive and grow strong so that they could try him, sentence him to death, and fry his ass in the electric chair at Huntsville.

And Daro wanted to be there to watch.

On the morning of the seventh day Mitchell was still being kept in ICU, but his prognosis was so greatly improved that there was talk of moving him to the police ward in the next few days under close guard. He hadn't spoken, but earlier that morning Mitchell had opened his eyes.

It was 10:00 AM when a nurse went to Mitchell's room to administer an injection. He was dead.

Between the time of his demise until the autopsy, Mitchell's death was a mystery. As soon as he uncovered the body, however, Doctor

Montgomery spotted a slight trickle of dried blood coming from Mitchell's left ear. A sharp instrument, probably an ice pick, had been inserted into the ear canal. Nobody saw or heard a thing.

"Come on, Mabel, think," an irritated Golden said to the nurse in charge of ICU. "Somebody had to have come in here. Do you remember anyone at all?"

Head Nurse, Mabel Ward was one of the old timers and knew all the cops. And she obviously didn't like Golden's tone. "I'm telling you, Goldie, there's not one swingin' dick comes in here without me knowin' it. Sure, there's been a bunch of cops traipsin' all over the place, dirtyin' up my floor with their big, flat feet, but there's not been one stranger - not one."

"Look, Mabel, somebody did this. Mitchell didn't punch his own ticket. Think, damnit."

Mabel turned her considerable bulk and matching wrath on Golden. "Now you look - we've got two doors into this place, and I can see both of 'em at all times," Mabel said, pointing a pudgy finger. "The way you came in by the desk and the other entrance through those two emergency doors over there are in plain sight of where I sit, and I can tell you there's been nobody in here I didn't know about. In fact, the emergency doors weren't opened a-tall. The only other people that's been in here is you, Killean, and that new guy - uh - Daro?"

Golden nodded. "Yeah."

"Besides you three, there's been that bundle of charm, Talmadge, and about fifteen harness bulls rattlin' and clankin' all over the place. Didja ever think it might be one a them?"

"Mabel, you may be a pretty good nurse, but when it comes to cop stuff you can really be full of it sometimes. We've been tryin' to catch this asshole, not murder him."

Mabel sighed and shrugged. "Have it your way. I'm just tellin' you that nobody came in here that didn't have a legitimate reason to be here. I know every damned one of 'em."

It didn't compute, and no amount of thinking that Golden and Killean applied to the problem seemed to help. The only possibility, as unlikely as it appeared to be, was that Daro was the murderer. But after comparing notes, the two detectives ruled out the idea since he had only been in the ward twice, once in the company of Golden, the other accompanied by both men. Besides – the timing was wrong. Mabel Ward agreed.

So the mystery remained. But beyond the fact that Mitchell had been murdered, the big question was why? Who, other than Daro and an outraged citizenry, would have a reason to want to get into a restricted area of a hospital, run the risk of being recognized or even caught in the act, and do away with some street punk? It was a real head scratcher.

"Could we be missing something?" asked a completely frustrated Daro.

"Obviously, but what?" answered Killean.

"I don't know," he said, spreading his hands apart. "I'm new at this stuff. But unless there's somebody else involved in this that we don't know about, it makes no sense at all."

Golden joined in. "True, but what's the motive?"

Daro shook his head. "I don't know. But something struck me the other day that's a real puzzle. Why murder my mom and dad where they did, but carry Sally off someplace else? They could have just as easily raped and killed her there. What was that all about?"

Killean and Golden looked at each other.

"You may make it yet, Daro," Killean said. "We've wondered the same thing. But the other two was done the same way, so it seems to be just part of their MO. They was young girls, too, just like your sister. You ain't gonna like what I say next, but we figure they took 'em off somewhere's else so's they could have all the time they wanted with 'em."

Daro couldn't have handled such thoughts until now. He interlocked his fingers and looked down at his hands. "Yeah, that's what I thought, too. You suppose there was someone else waiting for them to bring Sally there, and whoever that someone is might be afraid that Mitchell would finger them?"

"Could be," nodded Golden. "But that still leaves us not knowin' where that someplace is. And even if we did, it's been so long now that it probably wouldn't help us. I hate to admit it, but right now I'm stumped."

Daro opened his hands. "Well, it's obvious I'm in way over my head."

"Not really, Daro," Killean said. "You've been thinkin' pretty straight. At least, you've been thinkin' the same way we have. But zero plus zero still equals zero, 'cause we got zip."

"We may never know," Daro said.

Golden grimaced, "I hate to say it, but you're exactly right. But we're a far cry from done on this, even though Chicken Foot is ragging our ass to get on with other things. Oh - and another thing. You remember me telling you that morning that I wasn't gonna wake old Herm up because of what happened the last time I did?"

"Yeah."

"Well, this time I caught nine kinds of hell for *not* doin' it. Ya just can't win."

"It figures. But my problem is that I don't know if I can just drop it," Daro said, shaking his head sadly.

"Well, trooper," said Killean, "All life's a puzzle and it don't get solved real often. This just might be another one a them times."

• • •

7

Daro found it hard going back to work after Mitchell's murder. He reported for detail and walked quietly beside Lesher down Central Expressway South to the police garage on Canton Street. When they relieved the previous squad, both men stuck their billy clubs in the crack between the cushions in the front seat and placed their caps on the seat between them. Since Daro drove last on the previous shift, Lesher took the wheel of squad 43 and wheeled out Gaston Avenue to intersect Garland Road. Daro tried to keep his mind on business, but he caught Lesher watching him out of the corner of his eye.

"You okay, partner, or is somethin eatin' on you?" Lesher asked.

Daro shook his head. "I don't know, Lyle. I want more action on my family's murder and I'm not getting any."

"Moping around here like a bull with crushed nuts ain't gonna help. You talk to Golden and Killean?"

"Sure. They probably never wanta see me again."

"I doubt that - them's two good men. I've worked with both of 'em before they put on suits and I can tell ya they're straight arrows. Killean's got a pretty suspicious nature and a sharp mouth, but those ain't bad traits in a cop."

Daro grimaced and shook his head. "I know that, but the more I think about this thing the deeper the hole gets."

"For instance?"

Daro turned slightly in the seat so he could look at his partner. Lesher had a strong chin, almost as strong as his convictions. "Okay, why kill Mitchell? Who'd gain by that?"

Lesher shrugged. "Beats me. Maybe he had a partner."

Daro nodded. "Okay, say he did. What did they partner up about, rape? And even if they did and he was worried about Mitchell ratting on him, how did he get to the son of a bitch in the hospital without anybody seeing him? It's not making any sense."

"The way I figure it," said Lesher, "Mabel missed 'em somehow. Maybe she was givin' somebody a shot or wipin' someone's ass or somethin' and just plain didn't see 'em."

Daro nodded again. "I thought the same thing until I talked to her, but now I don't think so. That old gal doesn't miss a trick. She can tell you if a gnat farts on her ward."

Lesher shrugged, "Well, for sure he didn't ream out his own ear - not unless that ice pick had legs and walked in and out by its ownself."

"Yeah," sighed Daro. "There's something else, too. If Mitchell being dead was so important, why wasn't he killed long before he got crossways with a couple of cops? Unless I'm missing something, the danger to his partner or partners would be just as great before the shootout as after. There's no way they coulda known that six of 'em would get killed in a firefight. The more I look at this the crazier it gets."

Lesher opened and shut his mouth several times before he spoke. "Partner, can I say something without you goin' ballistic on me?"

Surprised, Daro said, "Sure."

"I think you're livin' in your own head too much. I mean, you gotta take some time for yourself when you ain't thinkin' all them heavy thoughts, you know? I think what you need to do is come out to the house and meet my family and let some of them kids crawl all over you for a couple of hours. You ain't even seen Carol but that one time at the Petroleum Club. Shit, I'll bet you can't even name my kids."

Daro smiled and looked over at Lesher. "What's their names?"

Lesher threw his head back and laughed. "Well, let's see now - there's Todd, he's thirteen and he just started his own acne farm. His voice cracks every other word and his peter's hard about ninety five percent of the time, but he is some kind of a whiz at math. Wants to be an engineer.

"Then there's Ruby, she's eleven. She's got red hair and green eyes - just started to notice that boys are different. She'll like you. When I seen that hair I kidded Carol about havin' a fling with our postman.

"And Jennifer, she's nine. A tomboy. Loves baseball. Wants to play first base for the St. Louis Cardinals. She don't know yet that only guys can play in the majors. That girl's got at least fourteen skinny arms and legs flying all over the place - my favorite, actually, but I'd deny I ever said it. She's pure devil. Pretty though.

"And then there's our accident, little Amy. She's three. So scared a strangers that she'll not hardly come out of her room if there's somebody other'n family in the house. Anyhow, you gotta come out."

Daro watched Lesher's face come alive as he talked about his brood. He hadn't noticed before but Lesher's sandy colored hair was beginning to gray at the temples and his hairline was receding. He felt a knot form in his throat and was afraid he couldn't speak.

"I think I might like that, partner,." He croaked.

Both men were quiet for a time as Lesher cruised up Buckner Boulevard. He made his way over to Lawther and followed the shoreline of White Rock Lake. The afternoon was inordinately mild for December. A gentle westerly breeze blew off the water and Lyle had his window rolled down, his left arm resting on the windowsill. Several sail boats tacked gracefully back and forth across the slightly choppy water. Normally Daro loved this drive, but he was too engrossed with his thoughts to notice. He even missed the several cars parked in secluded spots off the road in which couples joined together in intense, late afternoon games of slap and tickle, a precursor to the same, ever popular nighttime activity around White Rock Lake.

Lesher chuckled. "I wish I had the condom concession around here."

When Lawther rejoined Buckner at the north end of the lake, Lesher turned back south toward Garland Road. They were still several blocks north of their goal when a red MG-TC pulled onto Buckner Boulevard headed south. Blinded by the afternoon sun, the dark haired girl at the wheel apparently didn't see the black police cruiser.

She quickly accelerated through the gears until the pacing police cruiser's speedometer read fifteen miles per hour over the speed limit.

"You're up, partner," said Lesher.

Daro leaned over to get a better look at the speedometer and glanced at his watch. 4:30. "Okay, hit the lights."

Lesher pulled the switch for the red lights and tapped the horn to get the gal's attention. Typically, Miss MG looked in the rear view mirror and almost gave herself a whiplash looking back over her right shoulder to verify what her mirror had already told her. Grimacing, she signaled and pulled to the side of the road.

Placing his cap squarely on his head in the prescribed departmental manner, Daro got out and ambled up to the car, ticket book in hand.

Watching carefully from the driver's seat, Lesher picked up the radio mike and ran the car's plates.

The "no wants or warrants" came back long before Daro was through. In fact, he was taking much longer than usual. Just in case Lesher stepped out of the car and stood with his left arm draped over the top of the open door, his right hand on the butt of his old police issue model 10, S&W 38 special, it's retaining strap unsnapped. Everything seemed all right. He had removed his hat, his left arm on top of the MG's windshield.

Both he and the girl were all smiles. After some 20 minutes, and without giving her a citation, he patted the top of the car door, stuck his ticket book in his right rear pocket, and ambled back to the squad car. Lesher sensed a quiet excitement in his new partner.

"Took pity on her didja, hoss?" said Lesher, once more sliding into the driver's seat.

In addition to his elation, Daro seemed a little secretive. "Yeah, she was a friend of a friend."

"Right," Lesher said, giving him a broad smile. "I thought she was real cute, too."

Terri Silk thought she would burst with happiness. How could something so wonderful, so fantastic happen to her? Just saying his name gave her goose bumps. Danny Daro.

Never had there been anyone like him, over six feet tall, built like a wedge, and well over two hundred pounds. And those eyes, and that hair. She would kill for him, just say the word.

Terri had to laugh when she thought how they met. How magnificent he looked in his Dallas Police uniform, so straight and tall. It was love at first sight. He didn't even give her a ticket.

She did wish, though, that he had picked another place to meet. The Royal Cafe, just across Main Street on the north side of City Hall was too close to some of her worst memories. Terri was only twenty five years old, but there was no telling how many of the uniforms from across the street she had been with, at least a dozen - maybe more.

She shrugged. No more. Starting now only one man, Danny Daro, would tell her how pretty her blue eyes were, or how fine her body was and how good it felt under his hands, and how sexy her long, black hair looked fanned out on his pillow. No more of other cop's whispers in her ear as she watched a sweating, straining form moving above her. It always ended the same, lips pulled back in an animal snarl, almost like they were in pain.

She looked up expectantly as the cafe door opened. Not him. It was that loudmouth, Jack Perkins and his partner, Jeff Liggett. That Jack - ugh! She shuddered to think that she and he -. Too late she tried to pull back in the booth.

"Terri, baby," Perkins shouted, holding out his arms as if to give her a hug. "Long time."

Terri flushed. "Go away, Jack, I don't want to see you."

"Now, Terri," Perkins said in a mocking tone. "Is that any way to treat such an old and good friend? Here I've been worried sick about you since you went away and you treat me like this."

He laughed as the flush deepened, spreading over her dark, almost olive complexion.

"You're a real bastard, Jack, you know that?"

"Now you've gone and hurt my feelings," he said, placing his right hand over his heart. "But just to show you what a nice guy I am, give me and Jeff here a few minutes to get a cup a coffee and we'll go to your place and show you a real good time."

Liggett's face showed his discomfort. "Okay, Jack," he said. "Give it a rest."

Perkins laughed again, walked across to the counter, and plunked down on a stool.

Terri resumed staring into her coffee, stirring it slowly. Something in the cup caught the light. Absentmindedly, she fished out an eyelash with a long, red fingernail and tapped it loose on her napkin.

Where was Danny? She wanted out of here, away from Perkins.

Rummaging around in her purse, Terri fished out a compact and opened it to check her makeup. With a critical eye, she looked in the small, round mirror and blotted her full red lips against each other.

Everything checked. She tried a smile. Somehow it didn't quite come off. Too worried, probably. Was she really pretty? Lots of guys, mostly cops, had told her so, but then all of them had wanted something from her.

She tried not to think about all the different times and different guys. But Danny was so fine, so understanding. Marrying Danny Daro would be like marrying a god.

Where is he? Terri was worried. She checked the clock again - 11:58. The Royal closes in just a few minutes. Besides, he had the early detail.

For a moment her temper flared. He said he'd be here. Finally she swallowed her pride and went over to Liggett and Perkins.

"Hey, babe," Perkins said. "Change your mind?"

Terri knew she'd have to put up with a few of his jibes to get the information she wanted. "No," she said, impatiently. "And I never will. I just need to find out if either of you guys saw Daro in the locker room?"

"Daro?" Perkins asked, mockingly. "Danny Daro? Young guy, big; two tone hair and sort of funny looking eyes?"

She pulled herself up to her full five feet one inch. "I'll have you know we are engaged."

"Engaged in what?" Perkins asked, archly, poking Liggett in the ribs. He quickly ran his hand over her ripe behind, cupped in her skirt, and squeezed where the leg joined her bottom.

"Stop that!" she said in a stage whisper, slapping his hand away. "If I told Danny, he'd kill you."

"Sorry, babe, but I just can't help remembering. Your butt is as smooth and soft as your last name. You sure you don't want just one more session with me before you and Daro get married?"

Terri Silk had all she was going to take. Turning on her heel, she bounced off toward her booth. She didn't see Perkins' open appreciation, apparently drawing mental pictures about her and the six foot, four inch Daro. At five feet, one inch, and a hundred twenty five pounds, Terri was shapely, but slightly overripe.

The waitress brought her check and reminded Terri that they were closing.

"You know something, partner," Liggett said, checking his watch. "You can be a real horse's ass sometimes."

Perkins grinned. "Partner, if little Miss Round Heels over there had as many sticking out of her as she's had stuck in her, she'd look like a porcupine."

Disgusted, Liggett got off his stool and walked to Terri's booth and sat down across from her.

Silk looked up and frowned. "What's the matter, Liggett, your partner didn't say enough?

"Come on, Terri, I didn't feel your ass, that's Jack's department."

She shook her head. "Yeah, I know. Sorry."

"I just came over to tell you that I'm sure Daro was already gone when we got in. Our lockers are in the same row and he wasn't in the showers. I hate to rain on your parade, but he was on the early detail and Jack and I were on the late. He's gone."

Terri drew in a ragged breath, squeezed her eyes shut, and started to cry, noiselessly. Tears rolled down her cheeks, several dropping into her napkin.

Liggett got up to leave and Terri touched his jacket sleeve.

"Thanks, Jeff," she said, trying to smile.

He patted her hand. "Sure. No problem. And Terri, I've always liked you. I think you're a nice girl. I hope you and Daro will be real happy."

If Terri was a pup, she'd have wagged her tail. As it was, all she could muster was a grateful nod.

Waiting to be sure they were gone, Terri made repairs to her makeup. When she saw them drive away, she gathered up her things, paid the check, and left, bouncing off down the street to her car.

Her red MG was less than a block away. The little four banger caught on the first crank and without even looking, Terri pulled from the curb and raked through the gears, heading toward the Houston Street Viaduct and her Polk Street address.

It was half past midnight when she got to her apartment. Fumbling the lock open, she stepped inside and closed the door. She could feel hot tears start to flow. Running to the bedroom, she dropped keys, purse, and herself on the bed as the dam burst.

Sobs racked her as she made muffled, mewing sounds into the bed-clothes. Finally the sobs deteriorated into occasional, sharp intakes of breath which shook the bed. She'd made a decision. Getting off the bed she went to the bathroom and started a tub of very hot water. The clock read 1:30 AM. Disapprovingly, she glanced at the silent telephone.

It was 2:00 AM before Terri got through with her bath. She stepped from the still steamy water and patted herself dry with a large, beach size towel. Wrapping herself in a soft, full length robe she padded out to the living room to have a last cigarette. She curled up in her favorite chair, tapped a Camel on her thumbnail. Clicking her lighter she touched flame to cigarette and drew a billow of smoke deep into her lungs.

The telephone rang.

Nearly knocking the base off of the table, she grabbed the receiver. "Danny?" she shouted. "Danny, is that you?"

"Naw, babe, it's me," Jack Perkins said. "Just wanted to give you one last chance to get laid."

"You miserable son of a bitch!" Terri screamed into the phone. "Why can't you leave me alone?"

She slammed down the receiver, but not before she heard Jack's cackling laugh. Beginning a new round of tears, Terri went to the bedroom to dress.

Rummaging around in the bottom dresser drawer, Terri withdrew her special lingerie and dressed quickly. She stepped to the full length mirror and pivoted to the right, sucking in her abdomen.

Still a slight bulge. At least her milk had dried up. Even though it was fading, the three month old scar left by the Caesarean troubled her. Once again a thought brought her close to tears. Tonight she'd planned to tell Danny she could never have another child.

"No one loves me," she said, the sound of her own voice startling her.

Terri made a face and shook her head. It was time.

There was one last thing. Terri glided to the desk and jotted a quick note before returning to the bedroom. Seated on the edge of the bed Terri opened the drawer in the bedside table, removing a bottle of pills. The label read: Klein Discount Drugs, New Orleans, Louisiana, Prescription Number 516769, For : T. Silk, 09/17/55, Dr. Evans. Take as needed for sleep, Seconal Sodium, 100 mg. There were several dozen pills in the bottle.

Terri shook out a handful and downed them one by one between sips of water from her already filled glass on the nightstand. One quick check of the makeup, a small lipstick repair, and she lay down, carefully arranging her lingerie. Satisfied with the effect, Terri fanned out her black, wavy hair over the silk, ivory colored pillow. After intertwining her fingers over her abdomen, she closed her eyes. In minutes her breathing became slow and shallow. Body temperature lowered as she slipped into coma. At her last breath, the bedside clock read, 3:48AM. It was Friday, November 18, 1955.

Daro pulled his black and white Crown Victoria into a parking place by Terri Silk's apartment building just off Polk Street. The warm, morning sun felt good on his neck. He checked his watch. 10:35. Several police cars and an ambulance were parked in front, but he thought nothing of it. Another pretty day. Almost summer like.

Taking the front steps two at a time, he went to the elevator and punched the button for Silk's floor. When the elevator stopped and the doors opened, he almost ran into Detective Thomas Tines.

Not long out of Radio Patrol and a uniform, Tines recognized him. "Hi, Danny, what're you doin' here?"

Daro nodded. "Good morning, Detective Tines. I've got an appointment with someone. Or maybe I should say, I had one last night."

"Anyone I know?"

"I doubt it, her name's Terri Silk."

Tines blinked his owl like eyes. "Uh, maybe you better come with me."

Curious, but not asking questions, he followed as Tines led the way to Terri's apartment. He watched Tines speak to a short, cadaverous looking man he had never seen before. As the detective whispered in the man's ear, he turned and stared hard at Daro.

The whispered conference over, the man walked over, stuck out a hand, and flashed a set of horrible false teeth that clicked when he talked. His voice sounded like gravel on tin.

"I understand you're name's Daro."

He took the offered hand. "Yes, sir, and yours?"

"I'm Lieutenant Nathan."

"What's going on here, Lieutenant?"

"In a minute. But first I need a few answers."

Daro crossed his arms. "Fire away."

"How well did you know Miss Silk?"

He looked intently at Nathan, his expression clouding. "You talk like she's dead."

Nathan nodded and hooked a thumb toward the bedroom. "In there. We got the call about an hour ago."

Shocked and deeply disappointed, Daro asked, "How?"

"Sleeping pills, looks like. A friend found her. They were supposed to go shopping together."

"Oh, no," he said, bowing his head.

"When did you see her last?"

"Yesterday afternoon about four thirty."

"She seem okay?"

Daro shrugged. "Yeah, I guess so."

Uncomfortable talking up to the taller man, Nathan took a step back. "You know Jack Perkins?"

"You could say that. We've had a run in or two; worked together a couple of times. He and his partner have lockers on the same row as mine."

Nathan nodded. "Let's have a seat and talk this over."

They walked to the corner opposite the bedroom door. Nathan pointed to the couch for Daro. The Lieutenant took the leather chair and crossed his legs. "How well did you know this girl?"

"I didn't."

"Oh?" the Lieutenant said, arching his eyebrows. "I've been led to believe otherwise."

Daro snorted. "Lieutenant, you've been misinformed."

Not used to being so addressed by a common patrolman, Nathan flushed, but held his tongue. Rubbing his palms together, he leaned back in the chair, and looked at Daro.

"What's your first name?"

"Danny Daro."

Hell of a name for a grown man, thought Nathan. "Well, Danny, I've got me a serious problem here. I need to know all about this girl, in fact, anything at all you know about the case."

Daro looked at the Lieutenant and leaned back on the couch, resting his hands on his legs. "I don't have much to tell you. Do you remember the names Richard, Evelyn, or Sally Daro?"

Nathan furrowed his brow, "I've heard the names, but can't place 'em."

"They were my folks and my sister. They were murdered."

Nathan snapped his fingers. "Talmadge is handling it."

Daro laughed. "Yeah, I guess you could say that."

"I take it you don't care for Lieutenant Talmadge?"

"Let's just say, if you flushed him, he'd choke the toilet."

"That's plain enough," chuckled Nathan. "But how about we get back to Terri Silk?"

Daro ran his hand through his hair and changed positions on the couch. "Sure," he said. "I stopped her for speeding. She saw my name tag and mentioned that Betty, her younger sister, had gone to school with a Sally Daro. It didn't take but a second to establish that she was talking about my sister.

"Terri told me that Betty and Sally ran into each other the night Sally disappeared. She and my Mom and Dad had dinner and went to a movie, then talked awhile. I had a lot more questions than I could ask parked on the side of the road, so I arranged to meet Terri after work."

"That makes sense," Nathan said. "How long were you engaged?"

"Engaged? What the hell are you talking about?"

"Come on, Daro," Lieutenant Nathan said, sarcasm dripping from his voice. "And you were doing so well, too."

Daro smiled, all teeth, but no mirth. His strangely disconcerting eyes flashed a warning. "Lieutenant, I get the impression you're about to call me a liar. I wouldn't. As we sit here, I'm not a cop, but a private citizen giving answers to a police officer investigating an apparent suicide. After all the shit Talmadge has given me, I'm not about to take another ration from you."

Nathan was obviously taken aback. Daro watched the Lieutenant struggle not to show anger.

"Look, Daro, You remember I asked you about Jack Perkins?"

"Yes. I wondered when you'd get back to him."

"About thirty minutes after we got here, the phone rang. The girl who discovered the body, Paula Townsend, was still here, so I had her answer it. It was Jack Perkins. Since it was a girl's voice, he thought it was Silk. We got an ear full before I broke in. He like to have shit his pants. Anyhow, he told me all about last night."

He waited for Nathan to continue. When he didn't, he asked, "Is all this supposed to mean something to me?"

Nathan answered with a question. "Were you supposed to meet Silk last night?"

"Yes. At the Royal Cafe on Main, across from City Hall."

Nathan nodded. "Did you keep the date?"

"No, I got held up on a call. Didn't get off work until about eight forty five this morning. You can check that pretty easily with my partner

Lesher, or Captain Spencer, or a dozen other cops if you don't believe me. I was supposed to get off last night at eleven and then meet Terri."

"What held you up?"

"Missing kid. The one down in Little Mexico."

"Oh, yeah, the dispatcher rebroadcast it this morning. Dead?"

"Yeah. We found him in an abandoned refrigerator in this guy's garage. The kid got in, shut the door, and suffocated. The dumbass who owns it claims he didn't know he was supposed to disable the lock."

"Well, that explains part of it anyway," Nathan said. "Had you and Terri been having problems?"

"Lieutenant," Daro said, with a disgusted sigh. "I'm not getting through to you. Terri Silk was not my girl friend."

"Look, Daro, last night Perkins and Liggett went to the Royal after their shift. Terri was there," Nathan said, pointing toward the bedroom.

"Perkins made a pass - several in fact - and Silk told him somewhat more or less politely to stick it up his ass, that she was having none of it. You did know that Perkins was the father of one of her children, didn't you?"

Daro looked even more disgusted. "Lieutenant –."

Nathan held up a hand. "Okay, just hold on. Silk was in New Orleans for over six months waitin' to have her baby, her second, both given up for adoption. She got back to Dallas about a month or so ago. Last night Terri told Perkins and Liggett that you two were engaged."

Nathan coughed into his hand and continued, "Perkins said Liggett talked to her for a while, and she was crying and carrying on something fierce. It appears that she came straight home, got all dolled up, and took enough sleeping pills to kill a horse. But you say you don't know nothin' about that?"

"That's right, Lieutenant. We had an appointment to meet at the Royal after I got off shift. It wasn't even a real date. I was going to ask her out to my house to see what she knew about the night her sister had dinner with my family, that's all. I wanted to see if she knew anything at all that might help us find their killers."

"Wait a minute, here," Lieutenant Nathan said, puzzled. "Just how long have you known Terri Silk?"

Daro looked at his watch. It was almost noon. "At four thirty, today, I would have known her exactly twenty four hours".

"Son of a bitch!" Nathan exclaimed, throwing himself back in his chair. "We've been dealing with a nut case."

"I guess so," he said. "But, Lieutenant, what made you think I had any part in all this?"

"Carl," Nathan said, motioning to one of the detectives.

"Yes, sir?"

"You got the note?"

"Yes, sir," he said, "Right here in my pocket."

Lieutenant Nathan held out his hand. "Let me have it."

Reaching into his pocket, the detective removed a sheet of lavender stationary and handed it to Nathan. Without comment, the Lieutenant passed the note to Daro and watched his face.

It was addressed to him. His face all but burst into flame as the scent of Terri Silk's expensive lavender perfume was released into the room.

It was a simple note in a simple, almost childlike hand which read, "I LOVE YOU, DANNY."

• • •

8

At first Daro felt twinge of responsibly for Terri Silk's suicide, but he'd had no choice but to keep searching for the missing child. He kept reminding himself that Terri was an emotionally sick and terribly disturbed young lady. What happened had less to do with him than Silk's mental state.

In his bumbling, but usually effective way Lesher tried to comfort him, but the thing that helped him the most was when Lt. Nathan let him read portions of Terri's diary. The childlike scribbles were a successive litany of little girl fantasies about every policeman she had ever known. Each entry went into great detail of how she imagined her life would be, from marching down the aisle in a virginal white wedding dress to the three bedroom cottage with a picket fence. The only thing that seemed to vary with each transient new lover was the number of kids.

As it turned out, he was not unique. Daro just happened to draw the short straw when Terri finally dove over the edge. There was a moment of puzzled excitement as he ran across an entry about Sally, his sister; something about a telephone call. Terri's penmanship was neat, but fragmented. To whom the call was made and what it was about was garbled.

Daro felt as though he was being quickly driven toward paranoia. No matter where he turned, some obstacle blocked his every move, Terri's suicide providing a good example. Doors seemed about to open, then just as abruptly slammed shut, bruising his emotional nose. Each instance left him more angry and frustrated than if the door had never opened.

First Mitchell, and now Terri Silk - both dead and there was nothing he could do. It was as though the gods had taken him on as a personal project, trying to see how far down they could push him before he cracked. He made up his mind that no matter what, he would never give up searching for the murderers, the gods notwithstanding.

He knew that the course he'd set might take more than his lifetime and, with the lack of leads, would almost certainly use up the time remaining to him as a police officer. After all, he was a rookie cop and might never make detective. The thought was less than comforting.

Unable to question Terri, Daro's next goal was to interrogate her sister, Betty - if he could just find her. But somehow, somewhere, he would find the key that fit the lock to open a killer's door. It was frustrating to wait, but what other option did he have? The only thing of which he could be reasonably sure was a twenty year career on the force - if he kept his nose clean, that is. The only coin he had was time.

Through Sergeant Tines, Daro was able to locate Paula Townsend, the girl who had discovered Silk's body. It took several calls, but they finally made contact and he arranged a dinner date. He nervously drove to Townsend's Oak Cliff address.

It was seven o'clock on the dot when he rang the doorbell at Paula's apartment. She lived just a few blocks away from her former friend, Terri. When she answered the door, Paula turned out to be a tall, very thin girl with long, stringy hair of a nondescript brown color. She was obviously nervous.

Paula quickly scanned his face and shyly dropped her gaze to his feet. "Uh - hi. Come in. I'll get my coat."

She scurried to the bedroom before he could even answer. He looked around at the drab apartment, wondering why someone would choose to live in such a place. The only spots of color were the dozens of stuffed animals of every size and type spread about on the chairs, sofa, and even the floor. He had to remind himself that she might not have the financial wherewithal to do better. In a minute she came back throwing a frayed gray coat over hunched, thin shoulders.

When he tried to help her with the coat she trembled and pulled away.

"All ready, Mr. Daro," she said, still looking down.

He gave her his best smile. "My goodness, Paula, don't you think Mr. Daro is a bit formal? Please call me Danny."

She tried a shy smile, even allowing him to take her arm and escort her outside. "Okay - sure."

"Do you have a favorite place to eat?" he asked.

Paula brightened. "Yes I do. A little Italian place over on Jefferson called the Bella Napoli, if that's okay. It's a little expensive, though."

"I'm sure it will be fine. Tonight the sky's the limit."

After a short drive they arrived to find the restaurant almost deserted. The decor was attractive, small booths and rooms separated by lattice works interwoven with grapevine, but he was afraid that the lack of customers and the affordable prices listed on the menu were signals that he better keep the bicarb handy. So much for Paula's warning that it was a little expensive.

Paula ordered the least expensive thing on the menu. Getting Paula's approval he changed the order to Veal Parmigianino for two, and a split of Chianti. When their stocky waiter finished writing everything down, he scurried away as though his life depended on serving them immediately.

"Now," he said. "I know this must be hard for you, but do you mind if I ask you a few questions about Terri?"

Just the mention of her friend's name brought tears to Paula's eyes. She swallowed and said, "It's okay I guess."

"I understand you were real good friends."

Paula nodded. "Since grade school."

"Did you know her sister, Betty, too?"

Paula nodded again and adjusted her slipping glasses, looking up at him. "Yeah. She was younger and such a pest when we were kids. Used to follow us around 'til we thought we'd scream."

He smiled, remembering, and swallowed a lump. "Little sisters are like that," he said, softly. "Did Terri ever mention talking to Betty about the night my family was killed?"

"Yeah, she said something about it. Something about Betty meeting them downtown the night it happened. She said that Betty had called the cops - uh, I'm sorry, I mean the police - and gave somebody down there some information."

Daro felt a stir of excitement, but kept his voice steady. "Do you know what the information was and who she talked to?"

"Well," Paula said, furrowing her brow, "I'm not real sure. Betty said that it looked to her like someone might have been following your folks when they left the parking lot; a bunch of guys, maybe in two cars."

"Did she say what kind of cars, or write down a license number?"

Paula shrugged. "Maybe. I don't remember if she said so or not. But I do know that she called and talked to someone, so she must've had some information. I remember Terri tellin' me that nobody ever called Betty back or came out to see her. I guess what she had to tell 'em wasn't very important."

Keeping his voice nonchalant, he asked, "Where's Betty now?"

Another shrug. "I dunno. She's a wild one. Always gettin' in trouble, particularly with guys. When Betty's dad died, her mom kicked her out of their house up in Farmers Branch a couple of years ago and she lived with Terri for a few months. Terri's place is small - but you know that - and they had to share the same bed and everything. One night we came home from a movie and Betty had two guys with her - uh - in the bed and everything." Paula looked down into her lap, her face getting red. "Terri got real mad and told her to get out."

"Do you have any idea where Betty might be now?"

Paula shook her head. "No. Betty said she might go out to California, but I dunno. She left the next day with those same two guys. I haven't seen her since."

"How long ago was that?"

"Maybe six months."

Their dinner arrived and Daro discovered that he was starved. He had been so excited about meeting with Paula that he hadn't eaten that day. He also found out that his fears about the restaurant were groundless. The veal was excellent and, although he was not a connoisseur, the wine was also superb.

At home, Daro mentally ran over the night's events. Disappointed by the lack of detail, it was at least clear that some kind of information was passed to someone at the police department, and that the info - whatever the hell it was - apparently never reached Golden and Killean. He had no idea of what use such knowledge might be, but it could only add to the meager store he now had.

At first glance such an oversight smacked of either collusion or obstruction of justice, neither of which made any sense. Who would gain and what would that gain entail? The more he thought the more confused he became. He decided to sleep on it and get with Golden and Killean the next day. He briefly considered bouncing this new information off of Lesher, but he wasn't about to wake his partner in the middle of the night to ruminate over the telephone.

But Daro couldn't sleep, his mind refusing to turn off. Finally his thoughts turned to a honey haired, blue eyed blonde. Giving up at last, he called to make sure Jan was home and then drove over to her apartment. By the time he arrived every hormone in his body was awake. After all, he had not seen her for a couple of days.

His meeting with the two detectives the following morning was even less satisfactory than his evening with Paula Townsend. Like Daro, neither man could figure out why there was no memo of Betty's call.

"Look," Golden said, "there's not but a few possibilities; one, the memo got lost - but probably not in light of internal policy - or two, the information was too vague to be passed on or was maybe something we already knew. No matter what the call was about, though, all of 'em are written up and passed on to the team that has the case. Just the fact that we didn't get one makes me think there wasn't any call made. Maybe this Betty made it up - hell, maybe Townsend did."

All Daro knew was that he had arrived at another impasse. "Look, guys, is there some way we can look for Betty? I've got to do something about this."

"I reckon so," answered Killean. "You can talk to the girl's mother about filing a missing persons report."

"Can't we file it?" he asked.

Golden shook his head. "Nope. It's got to be a relative or a fiancé, or guardian, or something. If we file it there has to be a reason, like she was a witness to a crime, or maybe committed a crime herself - something like that. But if that was the case, it wouldn't be a missing persons, it'd be a warrant for her arrest."

Daro bristled. "You don't consider what happened to my family to be a crime?"

Golden looked peeved. "Come on, Danny, we're on your side, remember? But you can't file a missing persons unless it's within the purview of the missing persons law. Since none of the criteria fit, no soap."

"Well," said Daro, rubbing his hands together, "I guess I'll just have to talk to Betty's mom."

"You want us to go with you?" Golden asked.

"Thanks, but I'll take care of it," he said. He tossed them a semi-salute and strode out of the office.

Mrs. R. L. Silk was good enough to receive him after his telephone call. In less than two hours he knocked on her door in the small town of Farmers Branch north of Dallas. He was surprised when the door swung open to show a short, slightly chunky lady who could easily have passed for Terri's slightly older sister. Still, he knew she had to be in her late forties or early fifties. Her black hair was without a trace of gray, her pretty face unlined.

"Please come in, Officer – uh - Daro, is it?" Even her voice was like her dead daughter's.

"Uh, thank you, Ma'am. I really appreciate this."

"Not at all, Officer. Won't you please have a seat," she said, motioning toward a beige, overstuffed couch in front of a large picture window. Several evergreen trees and a juniper hedge lent the yard a spot of color. She sat down in a matching chair on his right and folded her hands in her lap. "How may I help you?"

He took the offered seat. "Mrs. Silk, I wonder if I could ask you a few questions about your daughter, Betty?"

Mrs. Silk stiffened, her mouth assuming a rigid line. "What has she done this time?"

He held out his hand in a stopping gesture. "I'm sorry, Ma'am, I didn't mean to imply she had. All I need to do is find her. She may have some information about another case. Do you by any chance remember the couple and their daughter who were murdered some time ago - Mr. and Mrs. Daro and their daughter, Sally?"

"I seem to remember reading about it in the paper," she said, her brow furrowed. Then her face cleared. "Oh my goodness - Daro - your name is Daro." She reached out and touched his arm. "I am so sorry, Officer Daro. They were your family, weren't they?"

He swallowed. "Yes, Ma'am, and thank you. You can help me out if you wouldn't mind. I need to find Betty to see what she knows about the night my family was murdered."

Mrs. Silk looked alarmed. "Betty has always been a bad girl, but I don't think she would be involved in a murder."

He shook his head. "No, Ma'am, she's not." He went on to explain what little he knew about that night. He further explained why it would be necessary for Mrs. Silk to file a missing persons report for the police to enter the case.

"I see," she said. "Then you just need to ask her some questions?"

"Exactly."

Mrs. Silk nodded and interlaced her fingers. "I will file the report first thing in the morning."

"I really appreciate that, Ma'am. Have you heard anything at all from her since she left?"

"I've had one postcard. She asked me to send money."

He became excited. "Was there an address? Did you keep the card?"

Mrs. Silk smiled sadly. "In spite of Betty's reprehensible actions over the years, I did keep it. I'll get it for you," she said, going into the next room.

Daro remained standing as he heard a drawer pull out and the sound of papers being rifled through. In a minute, Mrs. Silk returned and handed him the card. With trembling fingers he turned it over and found an address in San Francisco. Taking out pen and notebook he sat down at the coffee table and copied the street and number.

Mission accomplished, he stood to leave and warmly grasped Mrs. Silk's hand. "I can't thank you enough, Ma'am."

"Think nothing of it - there's just one thing. I'll be almost sorry if you find her. I find it hard to say about my own flesh and blood, but I never want to see her again. I'm convinced her antics were the direct cause of her father's death."

Her comment shocked him. Still, he understood that some children cause their parents great pain, and vice versa. "Ma'am, may I ask how long ago your husband passed?"

"Four years now."

"Mrs. Silk, this may be the most tasteless thing I've ever said to a lady. You are an absolutely beautiful woman in both form and personality. If you aren't dating, please find a nice single man and give him a chance to make both his and your life complete."

He closed the door on an astounded, but very pleased lady.

Daro left and drove his Crown Vic down highway 77 back to Dallas. He was taking a chance by not calling first, but Jan was home when Daro arrived, ostensibly for a cup of coffee. It wasn't long until he went on duty, but he didn't want to wait for Lesher. He was in need of an immediate, sympathetic ear. He lay on the couch, his head in her lap as Jan rubbed his temples and made appropriate clucking sounds while he thought out loud. He decided to cover all the bases by again hiring the detective agency. Calling from Jan's place, he gave them all the information he had, instructing them to enlist whatever help they needed both in Dallas and California. As to funding, he gave them carte blanche. When he hung up there was time for only one lingering kiss before he hurried down to city hall for his shift.

From the night of December 31, 1955 to the morning of January 1, 1956, Daro and Lesher went from swing shift to days. And two more tired cops had never lived. Not only did New Year's Eve fall on a Saturday, but it was the busiest day in the history of the police department. To further exacerbate the problem, he and Lyle got a radio call just before shift change; this in addition to being faced with a short turn around. They got home about 3:00 AM and were up at six to groggily meet a 7:00 AM detail. The only bright spot to their otherwise hectic night was a very quiet morning. Theirs was practically the only car on the street as they cruised District 71.

A common practice after short change-over was for one officer to drive and the other to snooze, switching drivers every so often. Daro was on the nod with Lesher at the wheel, cruising Main Street between Market and Record. When they passed the Green Door Bar, Lesher saw a light on in the back. Lesher made a U turn and parked down the block out of sight.

"Hey, Daro," Lesher said, punching his partner in the ribs.

"Huh - what's going on?"

"I dunno for sure," said Lesher. "There's some lights on in the Green Door."

Lesher had checked out the bar many times, a skid row hangout with ten cent draft beer and cheap wine. He couldn't remember ever leaving the place without arresting at least one drunk. But this was Sunday. By law, the bar was supposed to be closed.

It was 10:00 AM and still cool. The cruiser's windows were rolled up, but as soon as the officers opened their doors they could hear the juke box blasting away. As usual, Fats Domino was belting out his rendition of "Green Door", the unofficial song of the bar which bore its name. The bar was there years before the song however. Warily, both officers eased up to the front window and peeked inside. Even through the glass it seemed that Lesher could smell stale beer, sweat, and urine.

A party was in full swing, apparently a carryover from the night before. Two women and six men were behind the locked front door, one of the women asleep in a booth, the other staggering around the dance floor in the arms of an equally drunk man. Lesher immediately recognized the dancing woman as Darlene Miller, a snuff dipping whore from Little Rock, Arkansas. He didn't believe it at first, but

Darlene had once been a registered nurse before she began making her living on her back.

Lesher knew Darlene well, having booked her many times. Besides, there was no mistaking that hairdo. She looked like she had stuck her finger into an electrical socket, turning her into an aging Little Orphan Annie. Although dumpy now, at one time Darlene was relatively presentable. But she had fallen on hard times the past few years, turning two dollar tricks to make enough to buy a flop for the night and enough beer or wine to stay reasonably smashed.

It looked like it had been a good night for Darlene. From the smile on her face Lesher deduced she thought it would be an equally good day. She was reared back in her dancing partner's arms, grinding her pelvis into his crotch and grinning at him as though certain he was Mr. sperm du jour.

Lesher's baton tap on the window electrified the bar, the clientele snapping to attention as though hearing a pistol shot.

"Okay, Rafe, open up," Lyle shouted.

The bartender hesitated, indecision etched on his bloated face. When he made up his mind, Rafe put on what passed for a welcoming smile and waddled to the door. Opening it he wiped his hands on a once white tee shirt that billowed out over his belt like a wind filled spinnaker.

"Mr. Lesher, it's sure good to see you, sir. Come right in here."

"Well thank you very much, Rafe. I just know how glad you are to see us," Lyle said pleasantly. "We havin' a little party, are we?"

"Yes, sir, we sure are. Just a few friends, don't you see. Nothin' fancy, mind ya."

"Well, I'm so glad. You must have forgot my invitation 'cause I didn't see it in my mail box the other day."

Rafe shrugged and broadened his smile. "Oh, it wasn't nothin' planned, Mr. Lesher, it just sorta happened, don't you know."

"I can see that," Lesher said as both he and Daro edged further into the bar. "And as I live and breathe, isn't that Darlene Miller on the dance floor?"

"Howdy, Mr. Lesher, how the hell are ya," Darlene shouted, waving her arm in the air like a rodeo rider on an angry steer. She almost fell over backward when she took the arm off her dancing partner. "We've been needin' some new blood aroun' here."

Lesher grinned and nodded. "I can see that, darlin'. You been havin' a good time, have you?"

"You're damn right," she lisped. Darlene shifted her eyes to Daro and squinted. "And jush who the hell is that with you?"

"I beg your pardon, darlin. This here's my new partner, Officer Danny Daro. I want all you people to mark his name well 'cause he gets real pissed if you forget it. He'll like as not put somebody's ass in the jailhouse if they ain't careful."

The men shifted uncomfortably as Darlene cackled. "I'll bet I could simmer his ass right down, Mr. Lesher. Yes, sir, I'll bet I could jush do that."

Daro was already uncomfortable and Lesher seemed to be having fun watching his rookie partner's discomfort. He wanted to tell him to knock it off, but he knew that if he did, Lesher would pour it on all the more.

Lesher motioned toward the phone. "Partner, why don't you drop a dime and see if seventy two can give us a hand?"

Daro called dispatch from the pay phone on the far wall then came back. "They'll be here in about five minutes."

"Okay, people, you're all under arrest. Rafe, if you need to call someone to close up, you'd best get to it. You men hit the wall and spread 'em. You know the drill. Darlene, why don't you wait with Sleeping Beauty over there?"

"Sure thing," she said, happily. "I'll be right over here." Darlene staggered to the booth and plopped down across from the other woman who was still cutting zees.

Bishop and Nobles from District 72 arrived by the time the prisoners were shaken down. Lesher borrowed their handcuffs and placed them about the wrists of the four men he thought might be the most dangerous. He also handed over three illegal knives and a 25 caliber pistol found during the search. Daro watched the prisoners while

Lesher held a smiling, whispered conversation with Bishop. He should have guessed that something was up.

"Okay, Partner," said Lesher, "Bishop and Nobles are going to take the men and we're gonna take the women. You help Darlene to the car and I'll pour her compadre here in the front seat with me."

"Sure thing," Daro said, moving off to get his prisoner. Still seated in the booth, Darlene was humming softly to herself.

"You want to come with me, Ma'am?" Daro asked.

Darlene looked up, her eyes out of focus. "Damn right, darlin', you jush point the way."

He lifted her to her feet and helped her toward the door. Darlene clutched her purse to her chest as she teetered precariously on scuffed high heels. "You gonna come with me, sweet cheeks?" she asked, cackling again.

Embarrassed, Daro said, "Sure am, Ma'am."

"Thash jush great, darlin'," lisped Darlene. "Jush you and me, kid."

After Darlene staggered into the wall and bounced off both sides of the front door at virtually the same time, he got her into the left rear seat of the squad car. Right behind them came Lesher, all but carrying the other woman, half laying her on her side in the front passenger's seat. With Lesher driving, they set off for the city jail.

Arresting women was always a hassle. Since there were so few, the ratio of female to male prisoners being some thirty or forty to one, the City of Dallas had closed its women's jail, entering into a long-standing agreement between the City of Dallas and Bill Decker, the Sheriff of Dallas County. Even so, women were first taken to the city jail for booking before being transported to the County Jail.

Bishop and Nobles took the men up in the elevator to the men's jail, while Daro and Lesher booked the two women downstairs. The paperwork completed, they wrestled the women back into the cruiser and headed for the County Jail.

Lesher was barely off the vehicle ramp and out of the basement onto Commerce Street before Darlene started in.

"Say, Mr. Lesher, you wouldn't want to jush head to the boondocks an' play a l'il game a checkers, would ya?"

"I dunno how to play checkers, darlin'?"

"Hey, it's real simple. We jump each other and when you get to my back row, I king ya," she said, slapping her thigh and laughing.

"Better not, Darlene. You might give me something even penicillin couldn't cure."

The aging hooker started a whole new round of cackles. Turning to Daro she launched her rancid breath at him. "How about you, sweet cheeks, you wanta give it a shot?"

He felt sure his red face could stop traffic. "Thanks, Ma'am, but I better not."

"Damn, Mr. Lesher," Darlene said, reaching into the front seat to smack Lyle on the shoulder, "You sure trained this boy good. He's real polite."

"I did, indeed, Darlene; did it just for you. By the way, have ya showed my partner your bank?" Lesher asked.

"By damn I ain't," she said. With that, Darlene lifted her skirt to give Daro a flash of stretch- marked skin above an ample thatch of graying, oft plowed real estate. He already knew more about her than he wanted to know, but to that meager knowledge he added the fact that Darlene wore no underpants.

His face went to three alarms. "Damn it, Lyle, will you quit encouraging her."

Lesher was having a hard time with his face. "What's the matter, partner, ain'tcha interested in high finance?"

Fuming, Daro said nothing. Just about the time he decided things couldn't get worse, Lesher egged her on again.

"Hey, Babe," Lyle said, still watching in the mirror, "We're getting pretty close to the jailhouse. They ain't gonna let you keep your snuff."

"Like hell," said Darlene.

She opened her purse and took out a squat, tube-shaped tin of Garrett's snuff and popped off the silver top. Pulling out her lower lip, she stuffed a pinch of the finely ground, dark brown tobacco between her lower lip and gum. Replacing the top on the can, Darlene hiked her leg to reveal her favorite hiding place. Daro watched in absolute horror as the snuff can slowly sank from sight - a short, fat, cylindrical pessary now firmly ensconced within the confines of Darlene's bank.

• • •

9

Daro was still pissed when he and Lesher got off shift. Later, however, thinking about Darlene and her bank, he began to see the funny side.

Like Sunday - except for what came to be known as the Furry Federal Reserve Incident - Monday was also quiet. Pedestrian, automobile, and radio traffic were sparse, making time pass slowly. Boredom ate away at the pair, particularly in Daro's case since he had a date with Jan that evening, their first in several days.

"What's cooking?" Daro asked when he spoke to her that afternoon on the telephone.

"Funny you should ask," she said. "I want you to bring a change of clothes and a healthy appetite; something special is cooking for supper and I want you to stay the night."

"I'll see you in about two hours."

Expecting some exotic meal that required a long time to prepare, he was surprised when he reached the upper landing at Jan's. Smells from the kitchen were not of tarragon, oregano, or thyme, but smelled instead of bacon with just a hint of garlic. In light of their anticipated evening, he wondered about the advisability of that latter condiment.

"I'm in here," Jan shouted from the kitchen when she heard him come in the outer door.

Daro ambled back to find her standing at the sink, a plate in one hand and a dishrag in the other, an apron covering a pleated, powder blue skirt. Her show of domesticity brought a lump to his throat.

He came up from behind and encircled her with his arms, pressing his lips to her neck. Once again he was rewarded by a bumper crop of gooseflesh.

Jan hunched her shoulders and shivered. "Stop that, officer, or I'll call a cop."

He feigned fear. "I'm sorry, madam. Please spare me."

She turned within the circle of his arms and once again he met trembling lips. When they parted she rested her head on his shoulder. Sensing her need for quiet, he held her tenderly. After a few moments she broke contact and looked into his eyes.

"You are the sweetest man and you don't even know it."

Pleased, Daro flushed. "What brought that on?"

She shrugged. "I don't know. I'm just in a lovin' mood I guess. Now you get out of here and let me finish supper."

"What are we having?"

"Stuff you probably never had before - almost crisp fried flank steak with flour and garlic pounded into it with the edge of a saucer to make it tender - home made pinch-off biscuits dipped in bacon grease, and to top it off, flour thickened milk gravy. If my Daddy was still alive he'd crawl here from Tennessee."

"Is that where you're from?"

"Yeah, about a hundred years ago. Now git, so I can finish," she said, deliberately reverting to her southern accent.

After supper they cuddled on the couch, her head on his shoulder. Daro was stuffed and Jan was right, the food she served was a first. He decided that having a British cook was a good thing, but a lifetime of Mildred's cooking had caused him to miss out on a whole range of culinary arts he might otherwise have experienced.

When he spoke his breath rustled a wisp of her blonde hair. "You mentioned your dad, but not your mom."

"She died a long time ago. I was about three. I don't remember her."

"Did your dad remarry?"

Her chuckle was cynical. "Oh, yeah, to a real bitch. She drove me away and ended up killing him - not with a gun or anything, but she broke his heart. Dad's been dead since I was fifteen. I left home when I was fourteen."

"That's awfully young to be on your own."

She nodded, her hair brushing his cheek. Until now she had told the truth, but switched to one of her better, more often used lies.

"Yeah. I went to Memphis and stayed with Dad's older brother, Mike. Uncle Mike never married and I was his only niece, so when he died he left everything to me. I was twenty then and the bank administered the estate until I was twenty one. Without me even knowing it, he had set me up for life."

"What did he do?"

"He was a commodity trader - you know - wheat, corn, soybeans, and something called pork bellies. Doesn't that sound disgusting?"

Daro laughed. "It does, indeed. But if it wasn't for pork bellies there would be no bacon."

Jan pretended astonishment. "Is that what they are?"

"Yep. Little piggies that went to market. So, since you obviously don't trade commodities, what do you do?"

"Oh, a little civic and charity work - things like that."

Since that was exactly what his mother had done, it did not occur to him to question her further. In fact, the more he was with this fascinating woman the more he thought she might be the girl he was looking for.

"Are you up to a little civic or charity work right now?" he asked.

Her pouty lips broke into a smile as she once again moved into the circle of his arms. "Let's take a shower together and discuss it."

Arrival at the shower stall, sans clothes, was a tie. The hint of garlic turned out to be no problem at all.

Jan rolled onto her back and stared at the ceiling while Daro lay on his right side, loving eyes tracing her face. Hers was the first perfect nose he'd ever seen, just the right size and shape. He loved the way her nostrils flared when she was aroused. He caressed her profile with his eyes and, as if he were a coral reef, a wave of tenderness broke over him. A drop of perspiration - or was it a tear - scurried down her cheek onto the pillow. Without thinking he gave voice to a long forming thought.

"What do you think we ought to do about this?" he asked.

"About what?"

"About us, dummy." His smile removed any sting in his words.

She became very still. "What do you think?"

"Well, I think we should consider making honest people out of each other. Would it upset you terribly if we shopped for an engagement ring?"

More frightened than she could ever remember, Jan's heart pounded as though it might burst. She was convinced that Daro could hear it, that he could sense what she was, that maybe could even see deep within her soul and ferret out the filth she kept hidden there. Would he still want her if he knew? Should she tell him anything or let her lies stand? For sure she couldn't tell him much.

"I don't know, Danny. I love you, but there's a lot about me you don't know. You might not want me."

He pulled the bed sheet down to his waist exposing a well defined, hairy chest and lightly began to run his hand over her body. "Fat chance," he said, chuckling. "What deep dark secrets do you have up there?" he said, tapping a finger against her forehead.

She turned on her side and snuggled up close. "Oh, quite a few things," she said, her voice muffled against his shoulder. "Old friends, and places, and things. We've all got our skeletons, you know."

"Let's see, now," he said, assuming a stern expression. "Ever kill anybody?"

She smiled and shook her head. "Nope."

"Break any legs or arms?"

"Nope."

"Let's see, how about dogs, cats, or children - do you ever kick 'em?"

"Nope."

"Do you love me?" he asked, softly, laying a muscular leg across her hip.

Her smile went away and this time there was no doubt as to what they were when tears sprang to her eyes. "Oh, yes," she whispered.

"You'll make a wonderful mother," he said, covering her lips with his. He soon discovered that the night was far from over.

Jan fixed breakfast as Daro put on his robe and fetched the Dallas Morning News from the postage stamp sized front lawn. When he plopped down on the couch and snapped the string from around the paper, it unrolled in his lap. The headline read, 'Dallas Cop and Police Sergeant's Wife Slain.'

He nearly swallowed his teeth as his eyes jumped to the text.

'Early last evening at 5314 Stanford Street, the home of Helen Potter and Sergeant JD Potter, a ten year veteran of the Dallas Police Department, a single bullet fired from a Smith & Wesson, 357 magnum revolver took the lives of both Mrs. Potter and Officer Jack Perkins, a patrolman of the Dallas Police Department. The pair were found dead in the master bedroom of the Potter's home. Officer Perkins was shot through the back, the bullet entering his heart and passing out his chest, and subsequently through the chest and heart of Mrs. Potter. The bullet lodged in the floor beneath the bed. Both were killed instantly. Officer Neil Atkins at the scene was heard to remark, "Whoever did it apparently got two birds with one stone."

'At the moment, police officials will neither confirm nor deny that the couple was murdered, or that the husband, Sergeant JD Potter, is a suspect. According to Captain Louis Spencer, Sergeant Potter's Detail Commander, the investigation is proceeding normally. Several officers were overheard to speculate that the murderer may have mistaken Officer Perkins for the husband, Sergeant Potter. Arrests, if any, should be expected soon. The case will shortly be presented to the Grand Jury for possible indictment.'

There was much more, but Daro was too stunned to finish. He picked up the telephone at the end of the couch, but there was no dial tone. Jan had disconnected it before they went to bed.

"Jan," he shouted, "Your phone isn't working."

She heard the alarm in his voice. "What's the matter?"

"It's JD. His wife's been killed. I've got to get over there."

"Oh, Honey, no. Do you want me to go with you?"

Daro vaulted for the bedroom and his clothes. "No. I'll call as soon as I know something." Three minutes later he was out the door.

Storm Raney had a scowl on his face when he answered Daro's ring at Potter's front door . The scowl disappeared when he saw who it was. "Come on in," said Storm. "He's in the den."

"What happened?"

Raney shrugged. "Damned if I know. Perkins was over here throwing the blocks to JD's wife when somebody wasted 'em. I dunno who did it. JD sure is tore up."

"No clues at all?" asked Daro.

"Not that I know of. Whoever did it wiped the pistol clean and dropped it on the bed."

"Who found them?"

"JD. He'd been out to the pistol range doin' his monthly qualification 'til almost dark," said Storm, leading the way down the hallway to the den. "This here's some bad shit, hoss. We gotta help all we can."

"Where's Chief?"

"Him and the Missis are in Oklahoma on vacation; won't be back for three or four days. I can't even get him by phone."

"What can we do?"

"Not a hell of a lot 'cept be here for him," said a sad Raney. "There's lots of talk around the department that JD caught 'em in bed and did the number his ownself. but you and I know that's bullshit. The word's out and the rumor mill's already goin'. It's worse'n stomping on an ant hill - the more you stomp the more the little bastards keep popping out of the hole."

Potter sat on the couch, his head in his hands. He looked up when Daro and Raney walked in. For a moment his tear reddened eyes looked right through them before recognition came. He motioned for them to take seats as he took out a handkerchief and wiped his eyes.

"Thanks for coming, Danny. I guess it's all over the department by now," Potter said.

Daro shrugged and shook his head. "I don't know; I guess so. I just read it in the paper this morning."

"Well, it doesn't matter - I've made my decision. As soon as things cool down I'll resign."

Daro's and Raney's faces registered shock. The police department was Potter's life. Even though Raney was responsible for launching them toward police careers, he still insisted that Potter was the driver behind their decision to become cops.

"That's your ass talking, hoss," Raney said. "There ain't no way you'd do that."

"Look, guys," continued Potter, "I'm the prime suspect, and from what I've been told, there aren't any real clues. That means it's not gonna be solved and there'll be a cloud over me for the rest of my life. I don't have to tell you that clouds following cops around is not good, particularly if that cop happens to be a sergeant."

"Your fears are a bit premature, don't you think?" asked Daro. "It hasn't been twenty four hours yet. They'll get him."

Potter shook his head. "No they won't, not without a confession. He's covered his tracks. Besides, why are you so sure I didn't do it?"

Raney frowned. "Knock off the bullshit, JD. We know you."

Potter shook his head, a cynical chuckle refusing to escape his lips. "Such blind faith. At least I know who my friends are."

The three were quiet for a moment as Potter took a sip of water from a glass on the coffee table, stood, and said, "I guess I better get over to mom's. She's keeping the kids."

Without another word, he walked from the house, got into his 34 Ford pick-up, and drove away leaving his two friends to lock up.

Helen Potter was buried on Saturday, January 7, 1956. And JD Potter resigned one week later. Under rigid emotional control, Captain Spencer read Potter's resignation to his detail.

"Gentlemen, listen up," said the Captain, looking out from the dais over a sea of blue winter shirts. "I've got bad news. Sergeant JD Potter has submitted his resignation and I couldn't change his mind.

It is, therefore, with great regret that I'm forced to accept. I wanta read it to you."

Spencer fumbled with his glasses and set them halfway down his nose as he unfolded the single sheet of paper. He cleared his throat and in a choked voice began.

"It is with profound regret that I tender my resignation from the Dallas Police Department, effective immediately. All of us on the force have known sorrow and joy, but the bonds forged between us over the past ten years will be with me for the rest of my life. You are my friends - my brothers in deed, if not in blood - and nothing will change that. But everyone who has read the newspapers or watched television knows of the attacks being made on me and indirectly on the Department. I feel it is in the best interest of all parties that I remove the target of those attacks. May God bless you and keep you. Goodbye. Signed Sergeant JD Potter."

The Captain removed his glasses and strode silently from the auditorium. In a few moments an equally silent procession of officers followed, making their way to the police garage to relieve the previous shift.

Nothing Potter's friends could say or do made a difference. Since coming home from the Army after World War II, all he ever wanted to do was be a cop. At least with his college degree from SMU he should have no trouble finding a job. Still, Daro would sorely miss him. It was almost as though his reason for being on the force was gone.

Without saying so Daro wondered about his comrade. Potter was so methodical, a plodder. His sudden resignation was uncharacteristic. Daro could not believe that his friend was a murderer, even though what slim evidence there was continued to mount, all of it pointing in Potter's direction.

At detail Lesher looked disgusted. "Partner, you seen the paper this morning? Them bastards are having a field day. Accordin' to the headlines every swingin' dick from the mayor on down to dogcatcher is calling for our blood."

"Yeah, I saw it."

Lesher paused a moment then chuckled. "You know, it's kinda funny in a way. Them asshole politicians and the press love to jump all over the police, but they get real gentle when they get into some kind of personal trouble and need us - or the suspect is some well known dirtbag with a rap sheet that stretches from here to El Paso. Seems to me like the dirtier the suspect, the better the press treats 'em."

"That's a fact," nodded Daro. "I never noticed it before I got on the force."

"I don't know why this kinda shit surprises me anymore," said Lesher. "I got nothin' but contempt for reporters. You ever noticed don't none of 'em ever get a story straight?"

"Looks like it, doesn't it?"

Lesher winked and nodded. "You watch real close the next time we get onto somethin' that makes the paper. I've not seen even one investigation that was exactly the way it got reported; they always get somethin' fouled up, sometimes so bad you can't even be sure it's the same case. I think some of them lazy bastards make 'em up to please their boss."

"I thought all stories had to be verified," Daro said.

"You'd think so, wouldn't you? But they're not. They've been gettin' away with murder talkin' about JD the way they have. He's good people. Shit, they've even been poundin' on Chief Phillips tryin' to get him to resign - bunch of dirtbag bastards. The Chief's a good man, too. He was one of my first sergeants just before he made lieutenant. He oughta go down to both papers and kick ass and take names."

For external consumption, the police department presented a united front. Internally however there was a growing tide of resentment and confusion within the rank and file. Word circulated that Potter refused to cooperate with the Grand Jury, taking the 5th at every question beyond that of where he had been that day and what time he came home. As to what he found when he got there, he remained mute.

Hounded by the press and police investigators alike, Potter called a press conference. Thinking they might be the only ones from the department to show, Lesher and Daro attended to find the auditorium packed with cops. Potter maddened the expectant press corps and certain echelons of the police department by telling them that he had said all on the subject he intended to say.

"My reasons are simple," he said, reading a prepared statement. "It has been my experience that suspects who talk to the police, particularly those who are or were cops, whether or not they have done anything wrong, often get the dirty end of the stick, certainly from the press, and sometimes from a police department that is being hounded by self-serving politicians. At a time like this the motto appears to be, 'indict whomever you can, but get an indictment'."

He paused, looking out over his audience. "Over the years several innocent and well meaning officers have ended up in Huntsville Prison when they tried to do the right thing and cooperate with the investigation. They have often found themselves sentenced to a long stay in the penitentiary, euphemistically known as the 'Graybar hotel'. Although I have done nothing wrong nor anything to be ashamed of, my silence is the only way I have a chance of not meeting the same fate. In short, I have no intention of cooperating with you now or in the future only to join their ranks. As any other free citizen of these United States, I am innocent of any crime until proven guilty and the burden of proof rests with the State."

Every cop in the room understood on a gut level. They knew he was right, but they still wanted him to say more. Several would have settled for him merely to say, 'I did not do it.' But even that small thing he refused to do.

Singling out the press, Potter continued, "Based on my personal experience, whatever I might say would be deliberately misquoted in the newspapers or on television, and massaged or otherwise changed to make whatever political point you might wish to make at the moment. I have no intention of allowing myself to be tried in the newspapers, certainly not with my help. I have found virtually every member of the press with whom I have had personal contact to be without morals, honor, or principles beyond that of expediency. That's all I have to say."

As though to further irritate, he spoke not another word. Daro and Lesher were proud of their friend. He'd had the guts to say what most of them thought. The media were reduced to an ancient rehash of his war record, his Medal of Honor, and his considerable accomplishments as a ten year police officer. The rest was pure speculation.

And speculate they did.

But all of the press, most of the people, and a handful of cops were angered by his refusal to answer questions. Lesher remained incensed at Potter's treatment, telling everyone who would listen, that he wouldn't talk to the bastards either. One week after Potter's wife was buried Storm Raney escorted Potter to clean out his locker. With head held high, ex-police Sergeant JD Potter walked out of City Hall for the last time. The only ones to see him go were Raney, O'Neil, and Daro.

The recent renewal of his high school friendship with Potter made it all the harder for Daro to lose him again. Besides that, Potter's absence left a hole in Spencer's detail, an unfilled vacuum both in the police department and in the lives of Potter's other friends. Helen Potter's murder and his sudden resignation took Daro's mind off his primary goal, but only temporarily. When the furor finally settled, he once again tried to focus on his job; beat cop first, then that of finding out who killed his family. The task still loomed large. Worse yet, a check with Golden and Killean told him that they were still in waiting mode. Mentally, Daro slid back into a blue funk.

Two hours of silence with Daro behind the wheel of their cruiser was all Lesher could take. "I've had enough of this mopin' around bullshit, partner."

Miffed at Lesher's tone, he asked, "And just what do you intend to do about it?"

"Well, I could kick your ass, but it's real embarrassin' when a little man beats up on his great big rookie partner. This your last shift before break?"

He chuckled and relaxed. "Yeah."

"I wantcha to come out to the house."

"I've got a date with Jan."

"So bring her. You been tellin' me what a hot number she is. This'll be a good chance to show her off. Course, Todd may attack her. He's worse'n a pup tryin' to hump a parson's leg."

Daro laughed. "Six okay?"

Lesher smiled. "Perfect."

It was a few minutes before six and already dark when Daro grabbed the huge, hastily assembled Neiman-Marcus shopping bag from the passenger's seat of his car and walked to the door of the small, three bedroom house off Illinois Avenue near Kiest Park in Oak Cliff.

As he thought about trying to manage a home and family, Daro knew he'd made the right decision to have Mildred and Randall move with him. After he called the house it was Randall who arranged for his sack of gifts. Two of the items, a baseball glove and a revolver, were not available at the store, but the mere mention of the name Daro made heels click throughout the prestigious establishment. Calls were made and runners dispatched to get the requested items.

Daro was surprised to find Lyle's place so easily since he knew practically nothing about Oak Cliff. He never went there, except on duty, and even then it was rare. He punched the bell and waited.

Lesher answered his ring, a corn cob pipe in his left hand. It was the first time Daro had seen him smoke.

"So where's Jan?" Lesher asked, scanning the porch. He swung the screen door open to admit his partner.

"She had to cancel out. Some kind of meeting - some charity thing she's involved in. She sent her regrets."

Lesher shook his head. "Todd's sure gonna be disappointed."

Daro smiled. "That's the breaks. Maybe he can attack a chair leg?"

Lesher nearly choked on his pipe. He pointed the stem at Daro and said, "That's pretty good, for a rookie. Have a seat. I'll get the family."

There was a fireplace built into the west wall of the living room. A cheerful fire crackled on the hearth as Daro took a seat on the beige couch in front of a lively blaze and sat the shopping bag beside him on the floor. On the mantle above the fireplace was an old Seth Thomas clock. It began to chime at the same time one of the logs popped, launching a small, fiery projectile in his general direction. The ember bounced harmlessly off the fire-screen and back onto the hearth. To the left of the screen was a brass, three-piece fireplace set consisting of poker, broom, and shovel. Unlike Daro's almost identical set at home, Lesher's looked well used.

He stood when Lyle, Carol, and the three oldest kids came trooping into the front room from the back of the house. "Hello, Danny, I'm glad you could come," Carol said. "Supper will be ready soon. The potatoes have about ten minutes to go."

Carol Lesher was an 'earth mother' type in a print dress, pleasantly overweight with a pretty face, short, wavy brown hair and brown eyes, and a quiet, sensitive personality. Several times during their meal at the Petroleum Club, Daro caught her looking at her husband, her face a study in adoration. After only one evening with the couple, he understood why Lesher spoke about his wife in such glowing terms.

He walked over to Carol and took her pudgy hand between his, bringing it to his lips. "Thank you for having me."

She dimpled and colored slightly. "My goodness, how gallant. You could learn a thing or two, Hon," she said, glancing at her husband from beneath lowered lashes. Turning back to Daro, she said, "I don't think you've met the children."

Carol Lesher made the introductions, all except for the missing Amy. Todd's handshake was surprisingly strong and businesslike. Just as Lesher had predicted, Ruby began flirting almost immediately, tossing her long red hair for his benefit. Jennifer, wearing a St. Louis Cardinal baseball cap and chewing a large cud of bubble gum, acknowledged his presence, but her eyes were periodically drawn to the mysterious sack by the couch.

"Amy's in the den, afraid to come out," Carol said. "I fed her earlier. I'll swear, I've never known such a shy child. We have friends we've known for years and she won't have a thing to do with them."

Daro smiled. "Don't worry. My baby sister went through a shy phase, too."

"Let's eat," said Lesher as a timer rang in the kitchen.

After supper the reed-thin Jennifer eyed Daro's shopping bag. "Whatcha got it the sack?" she asked. "Is that really from Neiman's?"

Carol was seated in the rocker closest to the fireplace. "Jennifer, shame on you," her mother chided, softly. "You're not supposed to pry."

Jennifer made a face. "But, mama, he's got this big sack and I just thought –"

"Jennifer, you heard your mother," said Lyle.

"Oh, Daddy." Jennifer's voice was just insolent enough to make her point, but not enough to get her swatted.

Solemnly, Daro picked up the bag and moved it between his legs on the floor. "Jenny, maybe you better come over here and help me. I think I saw something in here with your name on it."

"Really!" she squealed almost flying to his side.

"Let's see, now," Daro said, making a production of going through the sack. He had Jennifer deliver a three pound box of imported chocolates to her mother, and a gift-wrapped package with their names on them to Lyle, Todd, and Ruby.

Hefting the heavy box, Lyle caught his partner's eye raising a questioning eyebrow. By the time Daro got to Jennifer's gift she was practically vibrating.

The nine year old tore at the wrappings, shredding them into confetti. "Daddy! Look! It's a first baseman's mitt with the official St. Louis Cardinal seal and everything. Oh, Danny, I love you, I love you!" Jennifer squealed, jumping up and down.

"Jenny, behave yourself," her mother said. "You're acting like a little savage."

"Oh, golly," Todd said, his Adams apple working up and down on his thin neck. He stripped the paper from the long, thin package. "It's a slide rule - a K&E. That's the best kind." He lovingly slipped the device from its leather case. "I'll need this in college. I'm gonna be an engineer, you know."

Daro nodded, happy that his gifts were so well received. "I don't know if your dad told you, but I'm an electrical engineer. If you like I'll teach you how to use it."

"Golly! Really?" He could tell by Todd's expression that he had elevated himself to god-like status.

Amy's present was still in the sack when Ruby began to unwrap her gift. She took great care not to tear the shiny golden paper. She obviously enjoyed being the center of attention as she worked each piece of clear tape loose. Jennifer could stand it no more and reached out to speed the process.

"Stop that," Ruby hissed, slapping her hand away.

"Daddy, Ruby hit me," pouted Jennifer.

"You had it comin', now leave her alone," said Lesher.

Ruby smiled at her father and continued to open her gift. After several minutes she slid a red velvet case from its protective box and opened it. She gasped when inside she found a gold vanity set consisting of comb, brush, and mirror. The initials RL were engraved on each piece in an ornate script, and the mirror and brush also had hand-painted, porcelain handles.

"Oh, Mister Daro, I - I -" Ruby was unable to continue.

"How about yours, Hon?" Carol said, trying to cover for her daughter.

"I don't know," Lyle said, again hefting the box. "Feels kinda like lead to me." He attacked the wrappings and opened the package to find a Smith & Wesson, 357 magnum and a box of 158 grain, jacketed hollow points. Like Ruby before him, Lyle too seemed taken aback.

"Why, honey," Carol said, "That looks just like the one you showed me in the store - the one you've been saving for."

Lesher's voice sounded choked when he said, "It is - it's exactly the one. Danny I can't take this from you."

"And why is that?"

"I just can't, that's all. It's way too expensive for one thing."

Daro shook his head. "Not so. They were having a sale and that was their last one. I got there just in time. They were practically giving them away. Besides - and help me out here, Carol - I've been riding you about carrying that pea shooter 38 the department issued you, and it's to my advantage that you have something better, particularly when I'm with you. It's for me, not you."

Lesher sniffed and wiped his nose while he fiddled with his pipe, all the while looking at the beautiful weapon with the satin blue finish. Daro waited, hoping he had phrased his spiel in such a way that Lesher could accept.

"I 'preciate it, partner."

Waiting for Lyle to recover, Daro thought he caught movement from the corner of his eye. Without being too obvious he watched the hallway leading to the back of the house. A small form stood watching from the shadows. He reached into the bottom of the sack and removed a stuffed brown bear about a foot and a half high and placed it on the floor where it could be seen.

"I'm glad you like it, Lyle," Daro said.

"Partner, you hadn't oughta done all this," Lesher said, but his eyes were still sparkling.

Daro knew he had instinctively done the right thing. He also knew there was no way Lesher could have afforded these things for himself and his kids. But because of what the gifts were, except for the baseball mitt and the pistol, Lesher probably had no idea of their cost, allowing him to get away with it.

As their conversation continued, Daro heard Carol gasp. From the look on her face, something extraordinary seemed to be happening. Careful not to look directly toward the hall, Daro turned his eyes to see a small child standing beside him, some three feet from the couch. He continued to make small talk with Lyle and Carol as the child looked first at the bear, then at him, staring for a long time at his profile. After several minutes she toddled over to the bear and picked it up. Looking it over carefully, she hugged it to her chest.

He expected her to take the prize and run, but instead she came around in front of the couch and crawled into his lap. She sat for a moment staring into his face as if to memorize every line. He found himself looking at a child with soft brown hair and eyes, almost identical to Sally's at that age. His heart felt like it had stopped in mid beat as he waited, afraid to move, afraid he might frighten her away.

After a time, Amy apparently found what she was looking for in his amber eyes. She stuck a thumb in her mouth, clutched her bear even tighter, and lay back in the crook of his left arm. Almost instantly her chin dropped to her chest and she fell asleep.

As if by signal the other children quietly gathered up their presents and left the room leaving Daro looking back and forth between two astonished parents. He felt a sense of release as he looked down at the top of this small child's head. Suppressed grief washed over him and he tried without success to swallow a lump roughly the size of Alaska.

He lowered his face into his right hand as he held his precious cargo with the other. Two happy parents looked at each other and smiled as Lesher busied himself with his pipe and new pistol. Carol took her knitting from a cloth bag beside her chair.

Until the old Seth Thomas clock on the mantle struck ten, the only noise in the room was the soft click of Carol's knitting needles and the occasional pop of another ember seeking escape from the hearth.

• • •

10

Daro had a new family. He tried not to be a pest, spending first one day with Jan and the next at Lesher's home, but he felt almost like an alcoholic who had just discovered where the booze was kept. When the kids weren't in school he worked with Todd giving him lessons on the slide rule. And always lurking about he would spot Ruby, looking at him with all the love in her eyes that only a smitten eleven year old can generate. Once in a while Jenny coaxed him into a game of catch, ostensibly to break in her new glove, but the majority of his time went to his major love, Amy. The little one was still painfully shy with everyone else, but when he arrived she was like a skin graft in search of a burn. Amy dropped whatever she was doing and ran squealing to her Uncle Danny. He in no way discouraged her attentions.

Days flew by, but the weeks dragged as he waited for word about the murder investigation. March, 1956 passed into April and it was hard for him to believe that his family had been buried for seventeen months. But it was even harder to believe he had been a policeman for almost a year, and that he wouldn't trade the job for any other in the world.

After booking a drunk their first day shift back on duty, Lesher scooted behind the wheel and nosed the cruiser west out of the basement of City Hall down Commerce Street. From long habit he almost turned north on Harwood, now a one way street south. In their infinite wisdom the city planners had decided that at midnight on a Saturday, Harwood should be changed from one way north to one way south. As usual, not everyone on the police department got the word.

Sunday morning, after the street had changed directions, the senior member of squad twenty two, an old time cop named 'Sus' Pendergast, finished booking a prisoner and came roaring out of the basement of City Hall onto Commerce, immediately hooking a right on Harwood Street. He smashed head-on into a southbound citizen. Both car's front ends were destroyed, but - other than a bump on the head and a few scrapes and bruises - the cops and the citizen were unhurt.

Shaking with rage, Pendergast jumped from the cruiser, steam spewing into the early morning air from the cruiser's smashed radiator and yelled, "You dumb son of a bitch, you're on a one way street."

"Yeah," yelled back the citizen, "But I'm going the right way."

For weeks thereafter a number of cops ended up with red faces as they forgot and turned north on Harwood only to come face to face with an irate citizen. Luckily however, none of these encounters suffered the same degree of violence as did Sus'.

Not wanting a similar incident, Lesher continued out Commerce. Low on tickets, he decided to hit the Commerce Street Viaduct, always fruitful ground for speeders. Lesher caught the green light at Industrial Boulevard and was driving through the intersection when he chuckled.

"What?" Daro asked, looking at his partner.

Lesher shook his head. "Did I ever tell you about breakin' in Johnny Reb? You know John Rebley, don't you?"

Daro smiled. "Sure. I've worked with him a couple of times. Nice guy. A real character, though."

"Yeah. I was his first training officer. You remember Sadie McNutt?"

"That whore we put in jail last month?"

"Yeah. She helped me train Reb right on this here viaduct. Sadie drives a gray, nineteen forty six Buick ragtop - and I do mean ragtop. It was all ripped to hell before she replaced it this year, and when she drove around it looked like she had New Year's streamers trailin' around behind her.

"Anyhow, Reb was brand new and I was clockin' Sadie across the viaduct here and she was doin' 'bout fifteen over the limit. I pulled the lights and tapped the horn, but she never even looked, just kept the hammer down. I pulled up right beside her and tapped the horn again, but Reb wasn't happy with that. I guess he'd been seein' too many movies 'cause he leaned out the window and pounded on the side of the cruiser - like to have caved in the door - and yelled, 'WHERE'S THE FIRE?'

"Sadie never turned a tap. She just cocked her mouth over to one side and yelled back, 'I'm sittin' on it, hoss! You think you got enough hose to put it out?'"

Lesher cackled, whacking the steering wheel with the palm of his hand as Daro joined his laughter. From the looks on their faces, several citizens in adjacent cars must have wondered what set the two officers off.

After their laughing fit, Lyle continued. "Ain't that some shit, partner? I wish you coulda seen Sadie's face when she looked over at who she'd yelled at. I'll betcha she pinched two new holes in them seat covers on that old ragtop, probably at the same time."

Daro pulled out his handkerchief to wipe his eyes. "Did you stop her?"

"Didn't have to. You'd a thought she throwed out an anchor she stopped so fast. Hell, I had to tell her to get her car off the bridge."

"Did you give her a ticket?"

"Hell no. I thought about givin' her a medal. She really took the wind out of old Reb's sails. He shrunk down to about the size of a politician with the shit kicked out of him. Best thing that ever happened to him. He was such an asshole when he was a rookie - kinda like somebody else I know."

"Why, you horse's ass," Daro said, whacking Lesher on the shoulder.

"Watch it - watch it! You're fritzing with the senior partner of this here squad, boy."

"Yes, sir, Sahib. So sorry, Sahib," Daro said, holding his hands in front of his chest in a prayerful attitude and bowing from the waist.

"Well - that's a little better, You gotta watch that stuff, rookie, 'cause I'll bet I know something you forgot."

"And what might that be?"

"I'm still your trainin' officer and I've gotta make my final report to see if you get to stay on the force. It's been one year this month."

Daro continued his prayerful salute. "And what is your verdict, oh mighty prince?"

"Well, I haven't decided yet. Tell you what - I'll give you an oral test and then a field test. The next call," said Lesher, pointing at the radio, "No matter what it is, you're gonna handle by yourself. 'Till then I'm gonna ask you a question that nobody I know has got right yet. Let's see how you do."

"Shoot."

"This really happened, so listen real careful. There's a guy sittin' in his house on a Saturday night readin' the paper. He's got the blinds pulled down and his readin' lamp shows his shadow on the shade. This old boy and another fellow have been fightin' over somethin' - I don't remember what, but it doesn't matter - and this guy comes over to the house and shoots through the window at the outline. He misses, but the point is, he tried to kill this guy. What Texas law would you use to charge him so's he'd get the most time in the joint?"

Daro massaged his chin. "Well, let's see. That ought to be pretty easy except you said nobody got it right so far. Is that really a true story?"

"Yep, I was the arrestin' officer," Lesher said, clocking a Cadillac on the Commerce Street Viaduct. The driver was going seven miles an hour over the limit. Not enough. Lesher broke off the clock and turned back toward downtown. It was rare in the Radio Patrol Division to issue a ticket for less than ten miles over the limit. Not a policy - more of a tradition. The big shock for traffic offenders came on Christmas day. Except in cases where the driver allowed his mouth to overload his ass, no citations were issued.

Daro frowned. "Okay, this guy tries to murder the guy in the house, right?"

Lesher nodded. "Right."

Daro spread his hands. "Then the charge has got to be assault to commit murder."

"Wrong," Lyle said, shaking his finger at him. "I told you it was tricky. The asshole got convicted of burglary and got twelve years."

"Burglary? What kind of bull are you trying to feed me, Lyle? That's no more burglary than I'm the Pope."

"You go over to Huntsville and tell that to a guy named John David Koontz. He'll tell you different. Look - assault to murder carries a max of five years, but burglary can get you twelve. And they wanted to put this dirtbag in the jailhouse for as long as possible - long beef sheet don't you know. If you'll read the burglary law real careful, it says that if you, OR ANY EXTENSION OF YOU, enters another person's domicile, business, or whatever, you've committed a burglary. If you shoot a gun at somebody, that bullet is an extension of you, got it?"

"I still think you're pulling my leg, partner."

"No I'm not neither." Lesher was about to clock another car when the radio came to life. "Seventy one, meet a complainant about a parking violation at the corner of McKinney and Noonan."

Daro laughed and grabbed the mike. "Seventy one, Roger."

"Parking violation?" said a contemptuous Lesher. "Ain't that some shit. That ain't no kinda test."

"A deal's a deal, partner," he reminded him.

"Twenty one must be out of service," Lesher said. "Okay, rookie. Maybe it'll turn into a murder. I'll just sit back and take care of the call sheet. You handle it and I'll watch. Come to think of it you may not be ready for anything tougher."

"Thanks a lot, asshole."

Lesher shrugged. "Think nothin' of it."

Daro had handled a lot of calls on his own. He had even been senior partner several times when Lyle had the night off, and paired with an officer out of a later academy class. But even though it was a nothing call, the mere fact of Lyle calling it a test bothered him a little. Shortly Lyle was cruising up McKinney approaching the intersection with Noonan.

"Over here, Officer!" yelled a stocky, middle aged man, waving to them from the corner. He motioned to Daro and Lesher, pointing toward the rear of a cleaning and pressing shop.

Lesher pulled the patrol car around back and stopped at the curb. Daro spooled out and placed his cap squarely on his head. He and Lesher, walked to the complainant who was standing beside a black, 1949 customized Ford, its bumper nuzzled against a power pole like a nursing puppy.

"Just look at that," the man said, pointing at the car. It was obvious that the citizen was more than a little angry.

Lesher at five feet nine made the officers look like a uniformed version of Mutt and Jeff. At that, the citizen was shorter and considerably heavier than Lesher.

Daro was puzzled. "Yes, sir, what about it?"

"Well," said the citizen, getting even more angry, "Are you guys gonna let him get away with it?"

"Sir, you'll have to be more specific," Daro said, "I don't know what you are talking about."

"That damned car is what I'm talking about," the citizen said, the morning sun glinting off his bald head.

He tried a different tack, "Sir, may I have your name?"

"Of course, Officer," the citizen said, "I'm James Wainright and I own this place." With an expansive wave of a pudgy hand, he indicated the rear door of the cleaners. Daro nodded as Lesher started making notes on the call sheet.

"Sir, please spell your last name?" he said. The citizen complied as Lesher scribbled it down.

"Now then, Mr. Wainright," Daro said. "How can we help you?"

"You can get that damned thing off my property," he said, glaring at the offending automobile.

"Is it your car?"

"Of course it's not my car," said an irritated Wainright, "You think I'd own something that looks like that

"Whose is it, sir?" asked Daro.

"I don't know the punk's last name, I think his nickname's Bud, but he works over there at that sheet metal shop," said Wainright, poking a thumb toward a metal building about a third of a block down the angled street.

Wainright Cleaners faced McKinney Avenue with Noonan Street running off McKinney at a forty five degree angle in the rear. On the far side of the building, a street - more correctly an alley - formed the base of a right triangle, isolating the business as though on an island. McKinney Avenue, an old and narrow street, allowed no parking because of its width, and Wainright apparently already had a problem with customers wanting to pick up and drop off their cleaning. Since space was at such a premium, and Wainright had room for only three customer's cars, he could not allow indiscriminate access. As if to exacerbate the problem, parked at an angle across all three spaces was the target of his ire.

"Mister Wainright, have you asked him not to park here?"

"Yes, and the little bastard just laughed at me," Wainright said, "Are you gonna do something about it or not?"

Daro sighed. "I know this isn't what you want to hear, but I have some bad news for you. The car is parked on private property and there is not a thing the police can do about it."

"This is a joke, right?" Wainright said, his mouth half open, "Tell me you're not gonna leave it there."

"No joke, sir. I'm afraid we have no choice."

Wainright put his fists on his hips, "I never heard of such a thing. You mean that little shit can get away with this?"

"Yes, sir, he can, but I may I make a suggestion or two."

"Well, I wish you would," he said, disgusted.

"You see how he's parked?"

"Yeah."

"Well, sir, if I were you, I would make me a big sign that said, 'PARKING FIVE DOLLARS AN HOUR' and below that I'd paint, 'except for customers' and nail it to that pole. Then I'd get me a big log chain and an equally big padlock, and the next time he parks there - if there is a next time - I'd padlock his car to the pole until he paid his tab."

Mr. Wainright grinned, "That's not a bad idea. Can I really do that, I mean legally?"

"Yes, sir," Daro said, "Your customers will still have a place to park, but everyone else will have to pay through the nose, particularly your friend Bud down the street."

Wainright thought it over. "Officer, I'll take your word for it, but that still leaves me with the problem of not having enough parking for my customers. I really need to get him out of here and keep him out. He's a pretty husky little shit and I'm not as young as I used to be. Your way might lead to a lot of trouble."

"There may be another way."

"You just tell me."

"Well, if the car should happen to slip out of gear, or the parking brake slip, the car might roll back over the sidewalk and into the street. If that happened, my partner and I would have to tow it in for being illegally parked."

"Not much chance of that," Wainright said, pursing his lips and shaking his head. "Even if it did, this is level, there's no way. The car wouldn't roll."

"I understand that, Mr. Wainright, but if it did somehow happen, we would be forced to impound the car, and the owner would have to come bail it out. At the very least it would cost Bud a healthy towing fee and be most inconvenient for him."

"Officer, how the hell could that happen?" Wainright asked, looking at Daro as though he was crazy, "There's no way in hell a car could roll back like that."

"I understand, sir, but if it did?"

"Officer–," a disgusted Wainright began as Daro held up a hand.

"Mr. Wainright, my partner here, Officer Lyle Lesher, was just saying to me before we got this call that he sure needed a cup of coffee. I suddenly find that I need one, too, so we're gonna go get one."

Wainright was incredulous, "You mean now and leave this car here?"

Daro was as patient as though dealing a slightly demented uncle. "Sir, pay careful attention. Do you know anything about the controls of this car?"

"Sure, I owned one."

Daro opened the driver's door and shut it again, "I notice this door isn't locked."

"So?"

"So, my partner and I are going for coffee. That'll take about fifteen minutes I should think," he said. "When we get through, I am gonna to drive back by your place just to see how things are."

Wainright started to grin, "Uh, right officer. Well, thanks anyway, if you can't help - well, you just can't help."

Daro shook Wainright's hand and turned away, "Let's go, partner."

Daro folded into the passenger side of the squad car and Lesher fired it up, driving away. When they rounded the corner, Daro took off his hat and placed it in the seat between them, brushing a strong hand over his flat top.

"How am I doing?" He asked.

"No comment yet. Where to, partner?"

"I don't care. Do you want to get a cup?"

"Yeah, I'd kinda like one."

"You're driving."

Checking out of service with the dispatcher for a quick cup then back in service again, almost twenty minutes had passed when Daro and Lyle went back to see what might have happened. As they drove past Wainright's shop, the car in question had apparently slipped out of gear and rolled back across the sidewalk, leaving its rear end sticking into Noonan Street.

Daro popped the radio mike, "Seventy one."

"Go ahead, seventy one," said the dispatcher.

"We have a car blocking the sidewalk at McKinney and Noonan. Need a tow truck."

"Seventy one, Roger. Tow truck will be dispatched. Estimate twenty minutes."

The tow truck must have been close, it was there in less than fifteen. The operator went about his job with speed and efficiency, and in a matter of minutes the front of the Ford was hiked up and ready to tow. The operator filled out his forms and presented them to Daro for signature. Down the block, just as he handed the papers back to the driver, a young man came out of the sheet metal shop. He struck a match on the sole of his right shoe and lit a cigarette, glancing down the street.

"Hey," he yelled, running towards them, "What the hell's goin' on?" He was about twenty, brown hair, not bad looking, maybe six feet, 185, and he was mad. He skidded to a stop in front of the two cops. The dirty blue coveralls he wore had the name 'Bud' sewn in yellow colored thread above the left breast pocket.

"What the hell do you think you're doin'?"

Daro fixed him with a cold stare, "You talking to me?"

"Damn right," Bud said, almost breathing fire, "You ain't takin' my car."

"I have news for you, friend," Daro said, nodding toward the Ford, "If this is yours, I already have."

In case he was needed, Lesher started inching within striking distance on the young man's right side. Daro stopped him with an almost imperceptible movement of his head.

"Put my car down, now!" Bud ordered.

"Friend, let me give you some good advice," Daro explained patiently, "You'd best turn around and go back the way you came. I am not impressed by your anger or your attitude."

By now, a small crowd had gathered, the most pleased of whom appeared to be a grinning Mr. James Wainright.

"That's the son of a bitch that called you, isn't it?" Bud shouted, pointing at Wainright.

"Friend, you just tore your britches," Daro said, coldly. "You've used abusive language in public and are now disturbing the peace. I'm afraid I must place you under arrest."

"Like hell!" Bud telegraphed a roundhouse right, but Daro slipped the punch and delivered two quick left hooks to Bud's right side, following with a textbook right cross to the point of the chin. Bud went down with a thump. Wainright almost applauded.

Unconsciously Daro sucked on a skinned knuckle as Lesher freed his handcuffs from their case and snapped them around Bud's wrists. Once done, Lesher looked at his partner. "Not too shabby."

The officers picked up the prisoner and placed him in the back seat of the squad car, then waved the tow truck driver on his way.

A grinning Wainright walked over and said, "Officer, can I have your name and badge number?"

"Certainly. Danny Daro, badge 1293, but why do you want it?"

"Well," Wainright said, "I've never thought much about the cops, 'cept maybe when one of you guys gave me a speeding ticket, or something. I just thought I'd like to write a letter and tell 'em down at City Hall what I think."

"And what do you think, Mr. Wainright?" Daro asked.

"Hey, I think you guys are great and I think they oughta know."

"Mr. Wainright, I would appreciate it if you didn't."

Wainright looked confused, "But, why not? I thought it'd look good on you guy's records."

"Maybe not, Sir," he said. "We haven't exactly handled this according to prescribed departmental policy, if you catch my drift. Our superiors might develop a pretty severe case of heartburn over it."

Wainright paused a moment, chuckled, and said, "I think I understand."

"Good," nodded Daro. "You about ready partner?"

"Yeah," Lyle said, still looking at his rookie partner with renewed respect.

"Okay, let's go book a prisoner."

"Officer?" Wainright said.

"Yes, sir?"

"Who does your cleaning?"

"Majestic cleaners on Oak Lawn, why?"

"I know the place. Good people. But I'd like to do yours and your partner's, if you'd let me."

"I appreciate it, Mr. Wainright, but we're not allowed to accept any sort of gratuity."

"Not even at my cost?"

Daro laughed, "I suppose so, but all we did was our job."

"That may be, but it was one hell of a job. I'd at least like to shake both your hands."

Daro and Lesher took the offered handshake with a smile. Daro nodded to the grateful man and slid into the patrol car on the driver's side while Lesher parked himself in the back seat, his gun side away from the still groggy, handcuffed prisoner. Daro cranked the V-8, and stuck it into gear.

"Officer?"

"Yes, sir?"

"Tell all your cop friends - cost."

"I sure will."

Daro and Lesher waved as they pulled away, heading toward City Hall and the jailhouse.

Lesher was quiet for a few blocks, then said, "Nice day, partner."

"That it is, partner," he said. "That it is."

Becoming a full-fledged harness bull was almost anticlimactic. Daro switched from days to mids, working from 11:00 PM to 7:00 AM. On the fourth day after changeover, he'd barely got to sleep when the telephone rang. Randall took the call and tapped at Daro's door.

"Mister Danny, it is Mr. Ledbetter from the detective agency."

Instantly awake, Daro threw off the sheet and grabbed the extension. "Yes, Mr. Ledbetter, what've you got?"

"Good news, Mr. Daro, we've found Betty Silk."

Daro felt his heart skip a beat. "Where?"

"San Francisco. Not too far from the address you gave us. She's living in an apartment with several men and women, including those two birds with her when she left Dallas. Just as you ordered, we have men on her around the clock."

Daro ran a hand over his face, forcing his mind to work. "I have one more shift before a two day break. Be sure they don't lose her. I'll make arrangements for an extra day or two and fly out on Thursday."

"You can count on us, sir," said Ledbetter. Daro could almost hear the wheels in Ledbetter's head turn as he mentally tallied the bill for his most valued client. "Would you like for me to have one of our detectives meet your plane?"

"Good idea. I'll want to go to Silk's place directly from the airport. I'll call you when I know my flight."

"Very good, sir. I'll await your call," said Ledbetter as he hung up.

Daro almost dialed Lyle's number before he thought. No need to wake his partner. Instead he called Storm and made arrangements for the two extra days.

Daro was still tired when he boarded his 10:00 AM, American Airlines non-stop flight for San Francisco out of Love Field, Dallas. The sleek lines of the plane, a four engine, triple tailed, Super Constellation, never failed to stir him. The plane's outline somehow reminded him of a dolphin. He always wanted to learn to fly, but never had the time. He made a mental note to look into remedying the problem.

Two pretty stewardesses, a blonde and a brunette, were in charge of first class. Both noted the young, obviously successful passenger as they checked the name Daro off their list. The blonde smiled and winked at her friend, mouthing, "My turn."

The brunette sighed and nodded, noting the flattop with the white streak, the broad shoulders, the custom tailored Navy blue pin-striped suit which, by its very conservatism screamed money. He definitely did not belong in the cattle car - sometimes referred to as Robert Hall - a euphemism used to describe the men who traveled tourist class. Both girls had a three day layover in San Francisco before their next flight and neither had plans. Mr. Danny Daro looked like fertile ground in desperate need of their special cultivation.

Still, fair is fair - the blonde got the first shot since her friend the brunette got first crack at the last likely prospect. They would have saved themselves time and aggravation had they seen Jan Colmer kiss Daro goodbye at the airport from the open door of a chauffeured Rolls.

"Sir, how do you pronounce your last name?" asked a low, breathless voice at his elbow. He'd just finished tightening his seat belt when he looked up into a bright, smiling face with wide green eyes. A tag above her pocket gave her name as Karen.

He returned the smile. “It’s Daro, like dare with an ‘O’ on the end.”

“Thank you, sir,” she said, making a note on her pad. “Is everything all right - may I get you something?”

He shook his head. “No Ma’am, thanks. Maybe a cup of coffee later.”

“Certainly, sir,” Karen almost whispered, bending lower to give him the benefit of both cleavage and a very expensive perfume she’d received several months before from a now forgotten admirer. “As soon as we’re airborne if there is anything at all, you just let me know, Mr. Daro.”

“Thanks,” he said.

Robbed of sleep the past two days, the clock finally caught up with him and he leaned back in his seat, closing his eyes. Two frustrated young ladies could only watch as their target snoozed away the flight, not awakening until the plane’s wheels touched down in San Francisco.

As promised a detective named Chuck Kramer met the plane and whisked him away in a nondescript blue Ford, obviously a company car.

“Where you wanta go first?” asked Kramer, his Adam’s apple bobbing up and down on his thin neck. The tie-less Kramer wore a too-large, brown sport coat over a lighter colored shirt. A few scraggly strawberry blonde hairs peeked out over the shirt’s top button.

“That depends. Is Silk at her apartment?”

Kramer nodded. “Yep. None of ‘em hardly goes out. The girls turn tricks for money, mostly to buy a lid of grass and maybe a bottle of booze, but yesterday was Silk’s day to work. They’ve got some sort of shift arrangement worked out. This is her day off.”

“How many of them stay together?”

“Four guys and three girls are more or less permanent, but several others come and go - free nookie maybe.”

Daro wasn’t paying much attention to the city, concentrating instead on the questions he had for Betty Silk. Kramer took them into the heart of the city to a hilly side street in a rather scruffy looking neighborhood. When Kramer parked, the front of the car was elevated to the point that Daro felt like he was inside a rocket about to be launched to the moon.

"This is it?" he asked, distastefully scanning the rundown block.

"Yep," said a smiling Kramer. "Real homey ain't it?" Kramer pointed a bony finger at a dingy looking, red brick building across the street. "They've got an upstairs apartment right over there - number 38. How about I go in with you just in case?"

"Good thinking," he said.

When they got out of the car, Daro noticed another man in an identical black Ford get out and walk toward them. He wondered if it was as obvious to everyone else that the man was a detective. Kramer introduced him as Jake Fields, a thin man about the same build and height as Kramer, differing only in that he had black hair. Daro shook hands, surprised at the strength of Fields' grip.

"Anything cookin'?" asked Kramer.

"Nah. Same old stuff," answered Fields, shaking his head. "The one they call Jill is out working, but the rest are inside. They made a pot run about an hour ago so they're probably all higher'n a cat's back by now."

"Okay, Jake, you stay out here," said Kramer. "I'm goin' in with Mr. Daro."

Daro suppressed a smile at the detective's obvious attempt to make sure he knew who was in charge of the investigation. Fields nodded and walked back to his car as Kramer and Daro went inside and up the stairs to the dark, beat up door designated as 38. Originally secured by a nail at both top and bottom, the '8' had lost its top nail and was canted to the right at 90 degrees. To a mathematician, the door's number would have looked like 3 infinity.

His ear to the door, Daro listened for a moment, but could hear no sound from inside. Two loose wires hung where there once was a doorbell button. He rapped on the thin top panel with the center knuckle of his right hand. Like rats at home behind a hollow wall, his knock produced some scurrying sounds. He heard some whispers followed by a muffled, "Yeah?"

He didn't answer, once again tapping on the door. Kramer pulled back out of sight as a key rattled in the lock and the door opened a crack. A suspicious, bloodshot eyeball looked Daro up and down, taking in the expensive suit. "Whatcha want?" said a raspy voice.

"I came to see Betty," he said, smiling.

The door opened a little wider. "You one of her customers?"

He widened his smile. "You bet."

The voice grunted and the door swung open, filling the hallway with the unmistakable smell of marijuana. He stepped inside the dark room followed closely by Kramer.

In lieu of furniture, several threadbare pillows were strewn about the living room. Four men and three women lay on the filthy cushions, oblivious to the intrusion. In the corner, halfheartedly watched by one of the men, a naked couple groped each other, playing a slow motion game of slap and tickle. None of the group so much as looked up.

"Hey, wait a minute," said Gruff Voice, addressing Daro, but taking a step toward Kramer. "I thought you was alone."

"Just hold your water," said Kramer, putting his hand inside his coat.

Gruff voice's eyes got big. "What the hell - you guys cops?"

"I am," Daro said. But not in San Francisco. I'm from Dallas and I need to see Betty."

"Well, if you ain't San Francisco cops and you ain't got no warrant, you can haul your asses outa here."

Daro's eyes narrowed and he stepped up to Gruff Voice, glaring down from his height advantage. He poked Gruff Voice in the chest the same way Perkins had done him. Stealing Lesher's favorite line, he said, "You listen up, asshole - I'll wade through you like a kid through a mud puddle. You point out Betty Silk before I mess you up so bad your mama won't even recognize the remains."

Had he been there, Lesher would have been proud. Kramer's eyes got big and Gruff Voice's even bigger.

"Come on, man," said Gruff Voice, switching on a frightened smile. "There ain't no need to get your shit hot. She's takin' a nap - I'll get her."

"I'll help you," said Daro. He took Gruff Voice by the elbow and escorted him down the hallway off the living room.

There were three bedrooms in the old apartment, all without doors. Betty Silk was asleep in the last room on the right, curled up on a bare mattress which had been thrown down on the floor. She wore a long, faded print dress pulled up almost to her crotch.

The Silk genes ran strong. Even in her sleep, it was obvious that Betty was a smaller version of Terri. Gruff Voice beat a hasty retreat when Daro told him to leave them alone. He sat down on the edge of the filthy mattress and shook the sleeping girl's shoulder.

Betty groaned and licked her lips, her eyelids pressing together so hard her forehead wrinkled. "Go 'way," she muttered.

"I need to talk to you, Betty," he said.

Silk's eyes opened at the unfamiliar voice. Dazed, she scanned his face. "Who're you?"

"I'm Danny Daro, Sally Daro's brother."

Looking puzzled, Betty sat up and leaned her back against the wall, pulling her dress down. "You mean, from Dallas; what're you doing here?"

"Looking for you."

Her puzzled look turned slightly frightened. "What for?"

He looked down at the mattress, toying with a loose thread. "I've got some news you probably don't know. Terri is dead - committed suicide."

Betty seemed almost unaffected by the news. "I'm not too surprised. Her head wasn't screwed on too tight. Do you know why she did it?"

He shook his head. "Not really. I'm a Dallas policeman. I stopped her one day for speeding and she said that you knew Sally. We just started to talk and I made an appointment to see her that evening after I got off work. I needed to find out what she knew about the night Sally and my folks were killed."

Betty momentarily bristled when Daro mentioned being a cop, but her attitude soon went away.

"You know, I always wondered about that night," she said. "We just kinda met by accident and me and Sally and your folks all had dinner after the movie. When we got done we walked over to where we'd both parked - you know, that lot on the corner of Harwood and Pacific?"

He nodded and Betty continued. "Your folks and that other couple took off first and when they pulled out on Harwood, these two cars full of the same jokers I saw lookin' us over when we walked down Elm Street started following 'em."

"Other couple?"

"Yeah," Betty said. "These folks had parked in the same lot we did and their car wouldn't start. Mr. Daro recognized the man. I didn't catch the whole conversation, but he was some sort of business acquaintance. Anyhow, Mr. Daro offered to carry 'em home - someplace up in north Dallas. I didn't hear the address."

Daro was pleased by this small bit of information. Finally there was a logical explanation as to why his family was so far off course that night. He wondered if the couple had seen his parent's killers, and if they might have called the police.

"The cars that followed my folks - do you know how many guys were in them and what make of a car they were?" he asked.

Betty shook her head. "I'd say probably four in one and three in the other, but I'm not real good on cars. I think they was Fords, either black or a real dark blue. I got the letters and the first number of the first car's license plate - NA 4 something - and phoned it in after I heard about your folks." Betty placed a hand on Daro's arm. "I'm real sorry. I always figured that if I'd of called sooner - maybe, just maybe it wouldn't a happened. But after nobody called me back, I figured there wasn't nothin' to it."

When he heard the partial plate number, it felt almost like an electric shock passed through his body. Betty had given him the letters and the first number of the license plate on one of the dirtbags cars that tried to corner Marge Johnson and Charlie Goren on the Houston Street Viaduct. The full plate turned out to be NA 4363, a number that was forever etched into his brain.

Trying to restrain his excitement, he asked, "Do you remember who you called?"

More brow furrowing as Betty thought. "I'm not sure who I talked to first - it was some operator. She transferred me somewhere else and this real sour talking horse's ass answered. When I told him why I was calling, you'd have thought I just told him there wasn't no Santa Claus. He said that he'd have someone look into it and hung up in my ear."

"Are you sure he said that he'd have someone else do it or that he would?"

Betty shook her head. "No, he said he'd have it done."

"Do you remember his name?" he asked trying to keep the excitement out of his voice.

"Yeah. He called himself Talmadge. Lieutenant Talmadge."

• • •

11

Daro wasn't surprised that Betty's information pointed toward Lt. Talmadge. He had almost expected it, particularly since the Chief of Homicide was so seemingly competent in solving other murders.

Before leaving the apartment he took a hundred dollar bill from his billfold and handed it to Betty. The angry fire that lit her eyes took him by surprise.

"Damn you," she growled, hurling the bill in his face. "Sally was my friend. You've got some nerve trying to give me money."

He retrieved the bill and once more extended his hand. "I'm not trying to pay you for information." He said, softly. "When your gravel-voiced friend in there answered the door, the only way I could get in without breaking it down was to tell him I was a customer. If you don't have some money when I leave, we both know what might happen."

Gratefully, he watched the fire behind her eyes die out.

"You're right," she said. "But that's way too much. You got a twenty?"

He replaced the hundred and fished out five twenties, handing them to her. "Give old gravel-voice one of these and hide the rest for a rainy day."

From beneath lowered lashes Betty flashed him a shy smile. "I wish I'd met you before I got so stupid."

Leaning down, he gently kissed her on the forehead. "Me, too."

Daro almost had his anger under control by the time the plane landed in Dallas. When Betty gave him the word about Talmadge, his first inclination was to storm into the Lieutenant's office and tear his head off. But the long flight home gave him more time for sober reflection. He decided to wait until he got all of his recently acquired, but disjointed facts sorted out. Still, he was glad the Lieutenant wasn't in his office when he went in to see Golden and Killean.

"That's about it," said Daro as he finished telling his story to the two detectives. Golden questioned him at greater length about the couple his family apparently took home from the parking lot, but he had told him all he knew.

"Did Talmadge ever mention a call?"

Both men shook their heads. "Not a word," said Golden. "You think Silk could've made this up?"

"No, she was straight with me," he answered. "She wouldn't know who's in charge of what section - not by name. She even described our friend Talmadge as being a crude talking horse's ass, an apt description if there ever was one."

Both detectives smiled and nodded.

"True," said Killean. "But what have we got now that we didn't before?"

Daro shook his head and sighed. "Nothing, I guess. But I want to know why Chicken Foot didn't tell you guys about the call. Isn't there a record made of such things?"

"Supposed to be," said Golden. "There's even a regular form for it."

"I'm going to ask Talmadge," Daro said. "I want to look him in the eye and get an answer."

"Now, hold on a minute," Golden said. "You got off easy the last time, but this time might be different. Remember Herm's call to your Captain? Spencer may be forced to burn your ass."

"I'm just going to ask a question. What harm can that do?"

Killean snorted. "Askin' ain't the problem. It's you, personally, that gets Herm all wrapped around the axle. In case you hadn't figured it out, he ain't real keen on you."

Daro smiled. "Do tell. For your information, that's a two way street. To steal one of Lesher's favorite sayings, I think Talmadge is lower than whale shit and that's on the bottom of the ocean. I'll hold off, but sooner or later that gentleman is going to answer a few questions."

"I Understand," nodded Golden. "But you gotta remember who he is. It's not like we can drag him in here like some dirtbag off the street. If you'll give us a little time, maybe we can find out something first."

"You'd better make it quick. I'm not gonna wait long."

"I Understand," Golden said again. "But I've never known Chicken Foot to forget anything, certainly not something as important as this seems to be. And there may be a logical explanation - but if there's not, we'll nail his ass. We may at least get the asshole an official reprimand and a few days off without pay. That's worth a short wait, isn't it, Daro?"

Several weeks passed without further word and every molecule in Daro's body kept screaming for action. But something - a hunch - told him to do nothing. If he'd been a cop longer, he might have recognized that acting on a hunch is often a symptom of becoming a good cop.

Strange and impossible suspicions formed in his mind. Could it be that Chicken Foot was somehow involved? Ridiculous. What motive could Talmadge have?

Although he would never believe that Herm had a good reason for the telephone record omission, Daro went along with Golden's recommendation to cool it. Granting even this small concession went against the grain.

He shared his suspicions, fears, and anxieties with Lyle, a sympathetic ear if nothing else. At every opportunity they sorted through their scant information, trying to come up with a sensible working hypothesis. There simply weren't enough clues even to make an educated guess.

In the process, at least, they became true partners, fitting together like two spoons stacked in a drawer. And, like all good police partnerships, in some ways they were closer than man and wife. The only strange thing about the pair was that their "marriage" had grown more quickly that most. Daro had never given it voice, but in a different way he loved Lyle as much as he did Jan. Dear Janette - more and more she became part of his life.

Daro was convinced he couldn't make it without Jan. Each day she filled more of his heart and mind. She became the rock on which his forced tranquility rested, the reason he could stay sane. She cooked for him, made herself available at any hour of the day or night, and most comforting of all, held him when his grief overwhelmed him. She could not help him forget, but she was able to ease his pain - a salve over the festering wound of his loss.

The very worst times came at night - the nightmares, the scenes of cold, gray slabs in the morgue with the twisted, misshapen bodies of his family laid out side by side.

Jan's unreserved affection made him even more aware of his deepening love for this beautiful, caring woman, and he repeated his marriage proposal. She tearfully accepted. He had no idea her tears were partly fear. As far as he was concerned he had, in his bumbling way, found the right girl and no earthly power would keep her from him.

They set their wedding day for October 12, the same day his parents were married. Daro was both pleased and amused by Randall's and Mildred's reaction to the news. Both were beside themselves with happiness. In their eyes, Master Danny had at long last found a woman who would make him a proper wife. Mildred had yet to meet her, but Randall had sung such vociferous praises about the tall, blonde beauty with the smoke blue eyes that his chubby wife felt sure she could pick the future Mrs. Danny Daro out of a crowd.

It was almost as if he and Jan had started something. At virtually the same time four other police officers, two of whom Daro had worked with, announced wedding plans. Tommy Tinsley, the best known to him because they had paired up a couple of times on Lesher's nights off, scheduled his wedding in late May. Within days the customary invitation circulated throughout the police department, all comers were welcome to attend Tinsley's bachelor party.

Daro wasn't particularly thrilled at the prospect of another bash thrown by and for cops. He had been to several and all of them had turned out to be a booze and broads blow out. He liked an occasional fling, but as to parties, he preferred small, quiet, intimate affairs of three or four couples. Also, for some now obscure reason, it had become a police department tradition to give the prospective groom 'last rites' at the home of Elizabeth Carring. Liz, a prominent Dallas lawyer and twenty year mistress of a cop named Clarence "Roughhouse" Jones, was the only female - other than dancers or hookers - allowed to attend. When he arrived at 11:30PM after working a swing shift, the bash was just hitting its peak. On the first day of a three day break, and already three sheets in the wind, was Lesher who had been there since eight o'clock.

"There's my li'l ole partner," Lyle yelled when Daro strode through the front door. Lesher waved a bottle of beer in a 'come here' gesture. "Get your ass over here, Rookie."

Daro grinned through the blue, cigarette haze. "You mean ex-rookie, don't you? It was you who screwed up and sent in a favorable report."

"By damn you're right."

The smoky room was filled with cops, noise, and the smell of beer as Daro made his way into the front bedroom. He tossed his light brown sports jacket on top of the already mountainous pile on the bed and shouldered his way through the packed crowd. Lyle and his two friends had that 'out of it' look around the eyes. Having seen his partner this way before, Daro guessed his partner to be on his fifth or sixth beer.

"Hey, li'l buddy," Lyle slurred, throwing his arm over his taller partner's shoulder. "You got here jush in time."

Daro smiled. "Jush in time for what?" he mimicked.

"For the movies, dumbass. Ole Paulie got in a new batch," said Lesher, referring to Paul New, the Sergeant in charge of the evidence room and extensive library of confiscated porno films. "We're gonna be the first to see a couple of 'em."

Daro made a face. "I don't get real excited about watching someone else have all the fun, partner. I mean, why be a voyeur when you can be a participant?"

"Ain't that some shit," Lesher said, turning toward his immediate audience of drinking buddies. "Ya send a donkey to college and ya get a smart ass. What's that big word mean?" asked Lyle, carefully swiveling his head back to Daro.

"Voyeur? It means somebody that likes to watch other people participate in things like sex, but don't particularly want to be involved themselves - you know - dirtbags like you and Raney."

"By damn, thash me," Lesher said, laughing and slapping his thigh. "There ain't but one thing I like better, but since my ole lady ain't here right now, thash all I can do - watch."

"Do you think Carol would approve?"

"Now that jush shows how much you know, asshole," Lesher said. "She told me it was okay to get my battery all charged up so long as I come home to run it down."

His drunken partner sometimes made him uncomfortable, but he had to chuckle. One thing about Lesher, he was a straight arrow. In spite of his mouth, Lesher's wife, kids, home, and hearth were his life.

Looking around the room for Raney, Daro noted that the highest ranking officer was a sergeant. Just as well, he thought. Anyone of greater rank might put a damper on things.

"You seen Raney?" asked Daro.

"Nope. Late shift I reckon."

"When's show time?"

"Beats hell outa me. Somebody said that they was bringin' a sixteen millimeter projector 'cause three of them ole trashy movies has got sound. I heard that one of 'em's Candy Barr," Lesher said, referring to the well known Dallas stripper with the big jugs. "In case you ain't never seen her, Candy's built like a brick shithouse - pretty face, too, if your eyes ever get up that far."

Daro rolled his eyes. "Wonderful. I can't think of anything I want to watch less than a porno flick, unless it's one with sound. You're depraved, partner."

"There you go again with them big words. I think college just about ruined your ass. And speakin' about college, Todd's so worked up about them slide rule classes you been givin' him he can't talk about nothin' else."

"Look at the bright side, partner," he said. "Todd won't be a dumbass like his old man."

"You see," Lyle said, turning to his drinking buddies. "You see what I've gotta put up with since taking this pitiful mountain of flesh under my wing - slavin' away at makin' him a good cop. He ain't never gonna make it."

The rest of Lesher's speech trailed off as Daro walked out of ear shot. He went to the kitchen for a beer and found an amused Liz Carring pinned against a cabinet, fending off the clumsy advances of Vince Borland, a motorcycle officer about half her age and size. The graying brunette had kept her figure, but she looked her forty seven years. Borland was attached to her like a boxer pup on a date with the sofa.

"You're Daro aren't you?" she asked, peering over Borland's shoulder.

"Yes Ma'am."

"Will you take care of our little ball of passion here before I have to kick him in the nuts? Pour some water on him, or something."

"Okay, Vince," Daro said, taking the smaller officer by the arms and peeling him off Liz like wrapping paper off a Christmas package, "Give it a rest."

"Hell no, I want me a hunk of that," said a bleary eyed Borland. "I've had my eye on that all night."

"You better put your eye somewhere else before Roughhouse gets here or your arms won't be long enough to scratch your fat lip. This lady is private stock."

Muttering something to the effect that he was so horny he could hardly blink his eyes, a resigned Borland got another beer and staggered back to the front room.

"Thanks, Daro," Liz said.

"Anytime."

Carring began rearranging the tray of hors d'oeuvres she was working on before Borland's playful onslaught. "I hear you're getting married, too," said Liz.

He smiled. "Yep. In October - to a neat lady named Janette Colmer."

Daro didn't notice Carring's hands pause. "I may have met her. A very pretty blonde; lives in Highland Park?"

"Yes. You know her?"

"Oh, not really. We met at a party, I think. It was some time ago."

A commotion started in the front room and a cheer went up. Roughhouse Jones, Sergeant New, two projectors, and a box full of films had just come in the front door. Following that came eight more cops carrying eight cases of beer and several bags of ice.

"That's gotta be my honey," Liz said. "Would you mind telling Jones I'm in here?"

"Sure."

Daro waded through the mob gathered around the two officers. Roughhouse and New were breaking open the beer and ice, replenishing the two previously full washtubs in the front room before bringing the rest back to the kitchen. He slapped Jones on the shoulder and shouted, "Liz wants to see you." He pointed toward the kitchen.

Jones nodded, shouted instructions to New about the projector and films, and went to greet his long time girl friend.

"Hey, babe, you lookin' real good," Jones said, running a broad, calloused hand over Carring's ripe behind. It was his usual greeting, but he didn't get the normal response. Liz turned a troubled face.

"What's the matter?"

"Do you remember that stag film we saw several weeks ago, the one with the pretty blonde in it - the one I recognized?" Liz asked.

Jones nodded. "What about it?"

"I'm pretty sure she's Daro's fiance."

Jones looked stunned. "You're shittin' me - did you tell him?"

"Of course I didn't tell him, dumbass," Liz said, sharply. "I can't be sure without seeing her in person. But if it is, we can't just let him marry her without telling him, can we?"

"Shit no. I ain't gonna let a brother officer marry no damn whore, particularly after she's made a movie for the whole world to see."

"So what do we do?" Liz asked.

"How the hell should I know. He might not take it too kindly if I was to waltz up to him and say, 'Hey, Hoss, I think your girlfriend not only struts her stuff, but sells it too.' He's a pretty calm guy, but he ain't that calm. Besides, have you seen the build on that big bastard? That boy's got muscles in his shit."

"So much for what we can't do - what can we do?" Liz asked.

Jones scratched his lantern jaw. "Well, we could show him the film."

Horrified, Liz said, "That's terrible. How would you like to be sitting with a bunch of other cops and have a movie with me in it splashed all over the screen."

A twinkle came into his eye. "Well, now, that might not be too bad. You ain't never done some of them nasty old fun things to me, you know."

"Damn you, Roughhouse Jones, you -"

Jones gathered her into his arms and silenced her with his mouth. In a moment, Liz was wishing they were alone. Who knows, she thought, remembering the various antics shown in the film, it might be fun to try some new things.

Liz broke free. "We got no time for that, babe. What are we gonna do about Daro?"

Jones sighed and pulled on his lower lip. "Look, we've got no good options. We tell him and you're wrong, there's hell to pay. If we don't tell him and you're right, there's still hell to pay. And he's gonna find out eventually. Better now than later."

With the constant stream of cops traipsing through the kitchen for a beer, Jones and Liz migrated to the back porch where they could have their talk in private. The debate raged back and forth, but the discussion shortly became moot. Unknown to the pair, New and several willing helpers had put up the screen and cleared a small table for the projector.

"All right, you assholes, put a sock in it," yelled Sergeant New.

Like a pebble dropped into a calm pool, the circle of quiet passed outward from group to group as drunks shushed each other.

"We got some new stuff for you tonight," continued the bald, mustached New. "And one of 'em's real special. Ain't none of us seen a film like this before. The acting's real good. Not only that, it's in color and there's sound, too, so we're gonna show it first. Everybody ready?"

A roared "Yes" greeted the question.

"Where's Tinsley?"

"Here," Tinsley yelled, standing on the far side of the room, bookended by two scantily clad hookers.

"Well, get your ass over here, boy," New said. "You and your two friends have a seat on the couch - after all, you're the guest of honor."

A tipsy Tinsley, assisted by his two female companions, sat in their designated places as the film started to roll. Both girls began to blow in his ears and kiss his neck. When one of them unzipped his fly and inserted a hand inside his pants, Tinsley's eyes glazed over and a silly grin spread over his face. About half the cops were watching the action on the couch instead of the screen when the brunette's head lowered into his lap.

Feeling a call, an embarrassed Danny Daro was in the upstairs bathroom when Storm Raney arrived. Even through the bathroom door, he could hear the whistles and catcalls as he flushed the toilet and washed up. He had never liked these parties, but something about this one bothered him more than most. He decided to make his way to the back door and leave quietly.

As he descended the stairs into the hubbub of darkness below, the first film began. Shifting light patterns splashed off the walls onto the assembled officers making them look like clowns on loan from the nearest circus. Almost every face bore a drunken, silly grin.

"Holy shit," said a pointing officer, "Would you look at the whang on that guy?"

There was a burst of laughter and Daro instinctively looked at the screen.

She was small, a well shaped young girl, stripped of her clothes, spread-eagled and tied to the four corners of a bed. Her head was covered by a black, cloth bag. Beside her stood an immense man in full erection, hooded and dressed as an executioner in black leather. With practiced moves he untied the cord from around the girl's neck and stripped off the bag, revealing her face. At that precise moment the camera zoomed in.

Soft brunette hair fell from her pretty face, and terror filled eyes locked on to her tormenter. Her already enormous eyes got bigger. A primeval sound gathered in her throat, and from her ripped a scream that stood the hair up on every neck.

Raney's move was a blur. He pulled the power cord from the electrical outlet and the screen went dark. The only light left in the room came from the partially open door into the dining room. A sound almost like a growl circulated through the room.

"Hey, Sarge, why the hell didja do that?" asked an angry voice.

Raney whirled toward the questioner, his teeth pulled back in an animal snarl. Pointing a finger at the screen, he growled, "Because, you dumb shit, that's not a blue movie, it's Danny Daro's sister."

Someone turned on the lights. On the stairs, frozen in horror, stood Daro, staring at the now blank screen as though still seeing his beloved's tortured face.

What happened next was unclear. Storm later told Daro that both he and Lesher tried to keep Daro from leaving, but it did no good. He stomped to the projector and snatched the film, taking it with him as he stormed out. Several other friends considered trying to stop him, but they could see death in his eyes. Knowing him so well, Lesher was convinced that his friend would have killed the first man who tried to lay a hand on him.

It was morning before Daro came out of it enough to realize where he was. Like a migrating bird he had returned to Turtle Creek, almost directly across from his former home. Seated on one of several benches, he was surrounded by over a dozen tame ducks, year-round inhabitants of the gently flowing stream. Somewhere he had picked up a loaf of bread to feed the ever hungry birds, some so tame that they would take a crust directly from an outstretched hand.

He smiled, remembering the sweet young sister that had so loved this place - at first frightened of the noisy, quacking creatures. She later made such fast friends that the ducks would waddle up to the beautiful child, happily greeting her whether she had food for them or not.

As early as age three, Sally pestered him until he stopped whatever he was doing so she could go see the ducks. "Duk-Duk!" she would shout, tugging at his trousers and jumping up and down until he relented. Daro remembered taking her by a tiny hand to escort the youngster across the street to the creek. Instantly surrounded, Sally would pet her special friends, all the while crooning to them in a sort of musical babble. As far as he knew, Sally was the only human being the ducks ever allowed to actually touch them.

The sun was well up, it's rays softly kissing the quiet waters of Turtle Creek when Daro left his comfortable musings and stood up to stretch cramped muscles. He tossed the last of the bread to the biggest drake, creating a minor brouhaha as several noisy rivals rushed in to steal a portion. Walking slowly toward his car, he lifted tear-reddened eyes and softly whispered, "Why?"

He paused, seeming to wait for an answer - one that did not come.

"Hey, Danny, you okay?" interrupted a voice.

He hadn't heard the squad car drive up. The officer who called to him was Rocky Purcell, one of his fellow graduates from their police academy class.

"Yeah, Rock, I'm okay."

"Man, you had us all scared shitless. You need any help?"

Jarred from his comfortable thoughts made Daro's irritation return. "I'm okay, Rock, just leave me alone."

"Sure - sure. Hey, I'm real sorry about last night, Danny," Purcell said. "Sergeant Raney and Lesher was about ready to put out an APB on you. I'll radio 'em that you're all right."

"You do that, Rock," he said, immediately sorry for the sarcasm in his voice.

He saw Purcell pick up the mike and hold it to his mouth. Purcell listened to the dispatcher's reply then leaned out the window. "Hey, Danny! Captain Spencer wants to see you, pronto."

"Tell him I'm on my way. I've got a stop to make first."

Even though Daro hadn't seen Harold "Shutterbug" McMillan since he bought some camera equipment from him several years ago, he was sure McMillan would help. The brain of Daro's high school class, his friend had always been an avid photographer, so much so that he had continued his interest, foregoing college and opening a small camera shop and studio. Not long thereafter McMillan's prize winning photographs began to appear nationally, then internationally. His work became so popular that he closed the retail store and concentrated solely on his photographs, traveling the world in search of new and unique places, people, and wars.

The year of the big Dallas flood, Life Magazine gave McMillan his first real break, a six page spread. Done in black and white, McMillan's photographs centered on the victim's faces as they watched the flood destroy their homes and wash away their dreams. Their pain seemed to ooze from the page and permeate the reader.

One series in particular struck Daro. The photographs showed a black man watching his house wash from its foundation and break apart in the churning water. The most heartbreaking of all, however, showed another black man bending down and carefully locking the front door of his house to safeguard his meager possessions - a roofless house which had no other walls.

When Daro arrived at the studio on Oak Lawn just off Lemmon Avenue, McMillan was already at work. Completely bald, except for a narrow fringe of hair above his ears, he looked up when Daro pushed open the door.

"Well, my goodness, he said, rubbing his hands together, "I never expected to see you. How are you Danny?"

"Not very well, Harold. I've got a real problem - maybe you can help."

McMillan's brow wrinkled. "Of course. Let's go in back - I'll put on some tea."

McMillan puttered about the small kitchen, putting on the kettle and filling the tea pot with hot tap water to warm it up. All the while he watched his old friend. Harold had a thousand inane questions, but seemed loath to ask them, sensing somehow that Daro had not come to renew an old acquaintance.

"What is it - there's something terribly wrong, isn't there?" Harold asked.

Daro nodded, holding out a flat, circular container. "I found out why Sally was kidnapped."

Puzzled, McMillan took the film can, looking first at one side then the other. "A motion picture?"

He nodded. "Yeah. It shows her being raped."

Horrified, McMillan recoiled. "Sally? That's monstrous. You mean she was taken so someone could make a movie?"

"Apparently so. I need to see if you can make a copy of this for me; actually two would be better. The film is evidence so I'll have to give it back, but I want a copy in case something happens to it. Can you do it?"

McMillan opened the can. "Of course. It looks to be about twenty minutes long. I don't have the equipment, but a friend does. We'll do it today."

"Will the copy be good enough to make a frame by frame examination?"

Harold held the first part of the film up to the light. Nodding, he said, "Yes, I think so, but I can't say yet what the quality will be. It's new film and it hasn't been run much. What, specifically, are you looking for?"

Daro shrugged. "I don't know. Something - anything that might help me."

Harold nodded. "I'll do my best."

He put his hand on McMillan's bony shoulder. "I know it's against the law to develop this kind of film - you could get into trouble."

McMillan looked tight around the mouth. "The law be damned. You probably don't remember it, but several times at school you kept some of the other guys from kicking my ass. In fact, one time you knocked Carl Trejo down for messing with me. I never forgot. This is the first time I've been able to do something for you."

"Now I owe you, Harold." He slapped McMillan on the back, nearly knocking him down, and walked out the door.

Stopping at a pay phone, Daro called Captain Spencer. The Captain was very understanding. Pleading upset, he asked for and got the night off. He promised to guard the film with his life now that its existence was known.

"Are you okay, son?"

"Not really, but I'll make it."

"I guess you know that old Chicken Foot is about to blow a gasket," Spencer said.

Daro was puzzled. "Why?"

"Hell's bells, son, you've got the only solid evidence there is and he wants it yesterday. That silly son of a bitch even tried to convince me to have you arrested."

Suddenly angry, he asked. "For what?"

"That's what I asked him. I got no answer. Anyhow, you get some rest and bring the film with you to detail tomorrow evening. I don't want you to go near Talmadge. I'll take it from here."

Before he went to bed, Daro called Lesher to let him know he was okay. Dialing again he called Jan, filling her in on what had happened. She tried her best to get him to come over and stay at her place, but he wanted to be alone. Pleading exhaustion, he broke their date and went to bed.

Daro slept from early evening until nine o'clock the following morning, having dropped into bed like a stone the moment he completed his calls. Randall and Mildred knew something was wrong, but were too polite to pry. If they needed to know, they knew that Master Danny would tell them in good time.

At breakfast the next morning Daro could sense the tension. He called Randall and Mildred into the dining room and sat them down at the table before telling them what had happened to their little girl. Mildred dissolved into hand wringing sniffles, but Randall showed Danny a side he never knew he had before. The old man was livid. There was no doubt in Daro's mind that his servant and friend could have killed at that moment.

When calm returned, he called his photographer friend and was surprised to hear that the film had already been duplicated. He jumped in the car and hurried to the studio.

"How did it come out?"

McMillan grinned broadly. "Unbelievably well. My friend has this new film processor - but you don't want to hear about that." His smile faded as he remembered the film's subject matter. "Have you seen the whole film, Danny?"

Daro shook his head. "No, but I'll have to eventually."

McMillan swallowed hard. "To be honest it made me ill. It's horrible, absolutely horrible. I didn't know there were animals such as these in the world."

Daro's face was a pasty white. "Can you show it to me?"

"Yes, but I'm not sure you should see it."

"I don't have a choice. Can you run it without sound?"

"Sure," he said, threading the film and flipping an internal switch to suppress the sound track. He killed the lights and started the projector. Like a lighthouse beacon, the beam reached out and splashed onto the especially coated wall McMillan used to view his 35 millimeter slides.

Having seen the film's opening, Daro was prepared for the start, but not what followed. McMillan was wrong, it was beyond horrible. Try as he might, he could not find words to describe his revulsion. Watching his sister be violated in every conceivable manner by as many as three men at once, he was almost relieved when a garrote was slipped around her neck and the life snuffed from her body. The film ended with a close-up of Sally's tortured, contorted face. It didn't dawn on him until the film ended that one of the three men who participated in the sexual assault had a unique, star shaped scar on his upper right thigh, identifying him as none other than William P. Mitchell, the dirt-bag who had an ice pick shoved in his ear.

Something happened to him as the film ran. At first he thought he would be sick. But then a strange calm eased over him, a calm like that inside a hydrogen bomb a microsecond before it detonates. He knew with an absolute certainty that no matter what happened for the rest of his life he would never again feel such pain. He found that place within himself that his partner, Lesher, had so often talked about - a hard, impenetrable cocoon into which all good cops must sometimes retreat in order to withstand the horror of an unbelievably evil world. It took but twenty minutes of flickering lights on a wall to rip from Daro the last tattered shreds of his innocence.

• • •

12

Charlie Golden was alone at his desk when Daro walked in the detective's office.

Where's Killean?"

Startled, Golden's head jerked up from his paper work. As though it might give him some clue how to answer the question, Golden first looked at his watch, then at the uniformed Daro. "Uh, it's his day off."

"I gave the film back to Captain Spencer," Daro said, hooking his thumbs over his Sam Browne belt. Something about his informal stance and dispassionate statement seemed to embarrass Golden.

"I figured something was up when Chicken Foot lit out of here a couple of minutes ago," Golden said. "I heard his phone ring. Must have been Spencer."

Daro nodded. "I was talking to Cap when he made the call. Our resident asshole almost ran over me in the hallway before I could get out of Spencer's office. Cap said he'd keep him busy for a few minutes so I could come see you without having another major confrontation. Anything new?"

Golden shook his head. "Nope. I've been poking around trying to find even the rumor of a telephone memo from Betty Silk, but I can't find a thing. Starting from the date your folks got killed, Killean and I went over the log book covering the next thirty days. Nothing."

"Could Talmadge have torn it up?"

"Yeah, he could have. But if he did, there'd be a gap in the log numbers, and there's not."

Daro frowned and shook his head. "This isn't right. I'm missing something. What possible reason could that son of a bitch have for covering it up?"

Golden shrugged. "Damn good question and I intend on finding an answer."

Daro fell quiet, remembering something his father once told him, 'Some day you'll discover that without suffering pain there would be no growth or learning.'

At the time he didn't understand the growth part. But he sure knew about pain. Years later, while reading Kahlil Gibran, Daro ran across these words, 'Your pain is the breaking of the shell that encloses your understanding. And could you keep your heart in wonder at the daily miracles of your life, your pain would not seem less wondrous than your joy. And you would accept the seasons of your heart even as you have always accepted the seasons that pass over your fields. And you would watch with serenity through the winters of your grief.'

As far as he was concerned the winters of his grief had arrived. Daro could only hope that the serenity part would come with time.

What he did know was that from the moment the projector stopped and Sally's tortured features were finished being burned into his brain, a strange numbness gripped him. Almost instantly he had developed a tortoise-like armor to insulate him from a hurtful world.

Changing subjects, he asked, "Do you know how Sergeant New got hold of the movie?"

"Vice confiscated a bunch of stag films several weeks ago," Golden said. "Took 'em in a raid. The guy's been charged. His name's Gary Stroud - lives over in Oak Cliff. He made a deal with a projectionist to use the theater over on Jefferson after regular hours to show stag movies to a very select crowd of well paying dirtbags, several of 'em in the upper crust of Dallas society. It's enough to make you sick."

Daro kept an impassive face and saw his new friend squirm uneasily in his chair. Talking to a man about his sister, especially a sister who had been subjected to such an atrocity, obviously made Golden more than a little uncomfortable.

"Your sister wasn't the only one - they showed three movies a night, rotating the mix every couple of days. Some were kids, almost babies. Those bastards were charging ten bucks a head."

"Were the other movies the same as Sally's?"

"One was. The girl was raped on film, but not murdered until later. She's the one we found dead - cut up pretty bad and dumped in an alley. Except for some assorted pedophilia and one movie that showed a woman with various animals, the rest of the flicks were pretty straight stuff - simulated rape, murder, two on one, three on one, that sort of thing - obvious from the acting that the rapes and murders weren't real," Golden said.

"Do you know where he got the film?"

"Nope. But we didn't even know there was a film until Tinsley's party. This guy Stroud's straight out from under the nearest slimy rock - out on bond of course - but we know where to find him. We know the right questions to ask now."

"I wanta be there," Daro said.

Golden sighed, tilting his chair back on its two rear legs. His red tie askew, circles of sweat showed under the arms of his once fresh white shirt. "What would that prove? We already know that this isn't the guy who made the film. We haven't asked yet, but I can guarantee you he doesn't know who did either. I mean, whoever is making this filth knows their ass is grass when we catch 'em, particularly a film that could be used in a rape and murder investigation. This kind of crap - they call 'em 'snuff movies' by the way - costs big bucks to buy. And this one had to cost a lot to make."

"Why do you say that?" Daro asked.

"Figure it. Those seven assholes that Charlie and Marge blew away weren't smart enough to operate a box camera much less make a movie. But they weren't dumb enough to pull off a kidnapping for free, either. Apparently the guys were hired to find a girl of a certain age or size, maybe even of a specified hair color or some other such thing. Unfortunately - for whatever reason - your sister filled the bill, so they ran her down and grabbed her. Your folks being there was just icing on the cake for that type. That kind likes to rape and kill. They don't need any other reason."

With the index finger of his right hand, Golden began itemizing points on his left hand, starting with his thumb. "But whoever hired 'em had to pay 'em off, rent or own a place to make the film, buy cameras and such, pay the guys in the film, pay the cameramen, pay to have the film processed, and above all have some means of distributing the film that will insulate 'em from getting caught and at the same time let 'em recoup all that money."

"Sounds expensive," said Daro.

"It is," responded Golden. "But the big thing isn't the money, it's the getting caught. My FBI contacts tell me that films like this are getting more common, precisely because they do make so much money. They're illegal in the States, but there's a big market overseas. Straight sex sells, but not like a 'snuff' flicker. You can be damned sure that whoever made it will have several buffers between himself and the buyer so the film can't be traced back to him."

"I still want to be there when you question Stroud."

Golden shook his head. "No can do."

Daro poked a finger at his friend. "You keep missing something, Goldie - Sally was *my* sister."

Golden's color rose, but he spoke softly. "And you keep missing something, Daro, I'm in charge of this case and I'll not take any shit off you. And just to keep the record straight, the only reason I don't give you an administrative ass kicking is because I know the strain you're under. You're hurting. Who wouldn't be? But my decision isn't open for debate. I'll get to the bottom of it if you give me time."

Golden paused and sighed. "Now that we've got Stroud, don't you realize that for the first time things are beginning to break our way? But whether you do or not, if you get in my way - if you get too far out of line - I'll have you for lunch. Clear?"

If Golden had joined him in a shouting match instead of such a quiet, efficient ass eating, Daro could have maintained his anger. He wanted to strike out at something, anything, and Golden was handy. But as much as he hated to admit it, he knew that Golden had poured out his soul on the case. It was his turn to sigh. "Yeah, I got it. And you're right. Look, will you keep me posted?"

Golden relaxed and smiled. "You know damned well I will."

With a two finger salute to the bill of his cap, Daro turned on his heel and marched out. Golden's sorrowful eyes followed his new friend's stooped, massive back down the hallway to the top of the stairs.

Plunking the chair legs back down, Charlie Golden rolled his thin shoulders, trying to massage the tightness out of his upper body before once again assaulting the mountain of paperwork stacked up on his desk.

Walking back across the street, Daro wasted no time in contacting Paul New. The sergeant had his back to the door of the evidence room, hovering over a pile of papers at the front of his desk when Daro walked in. New was so intent on what he was doing that he didn't hear him until Daro cleared his throat.

Known for his nervous nature, New whirled around, his eyes huge. Seeing the uniform, New said, "Damn, officer, you scared me half to death."

"Sorry," Daro said. Even to himself the apology sounded disingenuous. "I need to ask a few questions."

Recognizing him, New flushed a bright red. "Look, Daro, I'm real sorry about the other night. There wasn't none of us knew that was your sister. Hell, we thought it was just good acting - we didn't know it was for real."

"I know that, Sergeant - I'm not here about that. I need to find out if you have any more films like it."

New shook his head. "No. There's the other girl - the one that was killed. The rape was filmed, but not the murder. Talmadge already has that one."

Thoughtfully, Danny pulled on his chin, then looked up. "How about any others with the same background?"

"What do you mean, background?"

"You know, the same wallpaper, same bed, same room, same people -any other films that might have been taken in the same place by the same people."

New looked as though a light had come on. "Hey, that's a damn good idea. I've got two with that same big stud in 'em - they're both eight millimeter. I don't remember if it's the same place or not, but there's another one that I'm pretty sure is. It's a different kind of film. You ain't never seen a build like the one she's got - a natural blonde - but you don't get to see her face until the end. I was gonna show it the other night before –" Remembering who he was talking to, New trailed off, his face taking on an even deeper flush.

"What do you mean you don't get to see her face?" asked Daro.

Warming to his subject, New's eyes glowed. "It's a masquerade thing. You know, everybody wearing masks. All dressed up like a hundred years ago. She's wearin' one of them hoop skirts like during the War Between the States, and he's all dressed up in tight britches. But that don't bother her none. She peels him outa those things like the skin off a grape. I'll tell you what, he's a real hoss. Not as good as that hooded guy, but damn near it. It's one of them deals where everybody takes off their masks at midnight. I just knew her face couldn't match her body, but I'm telling you, that one'd make strong men leave their happy homes. She's the prettiest thing I ever did see."

Daro was finding New's comments increasingly distasteful, but he hid his feelings. "Sergeant, I'm going to ask you for a special favor. I want to borrow those three films for a couple of days. You have my solemn word that nothing will happen to them and if you need them back beforehand, you call me and I'll have them here in less than an hour - agreed?"

A nervous Sergeant New went around back of his desk and sat down, a frown on his face. "I could get in some real trouble if anyone found out."

Daro put on his most charming smile for the already guilty feeling sergeant. "I'll make you a deal, you don't tell anyone and I won't either."

New gave him a bit more token opposition, but Daro left with the films, stashing them in the trunk of his car. After meeting detail with Lyle they relieved the previous squad and dropped by Daro's car. He picked up the canisters and Lesher drove out to McMillan's to leave the film.

"What are you lookin' for, partner?" asked Lyle when they resumed patrol.

"I want to do a frame by frame search for clues."

"To find what?"

Irritated, Daro said, "How the hell should I know, Lyle. Anything. I don't give a shit. Anything at all."

"Damn, hoss. No need to get testy. I ain't the enemy."

Daro nodded. "Yeah - sorry."

They were assigned to district twenty three, unusual since the normal procedure was to split partners, the senior man left on his regular beat, the other paired with another officer to patrol the unfamiliar territory. They checked in service and Lesher cruised up Lemmon Avenue stopping for the red light at Loma Alto. In a green Chevy, a man, his wife, and two cute, blonde headed girls waited beside them. Daro looked over and the couple waved.

"That's nice," Daro said, waving back as the light turned green and Lesher moved off. "Not many folks wave at the police."

"Yeah," agreed Lyle. "And them that do most likely don't use all their fingers."

Daro laughed. "Ah, yes - the old one finger salute."

The incredible happened. Not a single call all shift.

The day after Daro returned the films a tragedy struck that neither he nor his partner would know about for several hours. Lesher logged them in on district twenty one as Daro nosed the cruiser out Harry Hines toward Oak Lawn.

Partner," Lesher said, "I got me a little girl at my house that's damn near suicidal 'cause she ain't seen her Uncle Danny for so long. Furthermore, Carol told me she's gained ten pounds eatin' them three pounds of chocolates, I'm about to shoot myself in the foot with this new pistol Santa Claus gave me, Todd's flunkin' math, Jenny burned all her baseball stuff, and worst of all Ruby is threatenin' to run off with the piano player down at the Silver Dollar saloon. Now I wanta know what you're gonna do about it."

Daro was wearing his wrinkled grin before Lyle got half way through his diatribe. "Partner, I just don't know. Sounds like maybe you need old Doctor Danny to come over and bail you out."

"And when might this visit take place?"

"How about tomorrow. Jan and I have a date tonight."

"Fair enough," Lyle said, turning serious. "But don't bullshit me. Amy really misses you."

Daro had hardly got, "I'll be there," out of his mouth when a blue, 54 Ford Victoria ran the light at Oak Lawn narrowly missing their squad car. Daro pulled the red lights and hit the siren, simultaneously punching the accelerator.

"Stupid son of a bitch," yelled Lesher. "I'll betcha five bucks that pisswilly's drunk as a skunk."

"No bet," said Daro.

Daro chased the car up Oak Lawn and through the light at Maple before the driver lost control and slammed into the rear of a parked car. The Ford ricocheted off, spun around once as it slid up an incline and came to rest across the sidewalk of a chiropractic clinic just short of Cedar Springs. Lyle was out of the car and had the driver in cuffs before Daro hardly finished turning the key.

Lyle wrinkled his nose. "Good thing you didn't bet, partner, this sucker stinks to high heaven. Don't strike a match near the asshole, neither. If his breath caught fire he'd take out half a block."

"I'll put him in the car."

"Shit, no, hoss. In a few minutes it's gonna soak into this bastard what's happened and he's gonna puke his toenails up. I don't wanta have to hose out the car. Set him on the curb while I get the wrecker."

Daro tossed Lyle a salute. "You're the boss."

Lyle was right. Long before the wrecker arrived, the pisswilly tossed his cookies, carrots, and other assorted tidbits half way across Oak Lawn Avenue. After finishing their business they loaded their prisoner in the car and took him to jail.

Lesher and Daro didn't hear about the fire until after they had booked their DWI. It wasn't until the next day that they knew how serious it was.

The Fire Marshal suspected that the fire was deliberately set, not surprising since it took place in the police evidence room. Originating directly in front of the heavy steel cabinet, the flames were so hot that they completely destroyed the film locker. In the locker was film evidence to be used in over fifty felony cases, not to mention Sergeant New's extensive porno library. There were indications that some of the cans had been opened and the film taken off the reels to make sure their destruction would be complete.

Investigators had no way to tell which films were involved, but the Fire Marshal's suspicions of arson proved accurate. That fact however was not divulged to the general public.

Something in Daro's mind clicked. He didn't know why, but even before he learned that the probable target of the attack was either the film library or some other evidence stored in the immediate vicinity, a small cop voice kept telling him that there was a connection between his folks and the fire, two seemingly unrelated events. The problem? There was no way to prove it. Besides having no proof, who would listen to a rookie anyway, especially one with a vested interest in the case? When something happens once it can be an error, twice a coincidence, but three times is a pattern. The thought occurred to him that the most crushed person of all was probably Sergeant New, his precious stag films reduced to ashes.

Not since the murder of JD Potter's wife and his subsequent resignation was the press so happy. For the next week the media attacked the sloppiness of the police administration, speculating on how such a thing could have happened. But if the department thought that week was bad, the next brought down the wrath of an outraged community as the newspapers reported that case after case had to be dropped because the photographic evidence was destroyed. Therein lay another problem, that of narrowing the field of suspects since so many had so much to lose.

Without exception, the media assumed that the fire was deliberately set by someone wishing to destroy convicting evidence. They further assumed, falsely, that the evidence locker had been forcibly entered, particularly after Police Chief, Carl "The Body Snatcher" Phillips, refused to comment or give any details. Every reporter in Dallas, whether print, TV, or radio, speculated as to the origins of the fire, automatically assuming that a pending case was the cause of the arsonist's extraordinary measures. And who was to say which theory was correct?

The final straw came when Carl Wade, the District Attorney, was forced to drop an indictment involving the abduction and rape of a twelve year old child. The girl, still in a catatonic state six months after the sexual assault, could not identify her attackers. To make matters worse, her assailants were man and wife and the only convicting evidence was a series of still photographs taken by the wife of the husband and child during every stage of the assault. The only proof to convict the sick pair was destroyed in the fire.

Even Daro was outraged as he and Lesher checked in with the dispatcher.

"Seventy one in service," Daro said, thumbing the mike.

"Seventy one, Roger."

The paper that day had run a particularly damning indictment on the dismissal of the rape of the twelve year old, the majority of which he had to agree with.

"Tell you what, Lyle, it's bad enough that some of these dirtbags are gonna get off because of that fire, but this little girl is just tearing me apart."

Lesher nodded. "I hear you, but there's two rules no cop can afford to forget or let bother him. Rule one - lots of dirtbags never get caught. Rule two - cops can't do nothin' about rule one."

"Is that supposed to make me feel better?"

"No, sir. It's supposed to make you care enough to do your job in spite of it. Let me tell you somethin'. You've got pretty cold lately and I know why. Hell, I understand. But as cold as you feel and as much as you want to shut out the world, you can't do it and be a good cop. You gotta keep on keepin' on. You've gotta accept the hurt - feel it deep down - and at the same time act like you don't. How do ya think I feel? That little girl coulda been Ruby."

Daro was quiet for a minute. "I never really thought about it that way."

"I understand," nodded Lesher. "You ever hear the serenity prayer? They use it in Alcoholics Anonymous."

Daro shook his head. "I don't think so."

"I worked with a partner for a while who belonged to AA. Hell of a good guy. Won't tell you his name, but he used to say that prayer so often that I got know it too. Goes like this, 'God, grant me the serenity to accept the things I cannot change, the courage to change the things I can, and the wisdom to know the difference.' He used to say that ever time we got into somethin' that pissed him off, but couldn't do nothin' about. You might just take it to heart."

Good advice. Daro took it under advisement.

But there was still his family. And too many coincidences had struck too close to home for him to apply any degree of serenity. He was haunted by the film of his sister. No one but Lesher knew he had copies of the four films.

After the shift Daro set up his projector to view the two, eight millimeter films, but McMillan would have to borrow a friend's sixteen millimeter projector before Daro could see the remaining film.

The viewing over, he felt unclean, disgusted not only with their content, but the thought of the kind of mind which thrived on such filth. But he learned something. New was right - the huge man in both films was the same one that assaulted Sally, right down to the hooded executioner's outfit. The first film he ran, an eight millimeter without sound, depicted a simulated rape with some of the worst acting Daro had ever seen. Film number two was of a different girl, prettier and a better actress, but still not convincing as the "rape" progressed.

But the film ended differently. This time the girl was supposedly "killed" on camera. Again, the acting was bad, but better than the first film. In these films, however, the hooded man was the only other person.

After rewinding both films, Daro shut off the projector and sipped the coffee that Randall had brought him earlier. Cold.

But something bothered him. Although he couldn't explain why, he felt sure these two films predated the one showing his sister. He also got the feeling that they were either experiments that didn't quite come off or they were pilots testing for script feasibility. Could it be that these films gave the producer/director the idea to film an actual rape?

Then it struck him. The film Talmadge had, the one he had not seen, was of the first girl kidnapped to make a movie of her rape. Although she was not killed until later, it followed the same pattern as the first eight millimeter movie he had just seen. At least it did according to what he had been told. Not identical maybe, but the idea was there.

Then there was the second movie, the one which simulated the girl's murder. Sally was taken and a similar film made that ended in his sister's murder. This time however it wasn't acting. Except for the addition of more rapists, the theme was the same as the second eight millimeter movie. Could it be? He would stake his life on it.

But now what? Just because he thought he'd discovered what might be an important clue made him no closer to the killers. Should he take his suspicions to Golden and Killean, even though he was convinced they would think he was nuts? He had about decided against it when the telephone rang. An excited Harold McMillan told him to come over as quickly as possible.

"What's up?" he asked as he entered Harold's studio.

The bespectacled, bird-like McMillan was all but wringing his hands for joy. "I found something - something important."

The excitement was catching. "What?" Daro asked.

"You've got to see this," said a smug McMillan, walking to a back-lighted, translucent glass similar to that used by doctors to examine x-ray film. He snapped a switch and the fluorescent tubes flickered to life as McMillan stuck a slide under a retaining spring at the top of the strip. Handing Daro a magnifying glass, he said, "Take a look."

Daro fumbled with the magnifier, moving it back and forth between his face and the film until he found the right focal length. The single frame of film showed a man and woman, both wearing masks, lying on a bed in the process of undressing each other. In the background was part of a chair, and a closet with the door closed. "I don't see –"

McMillan interrupted. "On the back of the chair, right at the top of the film."

The chair was cream colored and covered with small, blue flowers which acted almost like camouflage. He saw nothing at first, but then part of a hand seemed almost to pop out at him.

"Do you see it?" asked McMillan.

"Yeah, a guy's hand."

"Why a guy?"

He thought a minute. "I don't know. No nail polish. Fingers kinda fat and stubby." He peered intently. "Hey - looks like there's something wrong with the little finger."

McMillan grinned broadly and slipped another slide in place for Daro to see. "Give that man a cigar. I took that area and blew it up real big, even though it gets more grainy the more it's magnified," McMillan said, circling the hand on the back of the chair with a thin index finger.

Daro again bent to the task, adjusting the glass to bring the new slide into focus. "It looks like there's something wrapped around his little finger. I can't quite make it out."

"It's some sort of serpent, or maybe a dragon," McMillan said. "I can't be sure yet, but I did a frame by frame examination of the film and the same hand is on three more frames. I'm gonna blow all of them up the size of a house if I have too. I'm hoping that one of the other frames will be clearer."

Daro shook his head. "I just wish we had the originals."

"These are the originals," said McMillan, eying his friend with a sheepish look. "The three I gave you to take back were the copies."

"Harold, I could kiss you. But whatever possessed you?"

"Well, hell," McMillan said, shrugging thin shoulders, "I couldn't see why the police department needed them - not just for evidence that a crime was committed; a copy is good enough for that. I mean, we needed the best we could get to look for clues and stuff, like this guy's hand."

"Harold, that's the best news I've had in my life. But there's one more thing. If you can - will you make another copy, just in case?"

"No need," said his friend. "I already did."

Daro shook his head. "You amaze me. I sure am grateful for that day on the school grounds.

"Elementary, my dear Watson," said a beaming McMillan. "Uh - no pun intended."

He could not have explained why, but he told no one, not Golden, or Killean, not even Lesher. He sensed that he must play this one close to the vest. His first stop was City Hall to check out the moniker file, the place where aliases, scars, marks, tattoos, and other unusual items of potential identification were religiously gathered, cataloged, and filed away. But frustration struck again. Mrs. King, normally the keeper of such records, was at home recovering from a gallbladder operation and was not expected to return for several days. He felt disappointed. His information too general for the temporary clerk to identify.

Daro had to wait two days before the call came. When he answered the ring, a voice said, "It's a snake."

The statement didn't register, but he recognized the voice. "Harold? Is that you?"

"Of course it's me. Did you hear me? It's a tattoo of a snake, and a most unusual one at that. It shouldn't be too hard to find."

Daro's book dropped to the floor as he sat up straight on the couch. "You're sure?"

McMillan snorted. "Of course I'm sure. We got even luckier. I did another run through on the masquerade film and found a frame that had about half of the little finger and the tip of the one next to it. This time the camera was closer so the definition was much better."

"Could you tell anything else?" Daro asked, breathing hard as though he'd just finished a workout.

"Well, we know it's the left hand - but we knew that before. We already know that the guy is a bit pudgy. At least that's what his stubby fingers would lead me to believe. And I can now report to you that he has very hairy knuckles."

"Harold, if the police department had an 'above and beyond' medal for civilians I'd put you in for it. Surely we can find this guy now."

After a few more minutes of pleasantries Daro hung up. Now that he was armed with much more definitive information, he was convinced that his man would be listed right down to name, rank, and serial number - a cozy package that would fall into his hands like a ripe plum. After all, how many men could there be with the tattoo of a snake wrapped around the little finger of their left hand?

Again it was not to be. Mrs. King had not returned to work, but her presence wasn't necessary to determine that such a unique identifier did not exist. Not, that is, on a person who had been arrested in the City of Dallas, Texas. He was sure this unusual marking would not be overlooked, but the file had nothing even remotely resembling such a tattoo. He even requested an FBI and State search, but those too came back negative. Once more Daro felt himself spiral downward into a frustrated depression.

• • •

13

Looking back, Daro didn't know why he decided not to tell anyone about the snake tattoo, not even Lyle. It wasn't so much that the discovery was a secret, in a way it was more. The clue, and the reasoning it spawned, was uniquely his own, the only information so far unearthed that he had developed strictly on his own.

Also, Daro was feeling pretty cocky about saving the film from the fire. But when he decided not to tell anyone about having the movies, he and Lyle had a small fracas. Lyle was certain Daro would get his ass in a crack as soon as it came out that he had them – and Daro didn't even want to share the news with Golden and Killean. Later he intended to tell the detectives, but for now he wanted to savor the discovery alone. He conveniently forgot that, while it may have been his idea to make a frame by frame search of the film, it was Harold McMillan who found the hand. Besides, Harold was the only reason Daro had any of the films at all, much less the originals.

Still, Daro harbored a special proprietary feeling toward this newfound clue. And what a clue. What puzzled him however was how both the Dallas Police Department and the FBI could have so many thousands of records and yet not one of them made reference to such a unique identifier. It had to be because the guy had never been arrested, but someone, somewhere, must know the dirtbag's name.

Once again Daro embraced his work routine as plans for the wedding began to solidify. He was both surprised and saddened that one part of his life was going so well, but his sense of well being seemed to suck his emotions dry. Often there were days when he would much rather have stayed in bed.

Their forty four hour a week ritual rolled around again as Lesher and Daro paired up on district seventy one. They relieved their squad and Lesher took first shift behind the wheel.

"Now look, partner," Lesher said, just after they went on duty. "You been flappin' your gums about this Jan Colmer, what a beauty she is and what a great gal she is, and like that, but neither me nor mine have so much as laid eyes on her. When are you gonna bring her over to the house? You know damn well that Carol's gotta approve or you can't get married."

Daro smiled. "Okay, big mouth, when do you want us over?"

"Tomorrow night."

"Done. Pull up at the next phone and let me make a call."

Jan's greeting from the Leshers was mixed. He could tell by the expression on Todd's face that the thirteen year old was ready to trade in his slide rule forever, provided they leave him alone in a room with her for at least thirty seconds.

Jennifer was ambivalent, but Ruby went on afterburner, immediately recognizing Jan as both enemy and competition. As usual, Amy ran. But he knew he could count on Carol who greeted Jan with quiet, sincere dignity. He thought they liked each other, but he wasn't that good at reading the subtleties radiated by females.

After visiting for a few minutes in the living room, Lyle said, "You kids go to your room now."

"Oh, Daddy," whined Jennifer as she made a face and went toward the back of the house, pounding a baseball into the pocket of her new first baseman's mitt.

Todd was barely able to tear his eyes away from the tall blonde, his eyes alternating between chest and hips. He reluctantly left, followed by a frosty Ruby, her head held high as she glanced fetchingly toward Daro and strode regally from the room.

Once again he heard the timer go off in the kitchen. This time Carol had fed the children early so the foursome had the dining room all to themselves.

After supper, and over the objections of Carol, Jan invited herself to help with the dishes. When well out of everyone's hearing, Jan gave Carol an uncertain smile. "I don't think Ruby likes me very much."

Carol patted her hand and said, "That's all right, dear, Todd likes you enough for the both of them."

Inserting the stopper in the right side of a double sink, Jan drew several inches of hot water and watched the suds form as she poured a small amount of detergent beneath the stream. She smiled at Carol. "I know what I'm about to ask may seem sudden, but I wonder if you would do me a big favor."

"If I can," Carol said, getting a clean towel out of a nearby drawer.

"Danny's and my wedding is coming up in October and I don't have any family left. I would be so pleased if you would consider being my maid of honor?"

Jan didn't know it, but in the living room, Daro had just asked Lyle to be his best man.

Daro was on a two day break and Lyle was paired up with Roughhouse Jones working district seventy three. Lesher checked them in service and Jones took the wheel, making his way over to Ervay Street where he turned south toward Grand Avenue. They had worked together several times and it didn't take long for Lyle to realize that something was stuck in Jones' craw.

"You wanta tell me what's gnawin' on your ass?" asked Lyle.

Jones sadly shook his head. "Man, I dunno. You might get just as mad as that big shit of a partner of yours."

"You got a problem with Daro?"

"Hell no. I like him. I don't know him too good, but he seems like a nice guy. Liz says he's okay and that's good enough for me. It ain't that, uh - you know his girl?"

"Jan? Sure. Some knockout, but then you don't know her, do you?"

"No. I don't," agreed Jones. "But I've seen her. I've seen all of her. She's a hell of a lot of woman - more'n you know."

"What's that supposed to mean?"

Jones squirmed in the driver's seat. "I guess there ain't no easy way to say it. Colmer's a whore."

Shock and anger rolled all over Lesher as he hissed, "You've got me by about forty pounds you miserable shit, but if you'll pull this squad car over I'll do my best to whip your ass right here in the middle of Ervay Street."

"Come on, Lyle," Jones said trying to sooth Lesher. "You think I'd make up a thing like that. She made one of them movies like we show at the bachelor parties. Colmer was all dressed up in old time clothes and wearin' a mask –"

"A mask?" interrupted Lesher. "Well, if she was wearin' a mask, how in the hell did you know who it was?"

"You didn't let me finish, partner. She took her mask off right at the end, and Liz and me both seen her real good. I could tell somethin' was wrong right off and I asked Liz what it was. She says she knows her. Met her at a party some time back and knows for a lead pipe cinch that she's a hooker."

"Look, Jones," Lyle said, "Just because Liz met Jan at a party, that don't make her a hooker."

"And I suppose the damned movie don't? Lyle, you can stick your head in the sand all you want, but I'm tellin' you that Colmer's a whore and your partner's about to marry her. Now that don't bother me none, but it might Daro. She was up there on the screen, and I mean there wasn't nothing she ain't done to that old boy - kissed all over him and blocked his hat to a fair thee well. But you can have it your way. All I'm tryin' to do is help. If Daro knows, that's okay - but if he don't, he's got a right to, and you better tell him."

There was an uncomfortable moment before Jones asked, "Does he know?"

Lesher knew the truth when he heard it and he willed himself to calm down. Besides, he'd known Jones for a lot of years and Roughhouse was a straight up guy, not the kind to carry tales. Lesher had to give him credibility.

"I don't know if he does or not. It's not likely that I'm gonna go up to him and ask if he knows his fiancé is sellin' her ass and makin' movies. Are you real sure about this? No bullshit now, Jones - do you know this for gospel fact."

"Yes, damnit, call Liz and see what she says. We was over to her house a couple of weeks before the Tinsley bash, sorta havin' a little private party of our own, if you catch my drift," Jones said, grinning.

When Lesher didn't return the smile, Jones sobered and continued. "I'd got the movie from New that mornin'. They hadn't got it but two nights before in a raid. It was real good with sound and all. And that's why we was gonna show it at Tinsley's party - it was one of the four New brought with him, but the one with Daro's sister come up first."

"Holy shit," Lyle said. "I just thought of something."

"What?"

"Carol just said she'd be Jan's maid of honor and I'm Daro's best man."

Both men were silent for a while, lost in their own thoughts. "At least there's one good thing about all this," Jones said.

"Tell me quick, I could stand some good news." Lesher said.

"I understand all them films was in the locker room when it went up. Maybe there wasn't but the one copy."

"Yeah, it was, but -" Lesher caught himself. He almost let it slip that Daro had copies of several films; a sixteen millimeter of his sister, two eight millimeter with the same stud in them that raped his sister, and apparently the one Jones was talking about, the one with the couple dressed in costume. Come to think of it, mused Lyle, since Danny had the film, why hadn't he viewed it? But what if he had? It would take a mighty big man to overlook such prior activity. If anybody could however Lyle was convinced it would be Danny. His respect for his partner was still growing. Anyone who could get close to Amy in only one session had to be all right.

Lesher thought back, but he couldn't remember his partner being in that bad of a mood recently. And surely if he'd seen Jan in such a film Lesher would've known it. Maybe Jan had confessed, and Danny had forgiven her. Even so, thought Lyle, surely he would have detected at least a momentary coolness on Danny's part. Lesher could remember nothing.

"I'm gonna have to give it some thought, Roughhouse. I'd appreciate it if you didn't say nothin' to nobody else."

It was Jones' turn to get mad. "What the hell kinda guy do you think I am, Lesher? I ain't told nobody but you and the only reason I done that is because you was partners and all."

"Sorry," Lesher said. "I appreciate it."

It was a time of meetings, first the Leshers and now Mildred. Jan already knew Randall and she knew that in him she had an advocate with his wife, Mildred. But she was still nervous. It had been her experience that women were much more territorial than men, and Daro had been Mildred's territory for thirty odd years. The servant's dislike, should it come to that, probably wouldn't break the engagement, but harmony at their meeting would be so much better. Besides, if the couple stayed on after they were married, Jan wanted no major waves on the pond of their marriage.

Jan's battle with herself as to whether or not to tell Daro about her former occupation was one sided, the decision not to tell winning out with great ease. But her decision created another set of problems. What to do if someone recognized her? It wouldn't be quite the risk if she hadn't made the film. But she had and there was no going back. Meeting a former client, particularly since Danny didn't circulate in her social circles, was far less of a problem than coming face to face with a stranger who had seen the film. If only she'd stuck to her original insistence that she not remove the mask.

In retrospect, taking off the mask seemed the final act of degradation, a penetration where none had ever been made before. If only the money for doing as she was told hadn't been so good. Besides, she was doing nothing more on film than what she always did - making it with another John, and Johns could be controlled. At the time she completely discounted the camera. It didn't involve her, just someone who looked like her. Sex for pay was an act, a small mini-play in which her soul played no part, a time during which her emotions were shut down. Her date might as well be in the bathroom playing with himself for all her involvement. Besides, except for that one lapse, her clientele was so restricted that she felt sure she could steer her husband around any potential problem areas.

Husband. She liked the sound of that.

Opting for damage control, Jan insisted that their wedding be small. There would be only a few of Daro's closest friends, but there would be none on her side of the aisle. If he thought anything about the oversight, he gave no sign, seemingly happy to give his bride-to-be free reign. Inviting family was no problem, both her parents were dead, but it did give her an idea as to how she might further influence Randall's and Mildred's opinion.

"You seem nervous," Daro said as he picked Jan up at her apartment and drove her to the Bryn Mawr cottage. She wore a light blue, silk halter-top, the skirt falling in soft folds and hemmed just below center knee. She also knew that the matching two and a half inch heels and seamed nylons flattered her legs. Parted in the middle, her honey blonde hair hung straight down, except for a slight inside flip at the ends.

"I'm nervous. Do you realize this is the first time I've met Mildred? I've never even been to your home?"

Her statement seemed to take him aback.

"I guess I never thought much about it, he said. Randall talks about you all the time and we've spent so much time at your place I almost feel like it's home. A large part of that time was spent in your bed if you recall?" he said, grinning

Jan smiled and squeezed his arm. "Yes, I do recall. Your place might be a bit awkward, though. I'm sure Mildred has seen your bare bottom, but I doubt if she has recently - maybe not since you were in diapers."

Daro laughed. "That's true, but she sure saw a lot of it then. She was sort of cook and nanny to me. I know this much, she's whipped my backside lots more than my parents ever did. She's probably the reason I'm a cop and not in jail."

"Aw, I doubt if you were that bad."

The porch light came on and Randall opened the front door as Daro and Jan pulled into the driveway. He helped her out of the car, taking her arm and matching her long stride as he escorted her up the walk. Dry, refrigerated air swirled from inside the house in stark contrast to the hot and humid outside.

The old man's smile was broad. He bowed slightly and said, "It's good to see you again, Miss Jan. Welcome home."

Jan almost ruined her makeup at his obviously sincere comment. The first name familiarity felt like a promotion, as well as the reference to home.

"How very gracious, Randall, thank you. Anything good to eat tonight?"

"You are being singularly honored," Randall said, his British accent crisp and clear. "I don't think even Mr. Danny knows this, but Mildred is preparing Miss Sally's favorite dish, Lobster Armoricaine. Mr. Danny I hope you don't mind."

"Quite the contrary, Randall. I think it's not only appropriate, but a kind thing to do."

After Randall seated them in the living room, Daro explained the significance of the dish. In a small way it was almost a breakthrough. In their many hours of pillow talk, Jan remembered him telling her about this favorite food. She also remembered that Mildred had supposedly retired the recipe.

In a minute Daro went to the kitchen to fetch the cook. Mildred washed her hands, nervously dried them, then smoothed her almost white hair at the temples, tucking in a few errant strands before leaving the kitchen. When he made the introductions Jan could see an immediate response in the old cooks eyes. Relief flooded her. She was approved. After a few minutes of small talk, he escorted Jan into the dining room and Randall began serving.

"That was wonderful," Jan said after the last course was cleared away. "I'm not a bit surprised you never learned to cook."

"Me either. Mildred and Randall have taken good care of me. I know they'll do the same for you after we're married."

"Then they've agreed to stay on?"

"You couldn't drive them away."

She was pleased, reaching over to cover his hand with her own. "Do you mind if I go out to the kitchen? I need to speak to them for a minute."

Daro seemed mystified. "Of course not," he said, getting up as she left the table. His puzzled gaze followed her back down the short hallway to the kitchen.

The old couple were seated at a small table, settling in with a cup of tea. Both leaped to their feet.

"Is there something I can get you, Miss Jan?" asked Randall.

"Not at all. Please - take your seats and I'll sit here with you for a minute if I may."

"Most certainly," said the butler, holding out a chair for her. "Mildred, why don't you get Miss Jan a cup of tea?"

The cook took a paper-thin cup and saucer of their finest china from the cabinet. Removing the tea cozy from the pot, Mildred poured a cup of the brownish, orange liquid.

Jan accepted the cup with a smile. "I have a very great favor to ask, but I want you to feel free to say no if it makes you uncomfortable. Will you do that?"

Mildred dimpled, nervously. "We'll try," she said, her voice unsteady.

"I want both of you to have a part in our wedding."

Both were obviously flabbergasted. "But - Miss Jan – we, uh, we are servants," Randall stuttered.

"No, you are family - the only family Danny has, and therefore my family, too. I'm not too sure but what he thinks of you as his mother and father now."

Always the emotional one, tears glistened in Mildred's eyes. For a moment both she and Randall seemed too stunned to speak.

"Miss Jan, It is very kind of you say this. You cannot know how much it is appreciated," Randall said.

Jan smiled. "Which leads me to my favor. My father and mother are both dead and I have no close relatives, just a distant cousin or two back in Tennessee. Would it be asking too much, Randall, for you to act as my surrogate father? I would be greatly honored if you would agree to escort me down the isle to give me away?"

Randall and Mildred had been married for over forty years and in all that time Randall had cried but three times, first for Mr. and Mrs. Daro, then Sally, and years before when they became naturalized citizens. This night made a fourth.

For Daro it was a time of both joy and frustration. His personal life seemed well in hand, but he was still stymied at work, unable to find the man with the elusive tattoo. He began to wonder if it wasn't some sort of giant hoax, one done for the expressed purpose of driving him crazy.

The wedding plans now solidified, Jan, Mildred, and Randall were heavily into planning the reception. Although the house was small, all three wanted to have it at home, hoping for good weather so that any guest overflow could be channeled out into the well kept grounds. Daro suggested they hire a hall and have the affair catered, but an irate Jan would have none of it.

Daro found Randall's actions amusing. Having been asked to play the role of Jan's father, his servant and friend began acting almost like she was his real blood, doting over her as he would a favored daughter. Daro kidded him one day, telling Randall that he was one up on the rest of the wedding party. He was the only one who already owned the proper attire. Everyone else would have to buy or rent their clothes.

The weather went crazy in August, the rain beginning with a vengeance on the fifteenth. For two months prior to that however the daily temperature was over a hundred degrees and it hadn't rained for seventy three days.

Daro and Lyle were back together, working district seventy one. They had just booked a couple of drunks into the jail and were finishing up the paperwork when Archie Raymond, a young motorcycle officer, clanged shut the gray-colored bars of a holding cell on a now sleeping DWI.

Lesher looked out the barred window to the street several floors below. The rain appeared to be falling at over an inch per hour.

"Hey, Arch, you're livin' kinda dangerous ain'tcha, ridin' a motor in weather like this?"

Raymond was short and stocky with the bushiest black eyebrows Daro had ever seen.

"Nah. They got us in cars. I got this old green, fifty three Ford that wouldn't pull a sick whore off a piss pot, and I couldn't see a damned thing. The wipers don't do nothin' but streak up the windshield. I thought I'd never catch that drunk asshole. He finally hit a light pole or likely we'd never of got him stopped."

Lesher laughed. "I'm surprised Nellie didn't just issue your car a ticket for not runnin' faster."

"Nellie?" interrupted Daro.

Raymond turned his dark brown eyes toward Danny. "Nelson Tremane. We call him Nellie. You Lesher's partner?"

"I'm sorry, Arch," Lyle said. "This here little fellow is Danny Daro. He does my light work."

"Please to meetcha," Raymond said, shaking hands. "You ain't missed much not knowin' Nellie. He's obnoxious and that's his good point. He writes more tickets in a day than most do in a month, which is why he spends half his life in court. He ain't learned yet that most citizens'll only take so much bullshit before they start bowin' their necks. But I guess ain't neither of you heard about me and Nellie," said Raymond.

"Heard what?" asked Lesher.

"Well," Raymond said, screwing his face up into a grimace, "Nellie got kinda pissed off at me. The other day him and me was ridin' Harry Hines Boulevard when Nellie spotted this truck without no mud flaps. Of course, you know how chicken shit Nellie is. That's damn near a felony in his book. So he stops this guy.

"The trucker tried to explain that since it's so damn hot, and it ain't rained since Noah built the ark, he didn't allow as how not havin' mud flaps was that big of a deal."

"You're shitin' me," Lesher said. "He really had the nerve to stop him for somethin' like that?"

"That's the gospel truth," Raymond said. "I don't know if you been out there, but there's parts of Bachman and White Rock Lake that's so dried up they look like an alligator's back. Anyhow, this guy tells Nellie that the reason his truck's that way is 'cause his parts man didn't know they was out of replacements before he took the old flaps off.

"But you know Nellie - he's such an asshole. He tells this guy that there ain't nothin' in the ordinance which says that it's got to be rainin' to be against the law not to have 'em. He keeps on givin' this big bastard a ration of shit, and the guy finally gets tired of it."

Lesher began to smile. "What happened?"

"Typical Nellie deal. He whips out his ticket book - you know, that leather job his wife got him for Christmas, the one he's so proud of ? I'll bet she's an asshole, too - and I know for a fact they're raisin' two more little assholes at the house. And instead of payin' attention to how pissed this guy is, Nellie gives him some more shit. Well, the old boy'd had enough; and I don't blame him. He pulls back a fist about the size of Montana and gives Nellie a knuckle sandwich right in the mouth."

"No shit?" said Lesher.

"No shit," Raymond said, starting to laugh. "I wish you coulda seen it. That dumbass partner of mine dropped like a turd from a tall cow's ass and fell over backwards in the ditch. From the look on his face you'd a thought he went brain dead."

Lesher was still laughing. "I wish I had of been there."

"Me too," said Raymond, "cause now I got me a problem. Nellie's got this asshole all stirred up and now he's lookin' at me. So the guy turns facin' me and I'm gettin' ready for most anything from comments to cannon fire, and he raises his hands. Can you beat that - he gives up?"

"That makes sense, Arch," Lesher said. "He ain't mad at you."

"I know that now, but when you're standin' there looking at somethin' that oughta be on a map, not have legs, it sorta gives you pause. When you whack a bobcat in the ass he don't much care who it was that whacked him, he's gonna get a chunk of the nearest ass and that was mine. Anyhow, this guy starts suckin' on a skinned knuckle and says to me between sucks, 'I know I hadn't oughta done that, but I won't give you no trouble.'

"I'm real relieved to hear that, and then I get to thinkin', why put this guy in the jailhouse? It'll go real bad with him if I do, even if it was Nellie. He's just standin' there, waitin'. So I says to him, 'Mister, it's too bad I was lookin' the other way and didn't get the license number on your truck before you drove off.'"

Raymond smiled and shook his head. "You know - I reckon he was about the world's happiest man. So, to answer your question - Nellie and I ain't partners no more."

For the next few weeks Danny fought his job, the weather, his partner, and the world. He damned all the gods that gave him so much grief, and he kept himself so tightly drawn that to twang him would have yielded a high 'C'. While on patrol he tried talking to Lesher, but the radio or some other such thing kept interrupting and he could never get time to talk things out. He even tried to talk to Jan, but she was so busy with the wedding and reception that to call her away seemed almost an imposition.

What he really needed was a cop to bounce ideas off of. Lyle was coming up to a two-day break, so why not then? Maybe he could make some mental progress away from the job.

When Lesher's break started, Daro called.

"Come on over," his partner said. "I'll put the pot on."

It was less than twenty minutes before Daro's knock.

"Come on in," Lesher said, stepping aside to swing the front door open.

"I'm sorry to interrupt your break like this," Daro said, strolling into the living room.

Lyle shrugged. "No problem. What's on your mind?"

"Is the family home?"

"Out shopping."

Decidedly uncomfortable, Daro sat down on the couch and searched for the right words. "I need to talk."

"I'll get us a cup," Lyle said. He went to the kitchen and brought back two steaming mugs, handing one to his partner. Daro took a sip and managed not to make a face. It was obvious that Carol had made all the coffee he'd had at the Lesher house before.

Lyle took his favorite chair and became all business. "What's on your mind?"

Daro cleared his throat. "I know you've heard all this before, but I'm at my wits end. There's nothing new on my folks and it looks like the investigation is getting further away rather than closer to a solution. It's a loose end that I'd like to get cleared up for lots of reasons, one of them being that I'd like to start with a fresh slate on my wedding day and not have this hanging over my head. But every time I get something that looks like it might be a lead, it either blows up in my face or goes nowhere."

"Like what?" asked Lyle, leaning forward.

For the next hour Daro bent his friend's ear, telling him everything, even plowing through all the old stuff they both knew. About half way through, he realized that he was using Lyle as a sounding board. Just the uninterrupted telling of it to another human being solidified the facts in his mind.

Lyle listened intently, only occasionally asking for a clarification. Once more Daro went over all the happenings from day one until the present. Accustomed to being secretive about his find, however, he again left out the snake tattoo.

From the way Daro talked, Lesher could see Daro's progress toward being a sound, intuitive cop. Unlike what most people think, being a good cop isn't the normal kind of intuition, it's being able to read between the lines of your mind and sense what's not yet there - to be able to add a column of flawed figures and arrive at the correct answer. Sometimes being a good cop requires the candidate to be illogical, reaching beyond order and structure and form, sort of like watching the end of a movie to see who the bad guy is, then playing it backwards in your head to pick up the clues.

"We've talked about it and it's pretty obvious you've been thinkin' a lot, but things still don't add up as far as I'm concerned," Lyle said.

"Then it's not just me?"

Lyle shook his head. "Not hardly. Chicken Foot is a real horse's ass, but when it comes to running a murder investigation, he's always been the best. And he ain't been the best on this one, not even close. I've never known him to be less than competent, but this case has more loose ends than a pile of barbed wire."

"I've about lost faith in the detective division, partner," Daro said.

Lyle nodded. "I know. Your morale's been lower'n whale shit. The only time I see you happy is when you're over here or talkin' about Jan."

"Yeah, everybody's been a big help, especially Jan and Amy, if you'll pardon me."

Lesher spread his hands and smiled. "Love me, love my little one."

Daro frowned and went back to the case. "I never did think too much of Killean, and I hate to say this, Lyle, but I've about had it with Goldie, too. He's not treating me like I think a brother officer should."

"Don't pay no attention to the way he acts. That'll be for public consumption and probably for Chicken Foot, too. In a case like this he's got to treat you just like any other citizen, maybe even more so. You can bet your ass that he smells something bad, too."

Daro heaved a sigh and for the first time Lyle heard a little self pity to creep into his voice. "Yeah, I hope so. It just seems like you and I are the only ones who care."

"Tell you what, partner," Lesher said. "I know we've had words about this, but you need to tell 'em both that you've got those films. I know you don't trust 'em right now, but you can trust me - they're both straight as they come. And I can tell you this, too, you're gonna see two detectives jump through their ass they'll be so happy."

In spite of his mood Daro smiled. "I've got a picture of that. Okay. Tomorrow. I'll tell 'em tomorrow. Anything else?"

"That's my question. Is there anything else you know that you haven't told me? Anything at all, no matter how strange or off beat? Even the littlest detail?"

Committed to his course, Daro hardly hesitated. "Nope. That's about it."

"Good enough," Lyle said. "Then I've got something to tell you, but I want you to promise me something first."

"What's that?"

"That you'll try not to get too upset. I've been puttin' this off 'cause I'm a coward to tell the truth. I don't wanta tell you but I have to."

"What about?"

"Jan."

"Forget it," Daro said. "I don't want to hear anything you have to say that's bad. In fact, I don't think there's anything you can say that's bad - not and have it be true. You surprise me, partner. I thought you were a better man than this."

Lesher sighed, rubbing his hands together. "Look, Danny, I'd rather take a whippin' than say somethin' to hurt you. You're the best partner I ever had. Hell, you're part of my family now. And when people are family you've sometimes gotta say things that'll hurt 'em. If there's even an ounce of love in me, I've gotta do this."

Lesher did not hear the hint of warning in Daro's voice when Danny said, "Lyle, let me tell you something. I think I'd have died if it hadn't been for Jan. That girl's a rock and I love her. Now, I know she's not perfect, but neither am I, and I'll not have you say anything bad about her. Please don't do that."

Both men were so intent on the conversation that neither of them heard the car drive up. Carol handed each of the children bag of groceries to carry into the house. They started for the front door just as Lyle took a deep breath and dove in.

"Partner, I have it on good authority, by people who know 'cause they've seen it, that Jan made at least one movie where she has sex with a guy. She may not be now, and maybe she did it only that one time, but Jan made one of them movies like we show at bachelor parties. I'd rather have my arm pulled off than to tell you, but if you don't know and found out later, it'd be my fault for not tellin' you. I couldn't handle that."

Time seemed to stand still before Daro shot to his feet and took a step toward Lyle. Lesher started to get up, but didn't make it.

"You're a lying son of a bitch!" Daro yelled. With all his strength he hit Lyle in the mouth, knocking him over in his chair. Compressed against his teeth, Lesher's lip split and blood gushed forth while his horrified family watched from the front door.

• • •

14

Lesher was still on break when Daro reported for duty. For a partner he drew a rookie and hardly said a word to him the whole shift. Daro's sole communication consisted of a few guttural grunts. By the end of the watch however he had made up his mind. Directly after Daro was relieved he went to see Captain Spencer.

Tapping on the doorjamb, Daro asked, "You got a minute, Cap?"

"Sure, son. Come on in and have a seat," said the Captain, leaning back in his chair. Spencer picked up an old briar pipe and tapped the ashes out on the side of the ash tray. "What can I do for you?"

"I need a new partner, Captain."

Spencer's eyebrows shot up. "Trouble in paradise is there, son?"

"You could say that."

"You mind tellin' me about it?"

"I'm sorry, sir, but I do. It's personal and it's deep. Let's just say that we've come to a parting of the ways and there's no way we can get back together."

Spencer fired up his pipe, apparently to give himself time to think. "What if you and I and Lesher have a little sit-down about it, would that help?" he asked between puffs.

"No sir. Just take my word for it, Captain, Lyle and I are quits."

"And if I refuse, what then?"

"You will have my resignation within the hour."

"Son of a bitch, you really are serious. I still think I could help if you'd let me."

"Thank's, Cap, but no thanks."

Spencer shook his head. "I never had two officers work better together. It'll be damn near like grantin' a divorce."

"I know."

"Okay, son, consider it done. I assume you want this kept as quiet as possible."

"Yes, sir. I know people will talk, but let 'em."

Daro got up and stalked off down the hall wondering how and what he would tell his fiancé and servants. But as disturbed as he was, no less so was a Captain of Police still seated at his desk pondering what to do. Nodding his head, Spencer opened his most recent duty roster, moved a finger down to the L's and dialed Lesher's number.

It was before 5:00 PM and the civil service cadre of the police department was still at work when Daro started to leave city hall. He hated himself for his weakness but he had to know. Taking the stairs two at a time, he went to the second floor to the arrest records section.

"Whatcha need, officer?" asked a gum snapping young lady with dyed red hair.

"Would you look up the name Janette Colmer, or Jan Colmer and tell me what you've got?"

"Sure, gimme a sec," said the girl as she wrote down the name and flounced off down the multiple isles of filing cabinets.

The girl was back in minutes. "Nothing by that name, officer. I got a Jane Colmer, Caucasian, age forty six, but no Jan or Janette."

The clerk had no idea why Daro's smile was so wide. "Thanks a lot. That's good news."

On the way out, Daro walked past the records section where the moniker file was kept. He wondered if Mrs. King was back after her operation. Stepping inside he went up to the bar-like counter and stood waiting to be noticed by a gray-haired lady standing with her back toward him, presumably Mrs. King. In a moment he cleared his throat and she turned.

"I'm sorry officer, I didn't hear you come in," she said.

Daro judged her to be about sixty, slightly overweight with white hair, but with a flawless complexion. She was pretty, much younger looking than her years.

"What can I do for you, officer?"

"Are you Mrs. King?"

"Why, yes I am. Do I know you?"

"No Ma'am, we've never met. My name's Danny Daro. I've only been on the force a little over a year. I came in a couple of times while you were ill to check on something. By the way, how are you feeling?"

She became even prettier when she broke into a smile. "A little sore still, but not bad. I tire easily. This is my first full day back." She pointed to the white streak in Daro's flattop. "I see you're trying to join me,"

He laughed. "Oh, that. No Ma'am, I've had it all my life. I got it from my grandfather. It's genetic."

"I see," nodded Mrs. King. "I hope I didn't offend you; it's most attractive, actually. But you didn't come here to see about my health or have me admire your hair. I'll bet you have business."

"Yes Ma'am, I do. I've already made a couple of trips up here, and I've been to the FBI and the State looking for a particular tattoo, but there's no record of it. I was wondering if there's another file system, or maybe another branch of government – anything actually?"

Mrs. King smiled sadly. "It's a weakness in the system. Every state and city has its own file, and unless it's a case that gets a lot of attention, there's not much traffic between them. Not that we wouldn't like to cooperate more, but the volume of paperwork necessary would literally drown us. I only have two assistants."

Daro sighed. "I understand."

"You know, most of my customers work across the street and wear suits instead of uniforms. May I ask what you are looking into?"

"Two rapes and three murders."

Mrs. King's hand went to her throat. "My goodness," she said. "Are there some detectives on it?"

"Yes Ma'am, Golden and Killean."

She nodded. "Good men. In fact, Golden's the best, at least I think so. He's such a nice boy."

Daro smiled at the 'nice boy' designation since he judged Golden to be about forty. At that, he was probably twenty years Mrs. King's junior.

"Is there something specific you were looking for?" she continued. "Maybe I can help."

"I doubt it, Ma'am. I was here twice while you were recuperating and your girls couldn't find a thing."

Once again the white haired lady turned on her motherly smile. "I don't mean to detract from my girls, but both are relatively new. Why don't you let me try?"

"Sure," Danny said. "If you don't mind me wasting your time."

He unzipped his soft sided leather pouch and removed an eight and a half by eleven inch brown envelope. Undoing the metal clasp, he slid several photographs out onto the counter and placed them in front of her. The topmost picture was one of the best enlargements Harold had made of the snake tattoo. None of the pictures showed the couple in the midst of their wrestling match on the bed. Daro wasn't watching her face, but he heard her intake of breath.

"Where did you get these?" she asked in a choked voice.

Daro looked up. Puzzled by her expression, he said, "A friend of mine found them in several frames of a movie. Why?"

"And you don't know who this hand belongs to?" She stopped and shook her head. "No, of course you don't; you're too new."

Alarmed, he asked, "What are you trying to tell me, Ma'am?"

"This is a picture of Lieutenant Talmadge's hand before he lost those two fingers in an accident."

It happened again, almost a blacking out, as rage enveloped him. Daro was halfway up the stairs to Herm's office with visions of a 158 grain, 357 magnum, jacketed hollow point screaming through Talmadge's chest at 1250 feet per second. Luckily, the Lieutenant wasn't there.

"Where is he?" Daro asked after walking down the hall into the Homicide squad room, empty except for Golden and Killean.

The detective's heads jerked up to see a snarling Danny Daro standing in the doorway, a small leather bag in his left hand, the right near his pistol. His stance looked like that of one of the participants at the OK Corral just seconds before hostilities broke out.

"What the hell?" Killean said. "What's eatin' you?"

"I want him - Talmadge - where is he?"

"He's off today." Golden said. "Simmer down, Daro, and get your butt over here. What's the matter with you anyway?"

Stiff legged, Daro marched to the chair by Golden's desk and flopped down. He balanced the leather bag on his lap and extracted the brown envelope, again slipping the pictures out and throwing them in front of the puzzled detective.

"Who's hand is that?" Daro asked, tapping the top photo with a staccato finger.

Golden looked at the series of pictures and brushed his thinning brown hair away from his forehead. "Where'd you get these?"

Daro shook his head. "Nope; me first. Who is it?"

Golden tossed the pictures to Killean. "That's easy, it's Talmadge. But where did you get 'em?"

Daro's lips formed a thin, bloodless line and he closed his eyes for a few seconds. When he opened them he asked, "You're sure about this?"

"Absolutely. They were obviously taken before he tore up his left hand, but they're Talmadge all right." Golden looked over at his partner. "When was that?" he asked.

Killean shrugged, still scanning the pictures. "Dunno for sure. Year and a half; two years, maybe. That's what got him the name Chicken Foot."

So angry with himself he could hardly talk, Daro murmered, "I'm such a dumb-ass."

He proceeded to tell the two detectives about the films, Harold McMillan, and the pictures of the snake tattoo. Both detectives sat open-mouthed until he ran down. He concluded the monologue by saying, "All this time wasted. It never occurred to me that Talmadge could somehow be mixed up in this. A certifiable son of a bitch, sure - but a murderer, or accessory to murder, no way. After being around him for about two seconds, I just thought he was an incompetent asshole."

Daro could tell by looking that both detectives were holding in a lot of anger, much of it directed toward their boss, but an ample share left over for him. Golden leaned back in his chair and hooked his thumbs underneath his belt. "Tell you what, Danny, I'm going to get a big chunk of your ass later, but right now I expect you're beatin' yourself up more than I ever could."

Daro nodded. "Yeah, but if you wanta dine right now be my guest. What really gets my goat is thinking about that fat bastard nursing his hand in the hospital while you two are at my house asking about my sister. He was in the room with her when all this was going on. I just don't know if I can handle this."

"You're not gonna handle it, Hoss, we are," said Killean. "It's because of what you ain't told us that this case ain't solved yet, so you're gonna stay the hell out from now on, do you read me?"

"Yeah, I read you," Daro said, but there was fire in his eyes at being spoken to in such a manner.

"Listen to me real careful," continued Killean, "I don't want you within a mile of Talmadge. You back way off and let us handle it."

Golden nodded. "That goes double for me. If you don't want your ass in a permanent crack, if you want to keep on being a cop, you keep your mouth shut and leave it alone. You're in way over your head."

Biting his tongue and forcing an outward calm he didn't feel, Daro asked, "What next?"

"Normally I could tell you, but this time I ain't real sure since nothin' like this ever happened before," Killean said. "What's for sure, though, we need more horsepower than the two of us got. We'll go at least to a Captain, and maybe an Inspector. Depending on what they say, we might go higher, maybe to a sub-chief or something. Hell, I don't know, maybe the Body Snatcher himself will get in on it," Killean said, referring to Chief of Police, Carl Phillips.

"What can I do?" Daro asked.

Golden sighed. "You're not gonna like this. You can wait. I know," he said, holding up a stopping hand when Daro opened his mouth and began to fidget in his chair, "that's the roughest part of all. But considering who it is we're investigatin', we can't have you messing around in the middle of it. Not with what we know now. You're gonna have to cool it."

"Isn't there anything I can do?"

"Not really," Killean said. "Where's the films right now?"

"I have a copy and McMillan has the originals."

"Have you seen 'em?"

"All but one. It's a sixteen millimeter and Harold doesn't have a projector for it. He found the hand by doing a frame by frame search. I looked at the two, eight millimeter ones though. That's where I got the idea that they were sort of pilots for the other films."

"That's a pretty good theory, sounds to me like," said Killean. "I seen the film of the other girl that was raped and murdered later. Sounds like maybe the fake rape might of give 'em the idea to make a real one."

"Which of the films are these pictures taken from?" Golden asked, pointing at the photographs of Talmadge's hand.

"They're from both of the sixteen millimeter films. Harold found the hand in Sally's film first, but these better shots - the ones that are closer and clearer - came from the other one, the one where the couple is wearing masks and costumes."

"Okay," Golden said, "I want you to go with me to this McMillan character's place so I can pick up the originals. We can't handle things the regular way because of Chicken Foot. Everything goes through his office so I'll have to find a safe place to lock 'em up after we talk to some of the higher-ups.

"Meanwhile, you do your job'" continued Golden. "Report to work just like before, but stay the hell away from over here, 'cause you and I both know what'll happen if you don't. You'd mess us up with Chicken Foot more than it's messed up already, and I really want to nail this piece of shit. There's nothing worse than a bad cop; in particular this bad cop. Can you imagine what the papers are gonna do with this?"

After a few more pointed warnings, Daro and Golden drove out to see Harold McMillan.

In spite of every cell in his body calling out for action and revenge, Daro lasted three days without making a move. As instructed he stayed away from the homicide division and Talmadge, but as each hour passed his feelings of isolation and betrayal deepened. He even began to wonder if there wasn't some giant conspiracy within the department. In the absence of any news, doubt took over. After awhile these feelings extended to the two detectives. When he could stand it no longer, he called Carl Ledbetter, the private detective who had located Betty Silk.

"Yes, Mr. Daro, how can I help you today?" Ledbetter said after his secretary buzzed him. The detective was delighted to hear from his most profitable client.

"I need you to follow someone for me, Carl."

"Certainly, who?"

"A police lieutenant named Herman Talmadge."

Ledbetter had visions of a lengthy, involuntary stay in the jailhouse during which time he would have the opportunity to interview the men locked up in the tank from an insider's point of view. "But, Mr. Daro," he sputtered, "I couldn't possibly do that. Do you realize what you're asking?"

"Yes I do and I understand your reluctance."

"It's not reluctance, sir, it's refusal. I doubt if I could get any of my men to do it."

"How would four times your standard rate plus double expenses sound? There'll be a further bonus the less time it takes." Daro said. "I had in mind ten thousand dollars if you get it done in one day, nine thousand for two, eight for three; I think you get the idea."

The voice of alarm sounding in Ledbetter's ear was muted by the musical sound of a cash register. "Tell me what you need."

Daro outlined his requirements and as soon as the call was completed, the rangy detective got his six best men working in separate cars around the clock.

Jan hadn't turned a trick for over two months, sorry now that she ever had. And what started as a job, to extract information from a client named Danny Daro and deliver that information to Lieutenant Herman Talmadge, had turned into a deepening love. In less than a month, Jan Colmer, former hooker, would be Mrs. Danny Daro. And the world would never dare shit on her again.

Just thinking about how Talmadge had tricked her made her angry. In spite of his blackmail, Jan would never have agreed to do the job for the Chief of Homicide had he let her in on the details.

But Herm was the cop who caught her dirty the first week she got to Dallas. For several years he had used this knowledge to get her to do the occasional odd job for him. Once he even decided he would cash in sexually. Jan rewarded his effort with the comment, "It would cost you a thousand dollars for me just to hold your hand."

After that Talmadge was tough with her for awhile, but Jan figured even the Lieutenant realized he couldn't get too heavy-handed since all she had to do was move to another town. Her product was mobile. She could be in business the second she rolled into a new town and he wouldn't have the slightest idea where she was. As one of her hooker acquaintances once said, "Ain't hookin' great? It's portable and it don't need much maintenance. Besides that, you got it - you sell it - and you still got it. You can't say that about cakes and pies."

As initially explained to her, Jan's assignment was a simple, well paying, straightforward job of finding out what Daro knew about his sister's death. As for Mitchell, she knew him - and quite frankly he scared her - but she had no idea he did more than procure a few low class girls for Herm's films. She certainly had no idea that he and his friends found special girls to abduct, rape, and kill to make a movie. That knowledge she acquired much later, piecing it together from what she saw and heard. The idea was so bizarre that, had she heard about it up front, she probably wouldn't have believed it anyway. After her first and only report to Talmadge, and their subsequent argument over the telephone, he had left her alone. An uncharacteristic miracle; if she only hadn't made that one film. It left her vulnerable.

Jan was happy, if fearful. Daro was good to her as no other man had ever been, but most of all he stirred her heart. And she'd thought that impossible.

When their sexual affair turned into love, Jan contacted her clients to tell them she was no longer available, offering to fix several of them up with a couple of her better competitors. Although still somewhat afraid of being found out, she was beginning to have more hope as the wedding day drew near.

"Something's wrong," Jan said. "What is it?"

Jan sat on the couch with Danny's head in her lap, stroking his temples with long tapered fingers. "Is your headache gone?"

He sighed. "Just about. I really appreciate everything you do for me?"

She bent down and placed a soft kiss in the middle of his forehead. "I know," she said. "Can you tell me what's eating you?"

"Too many things happening at once. I really shouldn't put it all on you."

"Honey, in less than a month we'll be married. Part of a marriage, as I understand it, is to share things, even bad things."

Daro snuggled his head down into her lap. "For one thing I had to ask my captain for a new partner."

"Why?" she asked, alarmed. "I thought you and Lyle got along great."

"We did, but something was said that can't be forgiven and that's the end of it."

Jan thought furiously, wondering what it could be. It couldn't be about her, she figured, otherwise Danny would already be gone. Besides, the chances of Lyle knowing anything about her were remote, at best. What could it be?

"But he's your best man."

"Was; not anymore."

She waited a moment. "You're not going to tell me?"

His head rustled in her lap, his eyes still closed, as he shook his head. "Nope. Just between partners. It's not important."

"That can't be all of it, hon."

"It's not," Daro said. He started to say more and stopped.

"Come on, sweetie," Jan said, tracing his nose with her fingertip and breaking into baby talk. "Let mama help."

Daro frowned. "Don't do that. This is serious."

She was taken aback. "I'm sorry, Danny, I didn't know it was bothering you that much."

He sat up on the couch and turned halfway around, placing the upper part of his leg beside himself in a half-lotus position. Brushing a hand across his flattop, he said, "I shouldn't, but I'm about to tell you some really confidential stuff that's driving me nuts. It's about the murders and who was in on it."

Jan felt an almost electric shock. "You mean you know?"

"I know part of it, not all." He told her about Mitchell being one of the men who raped Sally. He told her about all the clues, even confiding to her that he had hired Carl Ledbetter to follow Talmadge for him. He even told her about having copies of the films now thought destroyed. And he apparently misinterpreted her look of terror for one of shock when he told her about McMillan finding the snake tattoo on the film in which a masked blonde in an old fashioned gown made love to a man at a masquerade ball.

"And we know for sure," he said, wrapping it up, "that Lieutenant Herman Talmadge is in the middle of it right up to his filthy neck."

Jan felt like someone had punched her in the gut as tears spilled down her cheeks.

"Hey - hey, what's this?" Daro said, reaching out a hand and brushing away a tear with his thumb. "I'm sorry, darling. I had no right to put this on you. I should have kept it to myself."

"Then you've seen the film," Jan sputtered in between sobs.

"The masquerade film? No. I didn't have a projector. Harold borrowed one to show me Sally's film, but he had to take it back the next day. It wouldn't have mattered - I was so torn up I had to get out of there. Harold found the hand in both of the sixteen millimeter films as he was doing a frame by frame search. That's where he got the enlargements."

Jan lowered her head into her hands as sobs wracked her.

Reaching out, Daro pulled her to him. "Honey - honey, don't cry. I knew I shouldn't have told you. Hush now, I'm sorry."

Snuggling into the security of his arms, Jan gave vent to her terror as he shushed her, patting her back. Her sense of relief after thinking he had found her out had caught her unaware. It took several minutes to control her raging emotions.

"I must look a wreck," she said, pulling away and snatching a tissue from a box. She dabbed at her eyes and attempted to make what repairs she could while Daro watched and smiled.

"You amuse me," he said.

"Why?"

"Because you're always worried about how you look. It amazes me that you have no idea how beautiful you really are."

His words brought on a whole new series of tears as once again she sought comfort in his arms. This time however the tears were of relief.

Her crying fit over, Jan asked, "What now?"

"Well, for one thing, I've got to get out of here and go home for some sleep. I think we've had about enough for tonight."

"You could stay over."

"No. I'm too wrung out. I'll call you tomorrow. I love you," he said. He kissed her softly and pulled away as he quietly left.

Jan allowed herself the luxury of a few more tears before a returning terror forced her to make the call. She dialed Talmadge's number and waited through four rings before he answered.

"Yeah?"

Jan opened her mouth to speak, but couldn't force the words out. After the second 'yeah' from Talmadge, she hung up and flopped down on the bed. Only moments later the telephone sounded, startling her. It was too soon to be Danny. After ten rings it went silent.

It was a muggy day in Dallas, the low, threatening clouds promising rain. Daro hated the idea, but for the first time since he'd been on the force he lied and called in sick. In his mind, however, the lie was told in pursuit of a good cause.

When Daro made the call to the detective agency, he had no idea how long the surveillance would take, or even if Ledbetter could help him. He realized that Ledbetter's men would have to be ultra cautious in light of their target, therefore it was a shock when only two days later the detective called.

Dropping everything, he rushed down to Ledbetter's office for a full briefing. When the detective finished, Daro wrote out a check, adding an additional nine thousand dollars. Of all the work Ledbetter had done for him, this bill was the easiest to pay.

He called Jan to tell her he might be late, then drove to a predetermined spot on Commerce Street and switched off the Crown Vic's engine. Momentarily turning on the overhead light, he checked his watch. 7:00 PM. He was in position and ready. Time dragged. It was like waiting in the dentist's office.

Daro's grudging patience finally paid off. Just as Ledbetter's report had said of the two previous nights, exactly at 7:30 PM the stout, waddling figure of Lieutenant Herman Talmadge came out of the downstairs doorway leading to the homicide detective's office. Daro smirked ironically when the ever obedient cop looked up at the sky and shuffled down to the corner to wait for a green light. When the light changed, Talmadge waddled across the deserted street to the parking lot on the corner.

Talmadge paid by the month to park his car. With a wave of his good right hand to the attendant in the lighted booth, the rotund detective in the seersucker suit slid behind the wheel of his new Cadillac Fleetwood and cranked up the big 390 cubic inch V-8. From his vantage point down the block, Daro watched as Herm turned on the air conditioner and mopped the sweat from his forehead with a stained handkerchief. Pulling down his tie and undoing the top button of a wrinkled, once white shirt, Talmadge shifted into reverse and backed out of his space.

Daro knew that Talmadge had an expensive car, but it wasn't until now that he wondered how a twice divorced cop who seemed always in need of money could afford such a vehicle. If it was as he surmised, the explanation was simple. He had uncovered the man responsible not only for the murders of his folks and Sally, but also the elusive figure behind the porno and snuff films being distributed throughout the southwest. It would be a very satisfying arrest, assuming that Talmadge made it to the jailhouse alive. Daro was so engrossed in his own thoughts that he didn't notice the nondescript car pull into the light traffic stream behind him when he began to follow Talmadge.

Already down to a trickle, traffic got even lighter as Talmadge worked his way north. Fearful of being spotted, Daro hung back from the dark blue Caddy. The detective turned west on Ross Avenue toward the Trinity River and drove to an old warehouse district, making a right turn into Griffin Street. Certain of where the Lieutenant was headed, Daro turned north on Field then left into Hord. Only an hour or so before even an ant couldn't have found a place to park in this area.

He whispered to a stop on the narrow street behind a lone pickup. The walls of the buildings on both sides were close together, climbing upward toward an already darkened, lead colored sky. Daro felt a twinge of claustrophobia.

He sat for a minute watching the dark, brick warehouse on the corner of Griffin and Hord. He'd never been on these two streets before, a place of grimy old buildings, many of which were built at the turn of the century. As he watched, he thought he saw a light on the second floor come on - or was it his imagination? Faint streams of light seemed to be leaking through the grime of a second floor window. He opened the glove box and took out the two-cell flashlight he kept for road emergencies.

Stepping quietly from his car, Daro punched the lock and gently eased the door shut, bumping the latch closed with a hip. When the lock caught it seemed as loud as a pistol shot. Glancing over his shoulder, he stepped across the street and down to the corner toward the door.

The report from the detective agency had been comprehensive. After two previous times the private detectives had followed Talmadge, Ledbetter had taken it upon himself to have his people check out the building and its ownership, plus making a rough sketch of the floor plan.

The building had been up for sale for three years by its owners, two aging Greek brothers who had already sold their string of auto supply houses. A part of the second floor was leased from the brothers by a business calling itself T&A Enterprises. The building owners stated that a proviso of the lease was that if a buyer was found for the property, T&A would vacate within thirty days. A quick check of the local records came up with the name Russell Johnson and a post office box number. Daro ran the name and came up with four men named Russell Johnson, one of whom had a record for rape and child molestation. Because Johnson was such a common name however, he refused to get too excited.

He almost panicked when he rounded the corner onto Griffin Street to find it deserted. Talmadge's car was nowhere to be seen. He had either parked inside one of the buildings or left before Daro arrived.

He walked down Griffin toward Ross, checking for some means of entry. All the street level doors and windows were locked. Even the big, sliding doors into a section of the warehouse were bolted from the inside. Standing on tip toe, he could see through a small hole in a window pane. Parked inside was a dark colored Fleetwood. He couldn't make out the plate, but he was sure it was Herm's car.

Midway down the block was a fifty by fifty foot square loading dock, inset between the two halves of the block-long warehouse. A lone truck, locked and unattended, sat facing the street, its tailgate pressed against the dock in the first of three loading spaces. Some ten feet behind the truck were three, roll-up doors, their corrugated surfaces resembling a giant's teeth in desperate need of a dental cleaning. Above the center door a bare, forty watt bulb cast its dim glow, just enough light to form eerie shadows. He couldn't be sure, but he thought one of the second story casement windows was swiveled open. At least he hoped it wasn't a shadow.

But how to reach it? Above the loading dock stood a parapet like structure, an open mouthed gargoyle at each end to draw rain off of the overhang. He had no way of knowing how high the parapet stood above the roof, but he suspected it would be several feet short for him to reach the window. Looking around, he spotted a row of fifty five gallon drums along the side of the dock, apparently placed there as trash receptacles. He went over to check them out.

About half of the barrels were filled with trash. In one he found a coil of frayed, insulated wire, something over twenty feet in length. Selecting two empty barrels, he upended the first under the lowest part of the parapet. Through a hole in the side near the top of the second barrel, Daro threaded one end of the wire and twisted it securely, yanking on it several times to test its strength. Satisfied, he uncoiled several feet of the wire and heaved the remaining loops up over the lip of the parapet. The coil landed with a soft thump. Pocketing the flashlight and steadying himself against the wall, Daro jumped on top of the upended barrel. Testing the distance, he reached upward. The top of the parapet was still several feet away. He jumped back down and again went to the trash area. Using the flashlight, he found a stout wooden box which measured roughly two by two by three feet.

Almost certain it was not enough, Daro jumped back on the barrel and placed the box on top, open side down. But even though the combination of barrel and box together added almost five feet to his already six feet four, when he stood on the rickety arrangement, the remaining distance looked to be almost three feet.

The only thing left was to try the long side, but he was concerned about both the box's strength and the stability of the stack. Even so, he turned the box the long way. Gripping with his fingers as high as he could between the ancient bricks, he jumped on top of the box. The stack groaned and teetered beneath his weight, but the arrangement seemed more stable than he had anticipated. Stretching upward on tip toe, he was still almost two feet short of the parapet's edge. And he didn't dare add to the stack's height.

Without even thinking, Daro squatted and jumped, reaching upward for the top. In spite of his onslaught the barrel stayed upright, but the box fell over, clattering to the concrete loading dock as his fingertips caught on the edge. A slow motion battle began as arm and shoulder muscles knotted and strained to pull his bulk upward. Gaining an inch or two, Daro sacrificed a part of the gain to get a better grip, scooting his hands forward on the edge. In addition to his hands, he pawed with his feet against the rough brick face trying for a toe hold. All he succeeded in doing was to shred the tips of his expensive, Italian shoes.

The hot, muggy night added to Danny's problem as a river of perspiration burst from his pores as the sweaty struggle went on. Lips pulled back in a last, grunting effort, Daro fought with all his strength, finally managing to get his right elbow over the lip of the parapet. He pulled himself over the edge and rolled exhausted onto his back, his breath coming in ragged gasps. Just then a soft rain began to fall on his upturned face. Grateful for the relative coolness, he still didn't have the strength to move, even though the flashlight dug uncomfortably into his right buttock.

After several minutes his muscles twitched and jerked as life returned to his arms. He stood up and retrieved the coil of wire. Drying his rain-dampened hands on his handkerchief so they wouldn't slip on the wire's insulation, he lifted the barrel, swinging it until it stood in the middle of the second, recessed door.

After another rest Daro braced a foot against the parapet and pulled the barrel upward, carefully keeping it away from the wall. As the drum neared the top, he reached out and gave it an extra heave, clearing the edge without bumping it. He was still worried about the relatively soft noise made by the fallen box, but the loud boom of an empty drum banging against a brick wall in this otherwise quiet place could get him killed.

Killed? It was a new thought.

Daro carefully set the barrel down and leaned on it. As Coach Redman had taught him to do between plays during a football game, he forced himself to breathe deeply while he checked out the open window. A small jump from the top of the barrel and he could easily reach it. As far as he could see he had but two problems. Could he get the window cranked all the way open, and if he did, would he be able to squeeze through the opening? The only way to find out was to try.

Danny placed the barrel beneath the window and got on top. Straightening up, he bumped his head on the swiveled out casement, raising a small knot on the back of his head. Muttering, he rubbed the already sore spot, then turned his attention to his problem.

A screen covered the opening, but the window was open enough for him to slit through the mesh with his pocket knife. Reaching a hand through the cut opening, Daro found the crank and opened the window to its fullest extent. Locating the lower two tabs that held the screen against the inner facing, he released them. He couldn't reach the top two tabs, but was able to work the screen back and forth until it came free. To avoid even the slightest chance of noise, he turned the screen sideways and fished it out of the opening, standing it against the outside wall.

The window would be a tight fit. Daro swung his right leg up and over the window sill, grasping the sides to pull himself upward. With his right leg inside and his left on the outside ledge, Daro's hip slid through without much trouble. His chest, however, refused to pass. Finally, inhaling deeply then whooshing out all his breath, Daro jammed himself sideways into the narrow opening. Moving in a shimmying motion, he worked his shoulders half way through.

He would soon run out of air, but he knew that if he didn't make it through on the first try it was all over. If forced to draw a breath he would be stuck until the following morning. Placing his right hand against the wall behind him, and reaching up over his head with his left to grasp the window frame to pull, he gave a mighty heave. Finally his chest popped through and he drew a grateful breath. There was no doubt that he would be sore in a few hours.

At first the inside seemed to be in total darkness. The only light he could see came from the stars that sparkled before his eyes due to the extraordinary exertion. The stars soon stopped however and his eyes began to adjust. Shortly he could make out vague shapes.

An opening almost directly in front of the window some thirty feet away looked big enough for a forklift to use. He headed for it. Barely lifting each foot so he would not trip on an unseen object, Daro moved slowly forward until he stood in the center of the opening. He couldn't be sure, but it looked like a mound of trash piled in the far corner to his left. To his right he could make out two doors. It looked like part of the warehouse had been partitioned into rooms.

Starting toward the nearest door he heard the unmistakable sound of a cocking revolver.

"Welcome to the party, Rookie," said a familiar voice. "I've been waitin'for you."

Talmadge's nasty laugh came just before Daro felt a blow behind his right ear and he sank into unconsciousness.

• • •

15

Daro felt nauseous and his head pounded. Like bunched fireflies, small exploding points of light scurried about behind his eyelids. Then he remembered - and failure washed over him.

"I think he's awake, Mr. Talmadge," said a high pitched, almost squeaky voice.

Daro opened his eyes, trying to focus on the two-fold shape of a huge man standing in front of him. The man held a Winchester Model 1897, 12 gauge slide-action shotgun cradled across his chest, the hammer on full cock. Slowly the two images merged into one. On the lone table behind the man, Daro could make out his off duty weapon, a Smith & Wesson Model 60, its cylinder swung open, its 38 special cartridges placed beside it.

"Yeah, he's awake," said the squeaky voice, rising in pitch and excitement. "His eyes is open." The small voice sounded incongruous coming from so large a man.

"Well don't get your shit hot, Russ, he's cuffed," answered Talmadge. He waddled around in front of Daro and stood balancing on the balls of his feet, an insipid grin on his face. It was the first time Daro had seen him smile.

"Hello, bad ass," Talmadge said. "You happy now that you caught me?"

Daro didn't speak, his eyes hot on his captor.

Herm's grin broadened, his deep set, closely spaced eyes further accentuating his reptilian appearance. To further the resemblance his snake like tongue darted out to wet thick, effeminate lips.

"What's the matter, badass, cat got your tongue?"

Daro still refused to speak. Apparently tiring of the game, Talmadge shrugged and circled around behind him, going about his business.

It took several minutes for Daro's head to clear. His hands were cuffed behind him, legs tied to the chair, and he had a mountain of flesh standing in front of him named Russ carrying an ancient shotgun at port arms. He figured that Russ was probably short for Russell and that this particular Russell had the last name of Johnson, specifically the child molester and rapist he'd discovered when he ran a check on the name. As best he could remember the face looked about right, but older and no longer covered by a beard.

But as one mystery cleared, another developed. Although Russ was definitely the hooded man who had initially assaulted Sally, he was obviously retarded, his facial expression almost moronic, his speech slurred and halting. All the man needed to make his face a stereotype was a rivulet of drool from one corner of his mouth. Russ also carried an air of unfocused fear, deferring to Talmadge's every order, obviously unable to make decisions. Even so, as big as Russ was and as weak as Daro felt, he would have given his fortune to be turned loose alone in the room with him.

Although he expected it, Daro was shocked when he realized that he was being held prisoner in the same room where his sister's film was made. The wallpaper was right, the bed, the other furnishings. He was further jolted when he examined the armrests of his chair. The pattern was a match with the one on which McMillan found the hand and little finger with the snake tattoo. He felt a new fury.

"Tell me something, Lieutenant, how does it feel to murder an entire family?" Daro asked.

Once more Talmadge stopped what he was doing and stepped in front of Daro, feigning surprise. "Well I'll be damned, it speaks. Actually, I didn't have nothin' to do with that. All I asked Mitchell to do was get me some young stuff, see. I didn't tell him to go crazy."

Daro was still seeing double, and two of Herm was three too many. "And that makes it okay, does it?" His voice shook, dripping with sarcasm. "I once heard that in politics, shit floats. I guess that goes for Chiefs of Homicide, too."

Talmadge was deceptively fast for a fat man. His face flushed and he stepped forward, backhanding Daro across the mouth.

"I've been wantin' to do that for a long time, Rookie. It's the rich assholes like you that's been keepin' people like me down all our lives."

Fighting for calm and nursing a cut on the inside of his lower lip, Daro smiled. "You wouldn't want to take these cuffs off and try that again, would you?"

Surprisingly, Talmadge laughed. But his almost colorless eyes didn't follow suit. Shaking his head, He said, "I don't think so. I've got some other plans for you, see. Russ - come here." Taking Johnson by the elbow, Talmadge dragged his retarded cohort to the door and whispered some instructions in the big man's ear. Russ nodded, a side to side jerking motion as though his head knew only two positions, and turned to leave.

When Russ opened the door, Daro got another surprise. He was still inside the warehouse. He remembered seeing two doors on his right before Talmadge knocked him out, and apparently he was behind one of them. From what he could see of the door's thickness, he guessed the room was reasonably soundproof, a logical precaution in light of its use. He hadn't noticed before, but what looked like a window on the far side of the room was a fake. Attached to the back side of a box-like arrangement outside the window was a huge photograph of an ornately decorated Chateau or castle, giving the impression of looking out onto a European scene. Thinking back, Daro seemed to remember that same window in the photograph in which McMillan found the snake tattoo.

Scanning the rest of the room, Daro noticed that there were no closets or other doors besides the one entrance. Cool air was circulating however and he noticed several slotted vents close to the ceiling on opposite walls. By listening carefully he could hear air whisper inside.

"What now?" he asked.

Talmadge rubbed his hands together, the three fingered stump looking like some obscene mutation. "Russ is gonna check downstairs to be sure you was alone, then he's gonna get a projector and film out of the car, see. I feel like looking at a movie."

Daro's lips pulled back from his teeth in a snarl. "You filthy bastard."

"Now there you go," said Talmadge feigning wounded feelings. "I'll bet you thought I was gonna show you the movie with your sister in it. Hell, I wouldn't do a thing like that. I've got something that'll interest you a lot more. I know it will me."

Abruptly, Daro changed the subject. "You killed Mitchell, didn't you?" he asked.

He could see that the question caught him off guard, but Herm smiled and said, "Tell you what Rookie, I'll answer your questions if you'll answer mine, but I go first. How long have you known it was me?"

Daro considered whether or not to answer. But what did he have to lose? His life was subject to Herm's whim anyway. In a minute he answered, "Not long. A few days ago I found out about your hand and the tattoo you had around your little finger."

Herm looked confused. "So what? How could that put you on to me?"

"You see this chair I'm sitting in? You had your hand on the back of it while you were making some of your movies. "You stood right here and watched my sister being raped and strangled. I can't even begin to understand a mind like that - hell, I don't want to."

Herm laughed again. Once more Daro was surprised at the unexpected response. "Too bad, Rookie. All them films are gone now, see. Funny thing about that fire, isn't it?"

Daro nodded. "Yeah; real funny. I know something even funnier. I've got copies."

The whole range of human emotions seemed to flash across the Lieutenant's bloated face, ending in fearful rage. "Where are they?"

"Real safe, Lieutenant. And completely out of your reach."

"Who else knows about 'em?"

Daro missed a beat before he replied. "Several people, such as Golden and Killean and some others."

Herm was becoming a regular hyena. Misinterpreting Daro's hesitation, he laughed again. "You ain't real good at lying, Rookie. Not enough practice. My guess is you ain't told anybody at all, see. In fact, I'll bet there ain't even any copies, neither. Too bad; and you with all that money, too. Your ass is in a real big crack and there ain't nobody to help."

"How about my questions?" Daro asked.

Herm dragged up the only other chair and plopped his overstuffed body into it. "Okay, shoot."

"How about Mitchell?"

"Yeah, I got him. Pretty slick, too, don'tcha think? It was real funny to see you people trying to figure it out how that dumb bastard got an ice pick shoved in his ear while he's in ICU under police guard. None of them assholes that work for me could find their ass with a search warrant if it wasn't for me."

Daro scooted forward in his chair to take some of the pressure off his wrists. "How did you and Mitchell meet in the first place?"

The Lieutenant reared back in his seat and grabbed his left hand with his right, covering up the deformity. "You know, that was kinda funny. He was a witness for me at a murder trial, see. When I busted him on another charge he had a room full of these films - lots more'n somebody would keep around just to look at. Turns out he was a broker; bought from an outfit in New York and sold 'em all over the Texas. Not big time you understand, but the markup was three - maybe four hundred percent."

Daro snorted. "So you two went into business."

Like he was talking to an old friend, Talmadge seemed to warm to the subject. "Not right away. But later I got to thinkin' about how the real big money is in the specialized stuff - you know, bondage, snuff, and the like. And if you made 'em yourself, the profit could be real big."

His grin was nasty. "So I talked to Mitchell and we made a deal, see. I started makin' eight millimeter movies using hookers as actresses, but it didn't work out. They could make like they was enjoyin' gettin' hosed - hell, women been doin' that for thousands of years - but they couldn't act, all except one girl that is."

"Because of that," he continued, "the movies didn't sell too good. Then Mitch had this idea. Why not pick up girls off the street?

Somebody real young, see. She wouldn't have to act, it'd be the real shit. You know - Mitch was pretty smart for a dirtbag. That was a damned good idea. But I had a better one. It was my idea to upgrade to sixteen millimeter and add sound and color. I'm real proud a that."

"I'll just bet you are," Daro said. The sarcasm went over Herm's head. It took all Daro's will power to appear calm. "So that's how Sally was selected? At random?"

"Look, Daro, you and me don't like each other, but I ain't real glad it was your sister, see. But how was I to know? Mitch went against orders when his bunch chased down your people. We had an agreement that they'd just pick out one girl all by herself, see. No witnesses - no problems. But some of them other guys got ideas. They got greedy, figurin' your folks would have some cash."

"That's real kind of you Lieutenant," Daro said, his voice filled with irony. "How did Russ get involved in all this? Seems to me he couldn't find the door if you didn't show him the knob."

Herm chuckled. "He's perfect for this kind of work. He don't even have to act. You just put a hood over his head so's nobody knows he's a retard, strip a girl down in front of him, and he does a job on her, see. The only time I about had a problem with him was when I brought in some other guys so's they could have a threesome."

The Lieutenant moved his left hand to a coat pocket and began toying with a film canister with his right. "Russ like to have went crazy 'til I explained things to him. He thought all them girls was his private stock and he didn't like nobody else messin' with 'em."

Daro hated what he was hearing, but he had to keep the Lieutenant talking. What really baffled him was Herm's cavalier attitude toward rape and murder, particularly after all the stories about how he lived for catching murderers. The term amoral came to mind, but it was the first time he had ever met someone so afflicted. It was as though Talmadge could see wrong in others, but not in himself. Apparently he felt no remorse, no shame, indeed had no feelings of any kind except for his own financial gain. And when it came to talking about the assaults themselves, Talmadge was as calmly unemotional as though discussing the weather. Daro's sister, and who knows how many other girls, were simply meat for Talmadge's sexual table, to be filmed, killed, and thrown away like food scraps raked from the dinner plates.

Daro didn't know what good it might do, but any extension of time was preferable to what he knew was coming. "Aren't you afraid Russ is the weak link in your chain? He'll talk if he gets caught."

"No way," the Lieutenant said, shaking his head. "I doubt if he even knows we're making a film. All he's doing is what he likes to do best. Shit, he don't even know what rape is, see. She's just a sweet, young piece of ass to him. Besides, I told him that if he told anybody, his whang would fall off. The dumbass believed me." He laughed and slapped his thigh with his good right hand. "That'd make a hell of a thud when it hit the floor, wouldn't it?"

Daro had trouble breathing as bile rose hot in his throat. Seconds later Russ came back with a projector, a small screen, and a film canister.

"Things is okay outside, Mr. Talmadge," reported Russ. "I looked and looked and listened all over and ain't seen nothin'."

"Real good. Set up the projector, will ya Russ?"

"Uh - Sure." With the practiced moves of rote learning the hulk unfolded the stand and set up the screen. When he got to the film reel he looked puzzled, finally sticking it onto the wrong spindle. Looking pleased with himself, he waited for Talmadge to finish the job.

"Still can't thread the film, huh Russ?"

Johnson shook his head, swinging it in an arc in front of his shoulders, his voice whiny, "It's too hard, Mr. Talmadge, not like when you get me them girls." An excited light came into his eyes and he asked, "We gonna see me?"

"Not this time, but there's a real pretty girl in it you'll like. This is a very special movie just for our friend here," Herm said, placing his hand on Daro's shoulder.

"Aw, shoot," said Russ, his lower lip sticking out like a small angry child. "I like to watch me."

"I know you do," Talmadge said, transferring his hand to Johnson's shoulder. "I'll get you some more girls later, but right now we gotta take care of some business, see?"

Russ sort of growled and retrieved his shotgun, once again cradling it possessively to his chest.

In spite of his fear and anger, Daro was curious about the movie he was going to see. What did Herm hope to gain? If it was of Sally, Daro could - in a strange way - understand how such a warped mind might derive pleasure from watching him squirm, but Herm had already told him it wasn't. Could it be that he just wanted to look at some random piece of smut? Daro thought not. It made no sense.

In minutes the film was threaded, the lights out, and the projector rolling. Several frames of light and squiggly lines flashed across the screen before the film settled down to show the closed door of the room he was now in. Off in the distance was the soft sound of an orchestra playing a Strauss waltz. The camera panned the room showing the fake window, another confirmation that Daro was in the same room where the films were made.

Seconds later the door swung open and a muscular, costumed man entered, pulling with him an elegantly gowned lady, both wearing masks. He pulled her into his arms and kissed her, his right hand cupping a heavy breast beneath the blue, velvet-like bodice. In less than a minute both participants were undressed and on the bed, the woman coaxing her partner to full erection. Filled with disgust and horror, recognition came as Daro stared at the screen. Straddling the man who laid stretched out on the bed, the woman made a now famil iar hissing sound as she sank down on him. Daro didn't have to see her face as he thought, 'Lyle was right.' An animal scream of hurt and rage joined Talmadge's laughter.

"You pathetic piece of shit," he hissed, shaking his head as the bedroom scene went on in the background.

Herm was enjoying himself. Now that Daro could see he'd been had, he figured he could tell him the truth or a lie and Daro would believe him. Still mad at Colmer for refusing to continue spying for him, he decided to tell the biggest lie of all. "Your precious fiancé, works for me, dumbass. Ever time you so much as farted, Colmer gave me a three page report. You still wanta get married, Rookie?"

Tied to the chair only at the ankles, Daro launched himself at Herm. There was a satisfying crunch when his forehead crashed into the Lieutenant's nose. When the chair tipped over, he tried to use it as a weapon, swinging it at the Herm's legs. All he succeeded in doing was to cause his bindings to bite more deeply into his flesh. Once again, Johnson hit him behind the right ear with the shotgun. Almost mercifully, he sank beneath the waves of consciousness.

His second awakening was more painful than the first. Herm had removed the cuffs and substituted a fine, almost thread-like cord securing both his hands and feet. But Daro's vision was worse. His head felt as though a bomb was alternately exploding and imploding inside his brain.

He lay on a large square of cardboard on top of the trash pile he'd seen in the corner. Although he couldn't completely trust his vision, he could make out the room where he'd been tied to the chair, the door standing open, light spilling out into the warehouse.

Suspended from supporting beams far above, pale overhead lights barely broke the gloom. Two forms moved about the large room, casting ghostly shadows across the floor. The largest shadow seemed to be carrying two objects, one in each hand. The shadow stopped, sat down its burden, and Daro heard a twisting, scraping sound, like a metal cap being removed. Staring hard and moving his head from side to side, trying to dispel the double image, he could barely make out Johnson as he unscrewed the top on a jerry can.

In spite of himself a moan escaped Daro's lips.

Hearing the groan, Herm sauntered over. Daro was gratified to see that the Lieutenant's nose was much wider than before. He was still dabbing with a handkerchief at a trickle of blood from one nostril. Making sure Daro was awake, he sunk his fist into his stomach.

"That's for the nose, asshole," he said.

Trying not to let him know how much it hurt, Daro said, "Thanks."

Herm brightened. "Hey, Rookie, you didn't see the best part of the movie, the part where they take their masks off. I figured you'd wanta be in on that."

Since Daro's mind was already as numb as his tightly tied wrists and ankles, Herm's words didn't hurt nearly as much as his gut. When he began to recover, he tested the cords.

"I wouldn't pull on them things too much if I was you," Herm said. "That stuff's called lacin' cord. It's used to tie up electronic cables and such, and it's stronger'n steel. You ain't gonna break it and it'll cut you up real good if you yank around on it."

Still having trouble breathing, Daro choked out, "Why did you do this, Lieutenant?"

Misunderstanding, Herm said, "I couldn't leave you here with my cuffs on you, asshole. You know yourself that they're serial numbered and could be traced back to me."

"That's not what I mean - why the rapes and murders? Was it just to make films?"

"Come on, Rookie, you ain't that dumb. Money. I've got me two ex- wives and rent to pay, and I like to drive a nice car, see. Besides, don't you think I know what most all the other cops think of me? I ain't goin' no higher'n lieutenant, even though homicide calls for a captain."

"So that makes all this okay?"

"Damn right. I'm lookin' out for number one. Nobody else is gonna."

Herm turned to see what Russ was doing. Apparently satisfied, he nodded and turned back to Daro.

"Well, Rookie," he said, reaching into his coat pocket and pulling out a short candle, "I'm gonna have to leave you now. I'm gonna put this right over there in the middle of the floor just as soon as Russ gets through wettin' everything down. Near as I can figure, in about thirty minutes we're gonna have us one hell of a fire. The difference is that you're gonna be in it, so them films you say you've got ain't gonna do you no good."

He knew Herm meant it. Why not - he had killed for less. Daro again tested his bindings and found them secure. After Russ made a flammable circle of kerosene around the inside walls, he poured four trails from the room's edges to the center. Daro watched as Herm placed the candle in a paraffin saucer and added a small amount of gasoline instead of kerosene to the dish. Careful not to ignite the liquid, Herm lit the candle. After he blew out the match, he walked to the far wall and turned out most of the overhead lights, leaving one dim row on.

"We wouldn't want nobody gettin' curious as to how come there's too much light after hours now, would we?" he asked, walking back toward Daro. Herm was over half way there when he heard Lesher's voice.

Don't make no sudden moves, Chicken Foot," Lesher said.

Daro looked toward the opening through which he had originally entered. He could barely see a form in the dim light, using the barricade stance taught at the police academy. Lesher held his gun hand forward, the rest of his body behind the wall, exposing only a small portion of his head, chest, and hip.

Herm froze, but Russ panicked, bolting for the shotgun standing against the far wall.

"Freeze, asshole!" yelled Lesher. Because of the angle, he had to step out slightly from behind his cover.

Terrified, Russ continued to carry out his last orders - 'Don't let Daro escape.' When he reached the old Winchester, he picked it up and turned frantically toward Lesher. Already covering Russ, Lesher fired twice striking the man in the abdomen and chest. Both hits were solid, propelling Johnson backwards. As though planned, his arms flew open and the shotgun came spiraling out, crashing through a window and sending a shower of glass and the Winchester clattering to the empty street below. Johnson was dead before he hit the floor.

Seeing his only chance, Herm dove for the floor and pulled his pistol as Lyle swung back toward him. In the exchange, Herm took a slug in the lower left abdomen and one in the right shoulder, shattering the bone and rendering his good hand and arm useless. The hits were not fatal, but they put him down. Had Lesher still been using his old police issue 38 special, Russ probably wouldn't be dead, and Herm might still be in the fight.

But Lesher was not so fortunate. When Johnson forced him to break cover, the Lieutenant's shot caught him in an exposed portion of the chest, four inches to the right of the heart. Daro shuddered when he saw his friend go down.

"Lyle! Lyle! - you okay?" No movement, no sound. Daro felt sure his friend was dead, but he rejected the thought, struggling with his bonds which did indeed cut more deeply into his wrists.

On the floor some twenty feet from him, Herm writhed in pain. Animal grunts came from deep within his throat. "Daro, you gotta help me," he croaked.

In spite of himself, Daro laughed. "You miserable son of a bitch, I wouldn't piss on you unless it was gasoline."

Herm went on as though he hadn't heard. "Some way you gotta help me. I - I can't move my legs," he said, his voice hysterical. He scratched feebly at the floor with his destroyed left hand trying to pull himself toward the paraffin saucer and the small yellow flame which lightly danced above it. "We ain't got much time. The candle —"

Daro was so angry that he hadn't thought of that aspect. He squinted at the tiny flame trying to assess the remaining time.

Twenty minutes? Ten? He had no idea how long it took a candle of that diameter to burn down. He knew it was his imagination but it looked like the harder he stared, the faster the taper shrank.

He heard Herm cough and saw him grab his abdomen with what remained of his left hand, his face wreathed in pain. Once again rage passed over Daro all but blotting out his fear. "Don't you die you bastard. I want you alive."

This time Herm didn't even grunt.

Think, damnit. What to do? Daro might be able to get on his feet and hop, but there was no way he could get out unless he could free himself. His vision still wasn't clear and all he knew about the warehouse was that there were some stairs and a freight elevator somewhere.

He felt sure that if he tried to get out now he would certainly fall, possibly to his death. His only plan at the moment was to watch the candle and if it got too close to the kerosene he would have to try somehow to smother it. He considered trying to gain his feet, hopping over to throw his body across the flame in the hope it would smother before the gasoline caught. If not successful, Daro could only imagine the horror of what he would experience.

He looked around, shaking his head trying to clear it. He found that by squinting he could see a little better. In addition to the cardboard on which he lay there were various lengths of wire, wooden boxes, pieces of broken glass, some sort of electrical instruments, greasy automotive parts, and several old car batteries.

Glass. That was the answer. Daro squirmed off his cardboard and slid down the pile, landing with a thump which almost blew off the top of his head. He groaned and pressed his eyelids together until some of the pain went away, speeding up the process by reminding himself that time was even shorter than the candle.

It took but a minute to discover that his great idea was worthless. His hands tied with the wrists facing each other left him no room to maneuver no matter what piece of glass he selected. Once more he closed his eyes, wishing away the pain so he could think. He glanced at the candle. It was down more than half from when it was first lit.

A muffled scream from Herm got Daro's attention. The detective was on his back, trying to roll over, his ruined left hand making scratching gestures at the splintered floor, his useless legs nothing but a drag.

"You and me, Lieutenant," Daro said. "When the building goes up, you go too."

"Daro - please - help me," Herm squeaked.

He would have laughed, but it hurt his head. Instead he tried to concentrate. His eyes fell on the car batteries. He wondered. Why not try?

It took several minutes to find a piece of wire he thought would be suitable. He would have preferred insulation on each end, but settled for some rags which he planned to wrap between his fingers and the wire, assuming he could get it bent the way he wanted. In addition to the bindings cutting into his flesh, blood ran down onto his fingers, only adding to the difficulty of working behind his back. He could better understand how frustrating it must be to be blind. He never knew how slick blood was until now, like oil.

The tricky part was to get the wire wrapped completely around the bindings and working with numb fingers was no help. Sweat popped out on his forehead from both the exertion and his occasional glances toward the candle. He found that by bending the wire first he could begin the loop then finish the bend after placing it over the lacing cord. He was grateful for one thing. Lacing cord was strong, but it was made of waxed nylon. Now if he could just apply some heat –

He hadn't heard from Herm lately. When he looked he was surprised to see the Lieutenant looking back, his eyes like two tiny caves recessed into the side of a large melon.

"Whatcha doin'?"

"Trying to get loose so I can kill you, Talmadge."

The Lieutenant actually tried to smile. The smile turned to a grimace. "I'd almost be glad of that right now, Rookie. I'd lots rather take a bullet than what's comin'. You'd best go back to the glass. You ain't gonna be able to saw that cord through with no wire."

"I don't intend to," Daro grunted. He finished as best he could then, holding the wire so it would not come loose, rolled over to a group of car batteries. Selecting the newest looking one, he said a little prayer and jockeyed the ends of the wire over the positive and negative battery poles. Gritting his teeth he jammed the bare wire ends to the battery. Nothing. The battery was dead.

He repeated the operation five times, each a failure. Convinced he would fail again, he tried the next to last. The moment the wire touched the poles he knew he had found one with a charge. In an instant the wire turned cherry red. His lips pulled back from his teeth and he screamed trying to relieve the pain as hot metal seared his flesh. The smell of burning hair and skin rose up to meet him. An instant before he thought he could no longer stand it, the lacing cord parted.

His hands were free. But at what price.

For a moment he thought his hands and arms wouldn't work. Finally, hunching his shoulders forward, he dragged his arms into his lap and looked at his wrists. Cooked to the bone probably, at least they felt and looked like it, but no longer bleeding. Cauterized. But there was no time for such observations. After a quick glance at the candle, he found a sharp piece of broken glass and severed the cord around his feet.

Unsteady as a small child learning to walk, Daro got to his feet, swaying as though in the grip of an earthquake. The earthquake moved up to his head, starting a whole new round of throbbing.

The words sounded strained as Herm croaked, "You did it, Rookie. By damn you did it. Hurry up and get us outa here, will ya?" he urged.

Not even acknowledging his presence, Daro staggered over to Lesher and felt at the neck for a pulse. It was there - faint and thready, but it was there. And now that he was closer he could hear his partner breathe, a sucking sound from Lesher's chest wound. Herm's slug had obviously punctured a lung.

Daro muttered, "Don't you die on me you son of a bitch. Don't you dare die on me before I get a chance to tell you I'm sorry." He expected no response and he got none.

Even though helpless, Talmadge was still arrogant. "Didja hear me, asshole. You're about to get us both burnt up. Get me outa this damn place."

"Shut up you piece of crap before I come over there and kick it out of you," Daro shouted. "What gives you the right to claim my help?"

Pain left Herm's face to be replaced by fear. "You ain't gonna leave me here?"

Daro looked closely at the candle - any minute now. He'd have to hurry, but he was so weak. Knowing that Lesher couldn't make it without help gave him a much needed shot of adrenaline.

Tucking Lesher's revolver into his belt, Daro went into the phony bedroom to retrieve his handgun. Slipping the little five shot pistol into his pocket he wobbled back outside and over to one of the jerry cans. He shook it. Almost empty, but there was a small slosh left. Taking the can with him he walked back to Herm, calmly looking him over, a fat slug stretched out on the floor.

His head was frantically swiveling back and forth between Daro and the last millimeter of candle above the gasoline.

"Hurry, Rookie. Hurry!" pleaded Talmadge. "We ain't got no more time. You quit bull shittin' me now and get us outa here. This place is gonna go up any second."

Daro shrugged. "That may be Lieutenant. But that won't matter to you," he said as he inverted the can and poured the last few ounces over the Lieutenant's crotch.

"Oh my God - you can't do that! You can't –" His voice trailed off as he began to sob.

Daro stood watching for a moment, his face as immobile as Mount Rushmore. "You've got a better chance than you gave my sister. See you in hell."

Daro turned and almost staggered over to Lesher, bending down to pick him up. Normally easy, it took all his strength to shoulder the one hundred seventy five pound man. Locating the stairs, he took one last look at the terrified Chief of Homicide, turned and staggered away. He was almost to the bottom of the metal steps when he heard the whoosh of flames spreading above him.

Wasting no time Daro hurried to the Griffin Street door and jockeyed open the bolt, almost dropping Lesher in the process. As the door swung outward, he stepped through and was met by Golden and Killean, their revolvers covering him.

"Thank God," Golden said. He holstered his pistol and helped Daro hold Lesher . Killean elevated his weapon upward at 45 degrees in the ready position.

While Daro held Lester, Golden checked him over. "Get the car," he snapped. "Lesher ain't got much time."

Killean took off in a dead run up Griffin and turned the corner onto Hord.

"Let's get him down to Ross Avenue," Golden said. "If we can't get an ambulance right now, we'll take him in the car. This place is gonna be crawling with firemen real quick."

It took the two cops several steps before they fell into synch, giving Lesher a gentler ride.

"When we got back to the office there was a message from Lesher waiting for us," Golden said. "He called in over an hour ago. You wanta tell me what's going on?"

Before Daro could answer a sound came from above. It was hard to hear at first, much less identify. But Talmadge's screams rose in pitch and volume until he was reminded of a pig's squeals.

A puzzled Golden looked at Daro. "What the hell's that?" he asked.

Daro grinned, "Our friend Chicken Foot - he decided to stay for the wiener roast."

• • •

16

As soon as he got to the car, Killean radioed for the fire department and called for an ambulance. When he pulled around the corner, Golden waved him on to Ross Avenue.

As Jim Killean traversed the short half -block the radio came alive, "Detective Three, be advised ambulance on its way. Should arrive momentarily."

With a shaking hand he grabbed the mike and thumbed the transmit button. "Detective Three - Roger. Be advised our location is Ross and Griffin."

Parking on the far side of Ross Avenue, Killean opened the trunk of the unmarked car and removed a blanket, spreading it out on the hood. When finished, he ran back to help carry Lesher.

Killean grabbed Lesher's feet while Golden and Daro handled his upper body. They carried him to the squad car and placed him on the blanket.

Squad seventy two, Bishop and Nobles, were back in service after booking a female prisoner into the county jail. Only blocks away when the fire call came out, they rushed to lend a hand.

"Hey, Danny," yelled Bishop when he drove up. "Need any help?"

Both officers averted their eyes from Daro's stricken partner, as though to ignore him meant he wasn't there and therefore hadn't been shot.

Daro had thrown part of the blanket over Lesher to help keep him warm while holding a bandage against the wound in Lyle's chest. He could hear the wail of many sirens headed down Ross Avenue when the dispatcher's scratchy voice boomed from seventy two's radio.

"Chief One, be advised ambulance is crossing Harwood and Ross."

"Sheee-it," said Bishop. "Chief Phillips is in on this."

Only a few blocks away, thought Daro. "We got it covered," He yelled over the increasing noise. "Why don't you take traffic?"

"Gotcha," Bishop said as he stuffed the interceptor into low gear and dumped the clutch leaving a trail of rubber half way to Field Street. Squad seventy two was barely around the corner and out of sight before the ambulance came screaming up.

Daro and Golden gently laid Lesher on the wheeled gurney and the two attendants took over immediately. Daro slipped a soft pillow under his partner's head, barely getting out of the way before an impatient attendant brushed him aside. Skilled hands made quick work of the job.

"Remember, Lesher, don't you die," Daro said, his face twisting. "Don't you dare die on me."

Lesher was still unconscious, his face the color of soot as they loaded him into the ambulance. At least he was breathing. One attendant drove and the other got in back, swinging the door shut as the driver sped off, his siren cutting a swath through the rapidly assembling fire equipment.

Daro stood looking after the ambulance as the soft rain continued to fall and more police units arrived on the scene. Some long forgotten words came to his mind, 'Greater love hath no man that this, that a man lay down his life for his friends.'

Sunday school? He wasn't sure. But he hoped that the "lay down his life" part wasn't the case - he hoped his partner wasn't facing death for him, even though that's exactly what Lesher had risked by coming after him. He'd put his life on the line for a partner who had called him a son of a bitch, hit him in the mouth in his own house in front of his family, and had humiliated him by going to his Captain and demanding another partner - and for what? For telling him the truth.

"Danny, we need to talk," said a voice at his elbow. His thoughts interrupted, he slowly swiveled his head toward the speaker. It was Golden, a look of concern etched on his fire-lit face.

It took Daro a moment to bring himself back to the present. "Can it wait? I've got something I need to do," Daro yelled over the growing din.

"Not really," Golden yelled back, pointing a thumb toward the warehouse. "Are you sure Chicken Foot is in there?"

He nodded and chuckled. "Yeah. Roast pig for dinner. And a side dish named Russell Johnson."

Golden opened his mouth to ask another question when the gasoline tank on Herm's Cadillac went up, sending a ball of flame and a cascade of bricks and twisted steel into Griffin Street. It looked like the whole front wall was about to come down. The Fire Chief on the scene went directly three alarms and placed two more units on standby as Daro raced down Ross Avenue.

"I'll meet you at Parkland Hospital," Daro shouted over his shoulder as he turned up behind the warehouse on Field Street. He had to move his car quickly before his precious Crown Victoria got roasted. He barely got backed out onto Field before another fire unit roared up blocking his recent escape route. Shouting, but well drilled firemen, attached the connector to a hydrant and gunned off toward the fire, unreeling what looked like a mile of flaccid hose. At the signal a fireman slipped a keyed tool in place and turned on the water sending it gushing into the line. The hose jerked to life, engorging as though sexually aroused at the sight of the fire.

Parked up the block, afraid to hurry to the hospital for fear of bad news, Daro stepped out of his car to watch the inferno eat away at the ancient building until parts of the side and back walls began falling into the street. A wry smile played about his mouth. Dante had his inferno, and now Daro had his. Somehow he felt almost cleansed by the flames. But the destruction was leaving a loneliness he felt sure would never be filled. It reminded him that he had two things left to do, the first starting at Parkland.

It took a direct order from Chief One, Carl Phillips, to get Daro to leave the double doors outside Lesher's operating room and let the emergency room staff tend his wounds. They cleansed and bandaged his cuts and burns, concluding the treatment with both penicillin and tetanus shots, but Daro categorically refused the neurologist's advice to stay in the hospital overnight. He also turned down a shot for pain. It was imperative that his head stay clear.

Seated in a small alcove waiting room, Daro felt even worse when Carol came in. Somehow he hadn't even thought about Lesher's family. In cases like this a policewoman stayed with the children and another officer brought the wife to the hospital, placing themselves at her disposal for as long as needed. He was sure little Amy was going nuts with a stranger in the house. Daro's face had a stricken look as he waited for whatever Carol might say or do. But there were no cross words, only a soft smile that lit her face. She reached up to hug him.

"He'll be okay, Danny. He's got to be for both of us."

As miserable now as when Sally and his folks were killed, Daro sat down by his partner's wife while she held his hand and tears ran down his face.

It wasn't until 4:00 AM that the doctor told them Lesher would make it. Carol dried her eyes and looked into Daro's face. "See?" she said. "My honey's a tough man."

He nodded, giving her what he hoped passed for a smile and asked, "But what was he doing there - how did he know?"

Carol smiled. "After you asked Captain Spencer for a new partner, he called the house. Lyle told him what had happened and why. So the Captain took him off regular duty and had him follow you. I guess you must have led Lyle to the warehouse. The Captain had told him to find out what was going on and call either him or Golden. I understand that Spencer was out of pocket, and Golden and Killean were out on an early stake out. Lyle left a message and waited, but when they didn't come, he must have been afraid to wait any longer so he went in."

"Not only am I a fool, but Lyle wouldn't be in there if it wasn't for me," he said, pointing with his chin toward the stainless steel doors of the operating room. "Everything he told me and more is true."

"What are you going to do?" asked Carol.

Not really answering her question, Daro said, "We can't see Lyle for several hours so I'll be back as soon as I can."

Carol placed her hand on his arm. "You really shouldn't leave. You look about to drop."

He shook his head. "There's something I have to do."

"Nothing foolish, okay?" Carol said. "And be careful."

"I will."

Daro kissed her hand and left by the emergency room entrance to pick up his car. Driving out Oak Lawn Avenue toward Jan's, he passed an all-night drug store. He had an idea and pulled into the parking lot. A lone young man was on duty when he walked through the door. Daro was the only customer.

"You got a storeroom in back?" he asked.

He could tell by the clerk's expression that both his appearance and the question frightened the young man.

"Uh – yes sir."

"How about some leftover stuff from Halloween?"

The young man's Adam's apple bobbed up and down as he swallowed in fear. "Uh – I ain't sure, but I think so."

Daro outlined his request, followed by the glimpse of a twenty dollar bill. The clerk went scurrying to the storeroom in search of the item. In a few minutes he returned carrying a small bag and held it out to a dirty, disheveled Danny Daro, a man with a pistol stuck in his belt.

"Mister," said the clerk, his voice quivering as he held out the bag. "You don't need to give me no twenty dollars. Here, take it for free."

Daro's lopsided smile seemed to frighten the clerk even more. "Thanks, but a bargain is a bargain."

He looked inside the bag, nodded, and handed the young man the twenty before striding out the door. In seconds the clerk was on the telephone talking excitedly to the police.

Wrapped in a white, terry cloth bathrobe, an alternately angry and concerned Jan Colmer lay awake on the sofa when she heard a car door slam. A moment later she smiled when his key rattled in the lock.

She looked at the clock - almost 5:00 AM - and got up from the couch to greet him. Her smile quickly faded when he stomped up the stairs and strode through the door.

Too stunned to speak she took in the bruised lip, the bandage down the side of his head and neck, the burned hands and bandaged wrists. But her street smart years of sizing up Johns warned her not to approach him.

Daro stood swaying slightly just inside the living room door off the foyer. He brushed his fingers through his flattop and looked at his palm as though expecting some of the black to come off. Once again he fixed her with his eyes.

"I saw Lieutenant Talmadge tonight," he said. "In fact, we took in a movie together."

His flat intonation chilled her like nothing ever had. "Oh? Anything good playing?" she asked, trying to keep her voice controlled and light.

Apparently angered by her flippant answer, Daro stepped a little farther into the room and Jan could see death in his eyes. She felt as though her heart was circulating pure liquid nitrogen.

"Honey, what is it?" Jan asked. She reached out to touch his arm, but he pulled back, his face filled with revulsion.

"I hadn't made up my mind until now if I'd let you live," Daro said. His voice was low and level, but a slap would have hurt her less.

"Do you mind telling me what you think I've done?" she asked.

Without another word he handed her the bag and walked out. When she opened the package she found a black, twenty nine cent Halloween mask, a mask of the type that an elegantly gowned lady might wear to a masquerade ball.

THE END

26519466R00145

Made in the USA
Charleston, SC
09 February 2014